Magnolia Nights

Copyright @2017 by Ashley Farley

IISBN-13:978-0-9982741-4-0

Cover design: damonza.com
Formatting: damonza.com
Editor: Patricia Peters at A Word Affair LLC

Leisure Time Books, a division of AHF Publishing

Magnolia Nights

ASHLEY FARLEY

Also by Ashley Farley

Sweet Tea Tuesdays

Sweeney Sisters Series

Tangle of Strings
Boots and Bedlam
Lowcountry Stranger
Her Sister's Shoes

Adventures of Scottie

Breaking the Story
Merry Mary

Saving Ben

CHAPTER ONE
ELLIE

ELLIE APPROACHED THE antebellum mansion with caution. Thirty-four years had passed since she'd last been here. Time had not been kind to the house, as evidenced by the paint peeling in sheets off the wood siding and rotten newel posts on the first- and second-floor porches. With Pixie dancing around at her feet, she climbed the brick steps and removed the brass key from under the mat where the attorney had instructed that she'd find it. After a struggle with the jammed lock, the key finally engaged, and she swung open the oversize paneled door. Standing stock-still on the threshold, she stared down the wide center hallway.

Memories drifted toward her, and her knuckles turned white as she gripped the heavy molding of the doorframe. She heard echoes of voices—some demanding and others more soft-spoken—and saw snapshots of the people who had once lived and worked in the house. Her mother and grandmother. Sally Bell the cook, Maddie the maid, and Abraham, the old black man they referred to as the chauffeur but who was really a jack-of-all-trades. Who was the little girl with dark curly hair and eyes as black as a moonless night? A playmate? A distant cousin or close family friend? In this memory, Ellie and the girl were huddled together behind an open door, hiding from something or someone. Were they playing a game? She'd spent endless hours and countless dollars working with a therapist to summon these memories from the deep recesses of her mind where they'd been locked away for most of her life. The voice inside her head grew louder, cautioning her not to let the memories out. When she backed out of the doorway and onto the porch, the voice escalated to a scream that warned her to get out of Charleston while she still had the chance.

But where would she go? There was nothing waiting for her in San Francisco. That chapter in her life had come to an end. She slipped the key back under the mat, and inhaling a deep breath, she wheeled her suitcase across the threshold and closed the door behind her.

Pixie was eager to stretch her tiny legs after being cooped up in her carrier during the long flight from California and the drive into town from the airport. Ellie followed along as her little dog's button nose led them from one room to the next. To the best of her recollection, the furnishings hadn't changed since she was last here as a six-year-old, the day the father she'd never met came to claim her. Even back then, everything had been faded and frayed. She found the dark fabrics oppressive in shades of browns, burgundies, and blues and thought the heavy furniture—enormous antique pieces with little detail and zero charm—belonged in an abandoned Scottish castle. Ellie remembered the grape juice stain on the Queen Anne sofa in the living room. She'd been punished for much lesser crimes than spilling the juice—a muddy footprint on the kitchen floor, leaving the lid off the cookie jar, hiding under her mother's sickbed.

When Pixie grew bored with the living room, she ventured back to the center hallway toward the rear of the house. The red damask wallpaper that lined the walls of the hall seemed more suited to a parlor in a brothel. As a child, Ellie had never been allowed to go near the antique grandfather clock. Now she felt a peculiar satisfaction in opening the glass door and nudging the minute hand with the tip of her finger. The gears sprang into action and filled the hallway with the steady ticking and tocking of the seconds as the decades slipped away. Had the clock ever kept decent time?

She found Pixie in the dining room, licking at a spot on the oriental rug at the base of her grandmother's chair. "Uh-uh, don't do that. It might make you sick." She scooped up the wiggling Maltese and tucked her under her arm. They'd eaten every meal in this dining room with her grandfather's beady eyes leering down at them from his oil portrait above the mahogany sideboard. She knew little about the grandfather who'd passed away years before she was born. His name had rarely been mentioned by anyone in the house.

Ellie could hear her grandmother's stern voice instructing her to finish her dinner. "There will be no dessert for you, young lady, until you've eaten your peas." Night after night, Ellie had been forced to choke down every last pea. To this day, the smell of peas summoned the taste of bile.

Ellie had neither seen nor heard from her grandmother in thirty-four years, since her father had taken her to live with him in California. Perhaps her grandmother's declining health had prevented her from getting in touch with her all these years. She wanted to believe her grandmother had loved her. She'd left Ellie her entire estate. Surely that was a sign her grandmother still cared about her, that she hadn't forgotten her. Though if the woman had been as cruel as her memories suggested, why did Ellie even care how her grandmother felt about her? She was desperate, however, to know whether her mother had ever loved her. There was so much Ellie didn't remember, and her father refused to tell her about her past.

When she sat down in her grandmother's chair at the head of the table, Ellie experienced an odd sensation—a powerful awareness of something or someone monumentally important to her—that sent a shiver down her spine and left her gasping for air. Gripping her dog, she squeezed her eyes shut tight. "Why can't I remember?" she called out to the empty room.

Her therapist had diagnosed her with dissociative amnesia. Her memory bank wasn't empty. She remembered plenty of things about her childhood. But her inability to recall the traumatic events she'd experienced in this house had caused chronic headaches, stomach issues, and insomnia all her life. What could possibly have happened to her here that caused such irreparable damage to her psyche? When she'd told her father she was moving to Charleston, he warned her to stay away. Maybe she should've listened to him. But the therapist thought that being back in this house might trigger her memories. Somehow, someway, she was determined to discover the piece of the past that would make her whole.

The sound of the back door closing and the squishing of rubber-soled shoes against the linoleum floor brought Ellie out of her chair. She pushed open the swinging door and passed through the butler's pantry, a rectangular room lined with storage cabinets that separated the kitchen from the dining room. She spotted Maddie depositing two grocery bags on the Formica counter. Deep lines had developed in her face, and her hair had gone gray, but Ellie recognized the woman she'd once known from the high cheekbones and bridge of freckles across her nose. How old had Maddie been back then? Surely not more than twenty-five or thirty.

The housekeeper set her dark eyes on Pixie. "Missus Pringle don't allow no pets in the house."

"Based on what her attorney tells me, she's no longer in a position to object."

Of all the people who'd been a part of her life back then, Ellie remembered the most about Maddie—even more than she remembered about her own mother. The housekeeper had paid special attention to the skinny little girl with strawberry-blonde pigtails. She'd bandaged her boo-boos, nursed her when she got sick, and snuck her treats from the kitchen—brownies and fudge and frosted sugar cookies. Had her grandmother's stringent demands hardened Maddie over time? She would have to find a way to soften her up.

Setting the dog down on the floor, Ellie located a saucer in one of the cabinets, filled it with water, and placed it on the ground in front of Pixie. She turned to face Maddie. "Nothing's changed around here, including you." She gave the woman's stiff body a hug, and when she pushed away, she was rewarded with a tentative smile tugging at the corners of the woman's pale lips.

"It's good to see you, Miss Eleanor."

Ellie's memories of her mother were fleeting glimpses of a willowy redhead with wide-set olive-colored eyes. They reminded her so much of herself she often wondered if these visions were figments of her imagination intended to satisfy her yearning for the mother she'd known for only six brief years. On the top of the list of things she yearned to ask her mother was why she'd name her innocent baby after a strict old woman like Eleanor Pringle.

"Please call me Ellie."

"All right then, Miss Ellie." Maddie set about emptying her grocery bags. "Mistah Calhoun called earlier. He said to tell you he's gonna be a few minutes late. There's a casserole warming in the oven for your dinner and a fresh pitcher of sweet tea in the refrigerator. I picked up some orange juice and coffee cream for your breakfast." She unloaded the groceries into the ancient refrigerator. "I don't know your food habits yet, but if you make out a list, I'll go back to the market in the morning."

"I appreciate your efforts, Maddie, but I can do my own shopping. But thank you for the casserole. After my long trip, I'm relieved not to have to worry about dinner."

Maddie closed the refrigerator and folded the paper bags in half. She set her lips in a firm line. "That leaves me out of a job then, don't it? If you're planning to do your own cooking and cleaning."

Ellie wondered if she could afford to keep Maddie on. If she couldn't afford to pay her, Ellie couldn't afford to live in the house. "As long as I stay in this house, I want you to stay here with me. I won't know how long that will be until I meet with Mr. Calhoun about the estate. You worked for my grandmother for a long time, Maddie. If, for some reason, I decide to sell the house, I'll make sure you're well taken care of."

The tension left the old woman's body. "That's mighty kind of you. Thank you."

"You're welcome." Ellie refilled Pixie's saucer with water. "I'll make out my list and leave it on the counter for you in the morning."

"Yes'm. I put clean linens on all the beds upstairs and towels in the baths. They threadbare. I'm sorry about that. Lots of things are run-down around here." Maddie appeared embarrassed, as though the burden of maintaining the household fell solely on her shoulders.

"Don't worry; you and I will address everything that's worn-out around here in good time." Ellie hoped she'd have the means to address these things. The attorney had told her little about her inheritance—only that her grandmother had left her a sizable estate. She'd spent an afternoon doing online research on the real estate market in downtown Charleston. Even in its dilapidated state, because of its close proximity to the waterfront, the house was worth millions. What she didn't know was whether her grandmother had left her a bank account to go along with the house. "How long was my grandmother sick? Mr. Calhoun didn't say."

"A few weeks at the most. She didn't suffer none. Don't you worry about that. The stroke left her in a coma. Mistah Calhoun and me, we made sure she had plenty of help to keep her comfortable till the end." Maddie removed her handbag from the pantry and walked toward the back door. "All right then. If you don't need me anymore today, I'll be on my way."

*

The house was quiet again after Maddie's departure, except for the sound of Pixie's tongue lapping the water out of her bowl and the distant ticking of the clock in the front hall. Once she'd emptied the bowl for the second time, the dog looked up at Ellie with expectant eyes. "What say, Pixie? Shall we continue our tour?"

Needing no further encouragement, the dog pranced on ahead of Ellie down the short hallway leading off the kitchen. She came to an abrupt stop in the doorway to the Florida room. Afternoon sunlight streamed in through a wall of grimy windows onto more heavy furniture and dark fabrics. Bookshelves lined the wall opposite the windows, and the wall facing the door featured a full-length portrait of her grandmother, her face set in a scowl even as a young woman. Pixie growled and scampered away. Ellie snickered. "I don't blame you. She scares me, too."

They continued their exploration upstairs, starting in the gloomy bedroom at the back of the house that had once been her mother's. A flashback took Ellie by surprise—the soft mound of her mother's body in the mahogany poster bed, rising and falling as she drew her last breaths.

She opened the door connecting to the adjacent nursery, the only way in or out of the room. As a child, she'd felt comforted knowing that if anyone wanted to get to her they'd have to pass through her mother's bedroom first. Only slightly bigger than a closet, the room was spartan with white walls, an oval-shaped rag rug on the floor in shades of brown, and a child-size iron bed. She recalled lying in that bed night after night listening to her mother's soft moans, overwhelmed by the loneliness and confusion of a small child with no father, a dying mother, and an uncertain future. On her way back through her mother's room, she smelled a pungent odor— the stench of mildew and rot—that she hadn't noticed a moment ago.

Ellie closed the door on her memories and wandered

back down the hall to the corner bedroom in the front of the house—the guest room reserved for guests who never visited. Unlike the rest of the house, the guest room was cheerful, with a green patterned carpet and velvet draperies that matched the bouquets of yellow roses in the wallpaper. An antique gilded bed with a fluffy white duvet and square-shaped down pillows graced the center of the room. She had no bad memories associated with this room. Feeling at peace in here, she decided to claim the guest room as her own.

Pixie scurried off before Ellie could grab her, back down the hallway and around the staircase banister to her grandmother's room. As a child, Ellie had been forbidden to go anywhere near this room. It was strictly her grandmother's domain. The bed—a walnut monstrosity with turned posts, an intricately carved headboard, and a patchwork quilt of Betsy Ross vintage—took up most of the room. Sensible black dresses and shoes filled the closet, and a collection of sterling powder jars, perfume sprayers, and brushes cluttered the marble-topped chest of drawers.

The sound of a car door slamming on the street prompted Ellie to wander over to the French doors leading to the second-floor porch. Lifting back the velvet curtain panel, she observed a silver-haired man, presumably the attorney, remove his suit jacket and leather document folder from the passenger side of a Mercedes sedan before making his way up the short sidewalk. She turned away from the window to go and greet him, but when she crossed the room to the door, she discovered it locked. She didn't remember closing the door behind her when she came in. She glanced down at her dog, who was staring at the door with bared teeth. "What's wrong, Pix?"

Pixie offered a low growl in response.

The same vile odor she'd smelled in her mother's room assaulted her nose, and she yanked frantically on the knob without success. She bent over to inspect the hardware but could detect no locking mechanism. The doorbell rang several times. She hurried back to the window, where she discovered the knob on the French door was also locked. On closer inspection, she realized the door had been painted shut and all the hardware removed. Strange. Why would anyone permanently seal access to such a lovely balcony? She knocked on the glass, but the leaf blower in the yard next door prevented Mr. Calhoun from hearing her. She watched him ring the doorbell again and clang on the brass knocker before searching under the mat for the key. When she heard the tapping of his leather soles on the hardwood floor downstairs, she returned to the door and began pounding on it, first with her palm and then her fist. Her heart was throbbing and sweat dripping down her back by the time Mr. Calhoun reached her.

"What happened?" he asked. "Did you lock yourself in?"

She held her hand out toward the doorknob. "There's no lock on the inside. How did you get it open?"

He hunched his shoulders. "I simply turned the knob, and it opened right up."

"I don't understand." She examined both sides of the knob. "Why wouldn't the knob turn when there's no lock on the door?"

"I can think of any number of reasons in a house this old." He held his hand out to her. "You must be Ellie. I'm Bennett Calhoun."

She gave his hand a quick squeeze. "Do you know if my

grandmother passed away in this room?" she asked, still pre-occupied with the door.

He chuckled. "Please call me Bennett. And yes, your grandmother spent her last weeks in this room with a host of round-the-clock nurses. But I wouldn't go worrying about ghosts just yet. We'll get the carpenter to look at it when he addresses all the other things that need to be fixed around here."

His explanation sounded logical to Ellie, but she closed the door behind her just the same.

CHAPTER TWO
ELLIE

ELLIE HAD SPOKEN to Bennett Calhoun several times on the phone in the month following her grandmother's death, but she was not prepared for his extraordinary good looks—tall, lean, and tan, in an impeccably tailored pale-gray suit. She reminded herself that she'd sworn off men and this particular one was old enough to be her grandfather.

She was parched after the trauma of being locked in her grandmother's bedroom. "Can I offer you some tea?" she asked as they descended the stairs, even though she would've much preferred a glass of chilled white wine.

"I never say no to tea, as long as it's sweet and iced with a taste of lemon."

In the kitchen, Ellie retrieved the pitcher of tea from the refrigerator and located two glasses. She filled the glasses with ice and tea and handed one to Bennett. When he started toward the Florida room, she suggested they go to the library to talk.

"After you." He held his hand out, gesturing for her to lead the way. "I was heading that way out of habit. The few times I met with your grandmother, we sat in the Florida room. I got the impression she spent most of her time back there."

Ellie didn't remember much about the library. Maybe that's why she felt more relaxed in there. She took a seat on the sofa and Bennett in a leather chair across the marble coffee table from her. "I find this room more comfortable. The Florida room gives me the willies." A chill crawled across her skin, and she untied the gray cotton sweater from around her neck.

He chuckled. "It's the eyes."

She froze, one bare arm in the sweater. "I beg your pardon."

"Your grandmother's eyes in her portrait. I've noticed them before. They unnerve me in a way I can't quite put my finger on. I have portraits of ancestors hanging all over my house, but none of them affect me quite like Eleanor's."

She considered this as she slipped her other arm in the sweater and pulled it tight over her sundress. Ellie had studied portraiture as part of the MFA program at UC Berkeley. It wasn't the way her grandmother's eyes, as gray as a stormy day, followed her around the room. That much was expected from a master portrait artist. "I know exactly what you mean, Bennett. Her eyes convict and sentence you to death before you've even committed the crime."

He tilted his head back and laughed. "Spoken like a true artist. We're gonna get along just fine, you and me. I must introduce you to my wife. She was impressed with your work when I showed her your website. We fancy ourselves collectors even though neither of us has a lick of talent."

"I'd like to meet her," Ellie said, taking a sip of her tea.

"I can see the two of you as friends. As for the portrait, if I were you, I'd stuff it in a closet and forget about it."

Ellie studied his face and realized he was being serious. "I'm not sure I can do that to my grandmother's portrait when I'm living in her house."

"It's your house now, Ellie, to do with as you like."

Pixie jumped onto the sofa beside her and buried her muzzle beneath Ellie's thigh.

Bennett smiled at Pixie. "Your grandmother would roll over in her grave if she saw your dog making herself at home on her velvet sofa."

It was Ellie's turn to laugh. "And I quote, 'It's your house now, Ellie, to do with as you like.'"

He held his glass out to her. "Touché."

A bemused expression crossed Ellie's face. "Didn't you tell me my grandmother's body was cremated? If so, that would make it difficult for her to roll over in her grave."

"A figure of speech, of course. Eleanor's ashes are in an urn on the mantel in the living room."

Ellie imagined her grandmother's soul yearning for release from the confines of a decorative urn. "Did she leave instructions on where she wanted her ashes spread?"

"Not that I recall. I'll leave that to you to decide." Bennett sat back in his chair, crossed his long legs, and opened his document folder in his lap. "Let's discuss the details of the estate." He handed her a sheaf of papers and pointed to a number so large it made Ellie's eyes blink shut and her mouth fall open.

"Is this some kind of joke?" she asked when she discovered her voice again.

"Nope. It's all yours to do with as you please. Eleanor lived like Scrooge. She never spent any money on anyone, including herself or the house, as I'm sure you noticed. You can live like

Oprah Winfrey and you wouldn't put a dent in your portfolio. It'll take several months to finalize the estate, but you have plenty of money at your disposal until then. Whether or not you realize it, your grandfather was one of the founding fathers at the Peninsula Bank and Trust. Virgil Bates has been handling your grandmother's money for many years." Bennett handed her a business card. "He's expecting your call."

She clipped the business card to the papers and set them down on the coffee table. "Do you have any idea why my grandmother left everything to me? We haven't been in touch in thirty-four years. Surely she has other family members more deserving." Ellie had often wondered if she had a string of first cousins out in the world somewhere.

He shook his silver head. "Your mother was an only child. If there are other family members, distant nieces or nephews, I am not aware of them."

"Did she make any bequests to her staff or her church or any nonprofit organizations she was fond of?"

Again, he shook his head. "Her will is very straightforward. You are the only beneficiary."

"Not even for Maddie?"

"Unfortunately not. I encouraged her to include Maddie in her will, but she refused. In fact, your grandmother never once gave Maddie a raise in all the years she's been working here. If you plan to keep her on, I'd address that issue soon. She's as loyal as they come. I've been giving Maddie annual bonuses to make up for it."

Ellie was moved by his generosity. "That's awfully kind of you. I hope the estate reimbursed you."

He chuckled. "I added it to my fees. Eleanor never knew the difference."

"Tell me, Bennett, how much do you know about my grandmother?"

"Not that much, actually. She led an active social life in her younger days, but she became a recluse fairly early on. In her fifties, if I had to guess. If you want to know the truth, I was a little afraid of her with that jogging stick of hers always close at hand."

Ellie froze, her glass of tea positioned near her lips. She set the glass back down as she recalled the pain of that wooden stick with its silver tips whacking her thighs. She had a long list of questions for him, but at the moment, only one presented itself to her. "What if I want to sell the house?"

He paused a long minute before responding. "You have every right to sell the house, if that's what you really want to do. But I advise you to think long and hard about it before you make that decision. This house has been in your family for generations, since back before the Civil War. Don't let creepy portraits and sticky doors scare you off. Hire a decorator. Put your own stamp on it. I understand you're an artist. You said the Florida room gives you the willies, but if you think about it, that room would make a wonderful studio with the natural light streaming in through its windows and the magnificent view of the garden. Although I must say the garden could use some tending."

When she first learned of her inheritance, Ellie had jumped at the opportunity to move to Charleston. But now that her belongings were in a moving truck making its way across the country, she wondered if she was running away from her heartache over a recent breakup more than she was embracing a chance to start anew. "I thought I was ready for a change, but now I'm not so sure."

"You're tired, Ellie. And understandably so. You've come a long way in a day." He consulted his gold wristwatch. "You've been here for only what, three hours? Give it some time. You'll feel more at home once you get settled."

Bennett had a gentle way about him that put Ellie at ease. "I'm sure you're right."

He drained the rest of his tea and stood to go. "Maddie tells me there are a number of repairs that need to be taken care of right away—things that can't wait for you to decide whether you want to keep the house or sell it. I would start with the leaky roof. It's hurricane season, and several storms are brewing in the tropics." He pulled a sheet of computer paper from his folder and handed it to her. "Here's a list of names and phone numbers of the contractors your grandmother used for repairs and maintenance. I added a few of my own. I suggest you let Maddie help you with this. She's very resourceful, and she knows the house better than anyone."

She placed the list along with the stack of papers that made up her grandmother's will on the desk and walked him to the front door.

"Shall I have my wife call you for lunch?" Bennett asked when they were on the front porch. "Lucille can provide an introduction to some of the key people in our art world."

Ellie appreciated his kindness. She felt certain she would enjoy his wife's company if she was anything like her husband. His twinkling blue eyes suggested a playful side she hoped she would one day encounter. "I would like that very much. So this is what they mean by Southern hospitality."

He winked at her. "It can be off-putting for some at first. But you'll get used to it."

CHAPTER THREE
ELLIE

ELLIE WATCHED BENNETT drive away in his Mercedes before turning around to face the house. She stared up at the three stories of a maintenance nightmare—columns, porch railings, wood siding, and shutters, all susceptible to rot and termites and all in desperate need of stripping and repainting. Having the windows cleaned, alone, would cost her a fortune. The foundation shrubs were way overgrown, and the small patch of lawn on both sides of the brick sidewalk appeared to be more weeds than grass. The sidewalk itself was buckling in places. She'd never owned a house before. How would she ever keep up with a money pit like this one? She was pleased to see the brass on the front door, which included a knocker, knob, and mail slot, had all been polished to a shine. She had Maddie to thank for that and so much more. How did she manage all of it at her age?

Ellie wandered around the downstairs for another hour before returning to the kitchen. She felt disoriented in her new environment and craved a glass of wine or hard liquor like bourbon on the rocks to take the edge off. Her grandmother didn't drink, as evidenced by the lack of alcohol in the house. After a thorough search of the cabinets in the kitchen and the butler's pantry, she finally discovered a dusty bottle of pinot noir at the back of the pantry, which was no more than a glorified broom closet with a few shelves to store nonperishable food items.

The only thing she could find resembling a wineglass was a set of four Waterford sherry glasses in the dining room's built-in china cabinet. She opted for an everyday juice glass instead and filled it to the brim with wine. She recognized the California label, although she'd never visited that particular vineyard. With a hint of cherries, the wine tasted surprisingly smooth.

There was nowhere to sit in the kitchen—no barstools positioned at the counter or chair at the tiny desk area beneath the wall phone. Her grandmother had intended this kitchen for cooking, not loitering. Ellie located a step stool in the pantry, set it up near the paned back door, and sipped her wine as she studied the sliver of lawn outside the window. The Florida room extended out the back of the house, cutting the yard into two sections—the larger garden area including the bluestone terrace off the Florida room and this patch of grass that provided enough room to expand the kitchen if she decided to do so.

Ellie's favorite place to hang out had been the kitchen in every place she'd ever lived. Come to think of it, she'd spent a lot of time camped out in this very corner by the back door, hiding from her grandmother, who felt it beneath her to enter the part of the house meant for the help. In Glen Park, the neighborhood where she'd grown up in San Francisco, she and her father had met for heart-to-heart talks in the kitchen of their modest home after her stepmother and stepbrothers went to bed. And for the past five years, she and Jake had spent most of their evenings together, cooking and sipping wines purchased from local boutique wineries and making out in the tiny kitchen of her studio apartment in San Francisco's Mission District. If she stayed in this house, she would remodel the existing kitchen and add on more square footage out back. An island would give her more counter space, and a banquette built into a wall of windows would afford her a sunny place to drink her coffee in the mornings and gather with friends for casual suppers in the evenings.

Slow down, Ellie, she thought. *You're getting ahead of yourself. First you need to make some friends.*

For the time being, she'd have to learn to live with the house as it was. She couldn't see herself eating alone at the dining room table. The living room was too formal for much of anything. The library was a cozy spot for curling up on a winter's day, but she found the dark paneling dreary. The Florida room would be ideal, if not for the constant presence of the woman who'd terrified her as a child.

Draining the rest of her wine for courage, she folded the step stool and dragged it down the back hallway to the Florida room. Lifting her head high, she stepped over the threshold and marched across the room. Then, teetering on the stool, she wrestled her grandmother's portrait off the wall. She set the portrait on the ground and leaned against it for support while she caught her breath. She looked around and noticed how the paint had yellowed over the years everywhere except where the painting had hung. *I'll need to do something about that*, she thought. *Along with the million other things that need addressing.*

She carried the large canvas in its ornate gold leaf frame up to her grandmother's bedroom. The door was stuck again, and she had to force it open using her body. She then held the door open with her foot while she maneuvered the portrait inside the room. She leaned it against the wall and quickly shut the door again, brushing the frame's dust off her hands.

Returning to the kitchen, she refilled her juice glass with wine and scooped a heap of the still-warm eggplant casserole onto a small plate. She didn't normally like eggplant, but she found Maddie's recipe with tomato sauce and melted cheese quite tasty. While she ate standing at the counter, feeling guilty for being so mean about her grandmother, she racked her brain for fond memories of Eleanor Pringle. She couldn't think of a single one. Surely those years hadn't been all bad.

After eating and realizing with dismay that there was no dishwasher, she rinsed and dried her plate. Ellie found an ink pen and a notepad on the counter beneath the rotary dial wall telephone and took them outside to the front porch. A gentle breeze made her grateful for her lightweight sweater. She sat down on the steps and commenced writing. Her grocery list included red wine and dog kibble. Her list for household repairs was longer. She would call the roofer first about the leaks, followed by the lawn service about bringing the yard back to life and Goodwill about the furniture from the Florida room she planned to donate. And she would ask Maddie about a handyman who could fix whatever was wrong with her grandmother's bedroom door.

She'd had a long day, and the wine had made her sleepy. She decided to turn in early, even though it was still light out and not yet five o'clock in California. She went back inside, turned out the lights, and locked the doors. She left the grocery list on the counter for Maddie and wheeled her suitcase upstairs to the guest room. She went to the window and stared out at the people and their pets across the street in the park. From this vantage point, they looked like ants crawling around on the ground. She experienced a sense of déjà vu, of deep sorrow and loneliness. She felt certain she'd stood in this spot many times before watching the world go by outside her grandmother's house. She reached for the knob on the French door leading to the porch. But like the one in her grandmother's room, it, too, was sealed shut. There was something more she was supposed to know about that, but she was too tired for it to come to her tonight.

She wedged the chair from the dressing table under the doorknob and stretched out on the bed beside Pixie. She doubted sleep would come easily with her mind reeling from so many changes, but she closed her eyes and was out within minutes. At eight the following morning, she sat bolt upright to the thundering of heavy footsteps pounding the stairs.

CHAPTER FOUR
ELLIE

MADDIE BANGED ON her door. "Miss Ellie, Miss Ellie, come quick! Are you awake in there?"

"Just a minute!" Ellie called and rolled out of the bed. She caught a glimpse of her reflection in the antique gilded mirror above the dresser. She looked a sight with hair matted and makeup smeared, the indigo-blue linen sheath she'd worn on the plane from California now a wrinkled mess. She pried the chair from beneath the doorknob and swung open the door. "What on earth is wrong, Maddie?"

"I'm sorry to disturb you from your sleep, but we've been robbed," she exclaimed, her right hand pressed against her ample breasts while her left gripped the apron of her old-fashioned gray housekeeper's dress. "Someone done stole Missus Pringle's portrait!"

"Calm down, Maddie. We haven't been robbed. I moved the portrait up here to my grandmother's bedroom. Come, I'll show you." They walked together to her grandmother's room.

"I didn't mean to upset you, but to be honest, the portrait makes me feel uneasy, and I wanted it out of the way."

Ellie held the bedroom door open while Maddie entered the room. Gripping the bedpost, she took several deep breaths as she stared at the portrait leaning against the wall. "Lawd, I thought someone broke in here and burglarized the place." Lines as thick as railroad ties appeared across her forehead. "But I know what you mean about the painting. I never liked her spooky eyes watching me while I worked, waiting for me to break one of her valuable possessions."

"We can both relax a little now that the portrait's tucked away up here." She gave Maddie a minute to calm herself. "Since we're here, I might as well ask you. I noticed this door"—she knocked on the door for emphasis—"has a tendency to stick. Do we have a handyman who can fix it?"

Maddie let go of her apron and smoothed out the wrinkles. "Oh no, Miss Ellie. There ain't nothing wrong with that door. That's your grandmother's spirit refusing to leave the house."

Ellie stared at the old woman, waiting for her to admit she was kidding.

"I ain't joking, Miss Ellie. We must take the spirit of the newly departed seriously. The Gullah people believe that a spirit ain't at rest until it passes into the afterworld. Missus Pringle and I have a battle going on over that door. I open it, and she closes it again, sometimes six or eight times a day. We need to keep it open so she'll know it's okay for her to move on to the great beyond."

"For the record, Maddie, I don't believe in ghosts. But hypothetically speaking, what happens if her spirit never leaves?"

"She'll keep building up energy until… well…" Maddie

fanned herself. "It ain't a pretty sight. I've seen spirits work themselves into furies. They break mirrors and crack floorboards. I even knowed one angry spirit who brought down a whole ceiling."

The rational side of Ellie didn't believe a word the woman said, but there was that other part of her, the part who'd experienced whatever traumatic event she'd experienced all those years ago, that was all ears. "Then by all means, let's keep the door open as much as possible." The sight of her grandmother's black dresses hanging in a neat row in her closet reminded Ellie of prison guard uniforms. "Would it help if we got rid of her clothes?"

"No ma'am! You can't get rid of her things until her spirit passes."

Ellie sighed. "We'll do it your way for now."

Maddie exited the room, and Ellie, careful to leave the door open, followed her into the hallway.

"Okay then," Maddie said, placing a hand on the banister. "I'll get your breakfast started. How do you like your eggs?"

"I don't care for eggs today, but thank you. I'll have some coffee and a bowl of fruit." She noticed Pixie at her feet, wagging her tail expectantly. "But I can get that myself. Do you mind running to the grocery store first thing? I left a list on the counter in the kitchen. I used the last of my travel supply of food. My little friend will be grumpy if I don't feed her soon."

Maddie looked over at the dog. "What's its name?"

"Her name is Pixie," Ellie said, picking the dog up and holding her out for Maddie to pet.

Maddie reached over to pet the dog and then snatched her hand back. "Do she bite?"

"She's never bitten anyone that I know of. Let her sniff your hand."

Maddie lifted her fingers to the dog's nose. Pixie sniffed several times and then began licking her fingers. She grinned. "Ooh. That tickles."

"Haven't you ever been around dogs, Maddie?"

"Not cute ones like her," she said, rubbing Pixie's head. "The only dogs I've ever known were mean."

Ellie waved the dog's paw at Maddie. "This little girl can be shy at first, but she's great company once she gets to know you." Pixie began to squirm in her arms. "I better take her outside before she has an accident. Let me get you some money for the groceries. I believe I left my purse in the kitchen."

"I can use the card Missus Pringle gave me for household purchases," Maddie said as they descended the stairs together.

"That'd be great. I'll straighten all that out at the bank. I hope to meet with them later today."

They parted at the bottom of the stairs, Ellie toward the front door and Maddie to the kitchen.

Once Pixie had concluded her business, Ellie showered and dug through her suitcase for a pair of dress shorts and a lightweight cotton sweater. She would need to go shopping soon. The remainder of her wardrobe would arrive with the moving truck, but most of her clothes were geared toward the cooler climate of San Francisco.

Maddie had already returned from the market with the dog food when Ellie went back downstairs. After she fed Pixie and devoured a bowl of berries, she took her coffee and her lists to the big desk in the library to make her calls. By the time early afternoon rolled around, she'd accomplished a great deal. The Goodwill truck had already come and gone.

She'd requested estimates for painting the exterior of the house from three different contractors. She'd scheduled an appointment at the bank for three o'clock that afternoon. She'd spoken to the lawn service about reseeding the grass, trimming the shrubs, and spreading fresh mulch in the beds. And the roofers were currently stomping around on the roof to assess the damage.

Her stomach growled, and ten seconds later Maddie entered the room with a pimento cheese sandwich, chips, and an icy glass of lemonade. Her grandmother's housekeeper was turning out to be a mind reader as well as a lifesaver. Maddie was on the way out of the door when Ellie stopped her.

"Maddie, did my grandmother own a car?"

"No'm, she didn't go out much." Maddie turned back around to face her. "I drove her in my car wherever she needed to go. She sold her Cadillac years ago after they took away her driver's license."

Ellie froze, her sandwich positioned near her mouth. "Why'd they take away her driver's license?"

"She ran over a fire hydrant one day on her way home from a doctor's appointment." Maddie's hand flew to her lips. "I know I shouldn't laugh, but I can still see Missus Pringle's face. She was fit to be tied that day."

"How'd she manage to run over a fire hydrant?" she asked, taking a bite of her sandwich.

"She was driving too fast for the speed limit. Tore the whole front end off her Cadillac. Water shot out of the hydrant like Niagara Falls."

Ellie laughed. "Okay, that is kinda funny."

Maddie grew serious, and tears welled up in her eyes. "That's when they discovered she had cataracts." She shook her head. "Stubborn old woman refused to have the opera-tion. She was nearly blind when she died."

Ellie had never considered Maddie's feelings for her grand-mother. She'd worked for her for more than forty years. Of course she'd cared about her, regardless of whether she liked her or not. With no family around to take care of Eleanor Pringle, the responsibility had fallen on Maddie alone.

Ellie pushed her chair back and came around to the front of the desk. "It must've been hard on you, watching her dete-riorate like that." She gave Maddie's arm a gentle squeeze.

Maddie sniffled. "It wasn't always easy, but we managed all right."

"Do you think that's why my grandmother ignored the repairs, because she couldn't see the house was falling down around her?"

"Trust me, she knew. I done told her nearly every single day." Maddie removed a tissue from her apron pocket and wiped her nose. "I don't mean no disrespect, but your grand-mother was stingy with her money."

"I'm learning that about her. I understand from Mr. Calhoun that she never gave you a raise. We're changing that right now. How much do you make?"

Maddie told her, and Ellie tripled the amount. "Plus, a week's salary bonus at Christmas."

"Lawd, Miss Ellie. You are too kind." She dabbed at her eyes with her tissue.

"You work hard, Maddie, and you were loyal to my grandmother, even though she didn't treat you very well. You deserve to be rewarded." Ellie made a mental note to ask the bank about the credit card Maddie used. "Were you able to make any home improvements using the credit card she gave you for household expenses?"

"Nah, that card was mostly for groceries. And doughnuts when your gramma got a hankering for Krispy Kreme. But she demanded to see every single receipt. She fussed at me if I overspent. Not that I ever did. I was scared to death of Missus Pringle. When her eyesight failed, she asked Mistah. Calhoun to read the bills out loud while I was in the room. She reprimanded me right in front of him more than once. She swung that old stick of hers at me." Maddie snickered. "Course, by then, she couldn't see well enough to hit me."

Ellie narrowed her green eyes. "I remember that stick."

Maddie walked over to the fireplace and removed a wooden stick from the mantel. "This belonged to your grandfather." She handed the jogging stick to Ellie. "Mistah Edwin used it to beat off the dogs on his way to his office or to church. Or so I've been told. That was before my time." She lowered her head and stared at the floor. "It's wrong of me to speak ill of the dead, Miss Ellie. I wanted you to know your grandmother's way so you'd understand how things got so bad around here. I tried to keep up as best I could."

Ellie ran her hand along the smooth walnut stick. The sterling tips shined as bright as every other metal surface in the house. "Thank you for telling me, Maddie. You've done an admirable job of keeping things up despite your limitations." She returned the jogging stick to the mantel. She would use it for kindling the first time she built a fire. Turning her back on the fireplace, she clasped her hands together. "I'm going to need your help. I've never owned a house before, and there's so much work to be done around here." *Starting with buying a car,* she thought, but she'd worry about that later.

"You can count on me, Miss Ellie. I know every inch of this house like the back of my hand."

"If you have a few minutes, we can brainstorm on what needs to be done," Ellie said, motioning her hand toward two chairs positioned in front of the desk.

Maddie nodded, and Ellie returned to her seat behind the desk.

"I noticed they hauled off the furniture from your gramma's sunny room this morning," Maddie said as she eased herself into the chair.

"A moving truck is coming with my things from California tomorrow. That seemed like the most logical place to put some of them."

"Be nice to freshen things up around here. Will you get rid of all Missus Pringle's books?"

"Not until I've had a chance to go through them." Ellie was eager to comb through the shelves. She suspected some of the books were valuable first editions and that some maybe contained her grandmother's personal documents as well.

*

At two thirty, Ellie left for her three o'clock appointment at the bank. Despite the midday heat and humidity, she enjoyed her walk up East Bay Street, taking note along the way of the restaurants, galleries, and boutiques she wanted to visit.

Virgil Bates, she discovered, was a jolly little man with pink dots on his chubby cheeks. He opened accounts and transferred money before she had a chance to sit back in her chair and cross her legs. He sent her on her way with a wallet full of cash and a promise that her cards and checks would be in her possession by week's end. In no rush to return to her grandmother's dismal home and feeling the need to stretch her legs, she walked several blocks north on East Bay before cutting over to Church Street. She ducked into a pet boutique and, on a whim, purchased a froufrou bed for Pixie—a fluffy pink mound fit for a puppy who thought she was a princess.

When she returned to the house on South Battery, she found Pixie bouncing around and barking excitedly as Maddie pretended to chase after her with the vacuum in the living room. When they noticed her standing in the doorway, Maddie turned off the vacuum and Pixie stopped barking.

Ellie faked a frown at her dog. "You've been holding out on me. I thought you hated the vacuum cleaner."

Maddie unplugged the cord and wrapped it around the upright unit. "I hope it's okay for me to let her out of her cage. I heard her whining—saddest thing I ever did hear."

"I don't mind at all, as long as she doesn't get in your way." Kneeling down, Ellie clapped her hands, and Pixie leaped into her arms. She nuzzled the dog's neck and received licks on her face in return.

"Not at all. She's good company." Maddie glanced at her Timex. "Lawdy, the day has gotten away from me again. Time for me to be heading home."

The day had flown by, but Ellie dreaded the lonely evening ahead. She trailed Maddie as she wheeled the vacuum down the hall to the utility room and then stopped in the kitchen, where she retrieved her bag from behind the pantry door. She stood at the back door for a long time after her housekeeper's old Chevy sedan backed out of the driveway. In California, when she needed company, she called a friend. She knew no one in Charleston to call, aside from Bennett, who wasn't the type of friend she had in mind. What she was feeling was more than loneliness. Could it be that she was still not over losing Jake?

Discovering Jake's secret life had shot a dagger straight through her heart. *You mean, his legitimate life,* Ellie corrected herself. His wholesome-looking, sandy-haired wife and her two snaggletoothed clones were the real deal. He'd kept Ellie hidden and out of the way. He'd been in the shower that morning when she decided to run down to the corner for the shirts he said he needed from the cleaners. She discovered the photograph when she'd gone to his wallet for money to pay for the dry cleaning. They'd never shared expenses, which should've been a red flag for her long ago. Jake had always visited her at her apartment in San Francisco but never invited her to visit him in San Diego, where he claimed to live. He rarely took her out to dinner, seldom offered to pay for their takeout, and never reimbursed her for the money she spent on groceries to cook him gourmet meals.

Six weeks and twenty-eight hundred miles offered a clearer perspective on their relationship. She'd never loved him. Well, maybe a little in the beginning. Somewhere deep down inside, she knew he would never ask her to marry him. How could she commit her body and soul to marriage when there was so much about herself she didn't fully understand? She'd been in mourning since their breakup. Not the loss of him, but the loss of too much valuable time. Most of her thirties—biologically speaking, her productive years. Some of her friends' children were already in elementary school. Some of her friends were already divorced. Jake had been her only hope for ever starting a family.

With her life in San Francisco over and her new life in Charleston yet to begin, Ellie felt like a displaced orphan as she wandered around the downstairs rooms in the house. Seeing that Maddie had set up a wooden card table and chair in the Florida room—what she now referred to as her studio even though her things had yet to arrive from California—warmed her heart and gave her hope that this mausoleum would one day feel like home. When she grew bored, she grabbed Pixie's leash and a couple of her doggy toys and headed across the street to Battery Park. The days were growing shorter, and a chill had set in—the tease of a new season on the horizon. She roamed the five-acre park admiring the civil war cannons and the Fort Moultrie monument. She read the monument's inscription: *To the Defenders of Fort Moultrie.*

She imagined herself as a child running barefoot in the grass, her mother sitting on a nearby park bench reading a novel. But it wasn't a memory. It was a fantasy. Had her mother been too ill to take her across the street to the park?

Ellie studied with an artist's eye the light filtering in through the live oak trees. When her supplies arrived from California, she would set up her easel in the center of the park and paint the row of houses on South Battery Street.

It was after six when she returned home. Ellie scooped a heaping spoonful of chicken salad onto a bed of leafy greens for her dinner. She poured a glass of pinot grigio from the bottle Maddie left chilling in the refrigerator and took her dinner to her studio.

While she ate, she watched a couple of wrens through the window, splashing themselves in the concrete birdbath outside. With the beauty of the garden as a backdrop, the room offered the sense of serenity Ellie craved. She hadn't asked for the house, but now that she'd inherited it, she might as well make it her own.

She finished her dinner and then took her plate back to the kitchen and poured another glass of wine. Returning to her studio, she set her glass down on the table and approached the bookcase, running her finger along the spines of the books on the bottom shelf. An hour and a half later, her wine untouched on the table, she was balancing on her tiptoes on the kitchen step stool as she reached for a leather-bound journal in the far right corner of the top shelf. She managed not to fall as she grabbed hold of the journal and climbed down from the stool. She opened the journal and read the first entry. The diary belonged to her mother.

When her hand began to tremble, she closed the journal and gripped it tight to her torso. She would read it for sure. But what was she hoping to discover? The key to her past? Confirmation of her mother's love? Her grandmother's love? Although that was seeming less and less likely, and less and less desirable. Was she ready to finally face whatever had happened to her here? She'd tried and failed for so many years. Could she do it alone with only her grandmother's ghost to comfort her? She locked up the house and headed upstairs to her room. She was ready to move on with her life. Of that much she was sure. But she was terrified of the experiences she might have to relive in order to do so.

CHAPTER FIVE
ASHTON

I ARRIVED HOME LATE on Saturday afternoon from the hairdresser to find James Middleton and his parents in the dining room with Mother, the silver tea service and an assortment of finger sandwiches on the table in front of them.

Mother rose out of her chair to greet me. "Come in, darling. Join us for tea," she said in a sugary sweet voice. She's never called me darling in my life.

She's mentioned James to me several times in recent weeks. She's got it in her deranged mind that we would make the perfect couple. I barely know the man. And he is a man—in his early thirties if my memory serves me correctly. He's awkward in both appearance and behavior. He lives at home with his parents on Gibbes Street and spends his days playing chess with himself on their piazza. Mother speaks often of his high IQ, as if that's any excuse for him not to have a proper job.

Mother says that James doesn't need to work. "Between

your money and his, your offspring for the next four generations won't have to lift a finger."

Phooey on her. Everyone should work regardless of the size of their trust fund. I refuse to be defined by another human being. I have higher aspirations for myself than being Mrs. James Martin Middleton V.

For the past month, after graduating from the all-women's college Mother had insisted I attend, I've been making the rounds of countless teas and luncheons hosted by Mother's friends and their daughters, many of whom were my peers at Ashley Hall from kindergarten all the way through high school. I detest these functions. I have nothing in common with these women, my supposed friends, who seem content to live the same life they've always lived. They sound like broken records, every one of them. They talk about marrying wealthy men, having children, playing tennis, and attending more of the same boring old parties. No thank you. That is not the life for me. I can't imagine sitting around doing nothing all day.

I have my future all planned out. Come hell or high water, I will go to New York and become a fashion model. One day I'll be featured in *Vogue* and *Cosmopolitan*. Last spring while I was still at school, I spent three months' allowance on a professional photo shoot. I sent the headshots to a handful of modeling agencies in Manhattan, and two of them wrote back requesting interviews. I'm still working up the nerve to respond. Every day I remind myself that I'm not getting any younger. A few more years and I'll be too old for modeling.

What's holding me back then? What am I so afraid of? My mother, of course. Eleanor Pringle would never approve of her only daughter flaunting her body in front of the camera in such a tawdry way. When she finishes beating me silly with my father's jogging stick, she will cut the purse strings with a butcher knife, leaving me without a dime. As much as I loathe my privileged lifestyle, I have no clue how to function in a world without money. Where will I live if I run away to New York? Who will I live with? What will become of me if I fail?

I sat at the table across from the Middletons and behaved like the young woman of proper breeding that I am. I planted a smile on my face, but I kept my mouth shut. I had nothing to contribute to the conversation. I felt James's eyes on me, but I didn't dare look at him. I stared, instead, at the portrait of my father above the sideboard. Edwin Pringle would've supported my decision to go to New York, God rest his soul. His was the only voice of reason I've ever known. I was only seven when he passed away from cancer, a year after his mother died of heart failure. I loved my Grandma Amelia. She was a sweet old lady who was no match for her daughter-in-law. Mother never showed any kindness to my father or his mother, and the minute they were in the ground at Magnolia Cemetery, she turned into a tyrant.

I plotted my escape while my mother gossiped with the Middletons about their mutual friends. I know the train schedule by heart, and I've put aside enough money from my allowance to live for a month without a job in New York. I'm a college graduate and grown woman of twenty-two. I feel ridiculous sneaking out of town under the cover of darkness to get away from my mother. But I'm willing to do whatever it takes. She can't force me to marry a man I don't love.

As they were leaving, James pulled me aside and asked if I would attend the Fourth of July party with him at the club on Tuesday. To avoid an argument with Mother, I told him yes, but I will be long gone by then.

Mother lectured me long and hard over dinner about the advantages of marrying into a wealthy family. I raked my fork through my mashed potatoes and bided my time.

I excused myself from the table and went upstairs to pack my bags. I emptied the jar of cash I keep hidden beneath a loose board beside my bed into my purse. After Mother retired for the night, I called a taxi to take me to the station to catch the overnight train to New York.

*

I arrived at Penn Station the following afternoon around three. Remember when I went to New York with my senior class in high school? We toured the city in a bus, visiting all the local tourist attractions, and the chaperones refused us any free time to explore on our own. But this time is different. I'm all on my own with no one to guide me. When I exited Penn Station, I was overwhelmed by the hustle and bustle of the busy city streets. Unsure of what subway line to take or how to hail a cab, I joined the throng of New Yorkers hurrying along the sidewalk to their destinations. I wandered the streets until I came upon a nondescript hotel advertising vacancy. Ignoring the creepy stares of the disreputable-looking men loitering in the lobby, I booked a room for three nights and took the elevator to the fifth floor. My room has a full-size bed with a floral-print polyester bedspread, orange wall-to-wall shag carpet with stains from liquids I can't bring myself to think about, and one window with a view of the building next door. I don't mind the squalid interior so much. The room represents freedom for me.

I went to the diner across the street for dinner. I ordered the blue plate special—fried chicken and biscuits smothered in butter—but the butterflies fluttering around in my belly prevented me from taking more than a few bites. I woke early enough to shampoo and blow-dry my thick hair. I chose a simple black sleeveless dress and matching patent pumps from the meager wardrobe I brought with me. I exited the revolving doors in the lobby of the hotel, and following the lead of the gentleman standing next to me, I raised my hand in the air to summon a taxi. The driver took me to the address I provided: an impressive stone office building on Fifth Avenue.

At the modeling agency on the third floor, I gave the receptionist the fake name I'd submitted with my photographs last spring. I'm now known to the world as Nettie Pearson. I want to start a new life with no strings attached to my mother or to Charleston. Creating a new identity for myself seems like a good way to go about doing that.

The matronly receptionist stared down her nose at me and asked if I had an appointment.

"Not exactly, but I have this." I slid an envelope across the desk to the woman and explained that I had submitted my photos to their agency and received a request for an interview in response. "I hadn't planned to be in New York today, but since I'm here, I thought I'd stop by on the off chance Mrs. Porter could see me."

The woman skimmed the letter, returned it to the envelope, and handed it back to me. She swept her hand in the direction of the adjoining waiting room and told me to have a seat.

The room was already packed with stunning beauties in all shapes, sizes, and genders. I experienced a sinking feeling in the pit of my gut as I made my way to the one available chair in the far corner of the room. A sheltered Southern girl like myself doesn't stand a chance against these sophisticated beings. The teenage girl to my right with vacant eyes and hollowed-out cheeks ignored me, but the young woman on my left, who appeared to be about my age, started jabbering away the minute I sat down.

"I don't know why I waste my time coming to these interviews," she said. "Even if I lost twenty pounds, they'd never pick me over someone like you. You're gorgeous. Simply gorgeous. I would kill to have hair this strawberry-blonde color." She fingered a lock of my hair—a gesture I would normally find offensive from a total stranger. But this girl's pert nose, bouncing white curls, and twinkling blue eyes made me feel at ease. She introduced herself as Louisa Whitehead.

I started to give her my name but caught myself. "I'm Nettie Pearson." The name sounded foreign and mysterious on my tongue, like I'm a Cold War spy.

"Say…" Louisa touched the tip of her finger to the dimple in her chin as she studied me. "I don't think I've seen you around before. You must be new in town. Are you by any chance in need of a place to live? Because I'm looking for a roommate. My last roommate gave up on her modeling career and moved back home to Ohio. I can afford the rent, even if I never land a modeling gig. I have a full-time job at an advertising agency. I live with two other girls in a two-bedroom apartment in the Village. You would share the other twin bed in my room. You'd have the room to yourself most nights. I have a boyfriend. At least for the moment. I'm not sure how much longer we'll be together. He's nice enough, but he's not exactly the marrying type. Not that I want to get married anytime soon. I'd rather be single than waste my time on a relationship with no future."

Louisa talked so much I was worn out from listening to her. I can barely remember what she said. But I liked her just the same. I've never met anyone quite like Louisa, so open and energetic. I asked her why she was interviewing at a modeling agency when she already has a career.

"It's not a career per se. I'm a secretary. I'm only twenty-three. I'm not ready to give up on my dreams quite yet." Louisa dug her fingers into my arm. "I know what you're thinking—what's she doing playing hooky from her paying job to come here? Don't worry. I don't miss work very often. I rarely get called back for interviews." She paused to take a breath. "So, are you interested? In looking at the apartment, I mean." She rummaged in her bag for a scrap of paper and jotted down her address. "Why don't you stop by around six tonight? It won't hurt to take a look."

I took the number from her and folded it into my bag. What did I have to lose? I have nowhere else to live.

For the next few minutes, Louisa spoke about the apartment and all the benefits of living in Greenwich Village. I was so mesmerized by her talk of life in the Big Apple, I failed to respond when the receptionist summoned Nettie Pearson.

Louisa elbowed me in the side. "She's calling your name ahead of everyone else. That's a good sign!"

With a quick glance around the room, I noticed all eyes were on me. "I don't understand. I was the last to arrive."

"But you're the prettiest one in the room. That's how these things work." She nudged me out of my seat. "Go. Good luck, and I'll see you tonight at six."

I followed the receptionist down a long narrow hall into a large office with a bank of windows overlooking Fifth Avenue. A rectangular table was positioned in front of the windows, behind which sat a young man wearing a black beret and an imposing figure I recognized right away as Olga Porter. She came from behind the table to greet me. Dressed in Chanel with her black hair piled atop her head, she was every bit as elegant in person as she was in the photographs of her featured regularly in magazines and on the news.

She circled me, scrutinizing me from head to toe. "You're lovely, dear. Very wholesome. Have you done any modeling?"

"No ma'am," I answered.

Olga raised a pencil-thin eyebrow. "Beauty pageants?"

I shook my head.

Olga brushed an invisible speck of lint off her Chanel suit as if brushing away a fly. "So you're just another Cheryl Tiegs wannabe from Minnesota?"

Despite the churning in my stomach, I looked Olga in the eye and held her gaze. "I'm not from the Midwest. I'm from the South."

"That makes a difference then. Did you hear that, Abbott?" Olga turned to the young man sitting behind the desk. "We have ourselves another Scarlett O'Hara wannabe." Her attempt at a Southern accent failed.

Abbott got out of his chair and approached me. Lifting my chin, he rotated my head one way and then another. "She has good bones. Why don't we see what the camera thinks?"

Olga peered at me over Abbott's shoulder. "I don't see it. But you're the genius. Go. Take your photographs." She shooed us off toward a side door. "But don't waste too much time on her. We have a waiting room full of wannabe somebodies today."

Abbott led me into his studio in the adjoining room. Closing the door behind us, he pointed to a bench in the corner. "You can put your things over there. You might feel more comfortable if you take off your shoes."

I dropped my bag on the bench, slipped off my shoes, and went to stand in front of his camera. I felt awkward at first, but Abbott's warm chocolate eyes, gentle smile, and soft voice instructing me on how to position my body and where to direct my eyes set me at ease. He's attractive despite his hawkish nose, which I think adds character to his otherwise ordinary face.

When he finished shooting, he asked me if I had time to wait for his assistant to develop the proof sheets. I smiled at him and told him, "Of course!" I was willing to wait all day for a chance at a job.

Louisa had already left when I returned to our corner of the waiting room. I thumbed through magazines while I monitored the comings and goings of the wannabe somebodies in the room. One by one, they were summoned for their audience with Olga, and one by one they exited her office. Most wore dejected faces, but one lucky lovely was given a clipboard with forms to fill out. I hadn't considered the application, the challenges ahead of living under an assumed name. If I'm fortunate enough to be offered the job, I'll speak confidentially to someone in the personnel department, explaining my need to protect my family's privacy. Fabricating a little white lie will add legitimacy to my claim. I'll tell them my mother is mentally ill. That should do the trick. A talent agency will certainly want to keep that skeleton in the closet.

My stomach rumbled for a stretch around lunchtime, but the hunger pangs eventually subsided. The last interviewee left around four, and I was beginning to think Abbott had forgotten about me when he finally emerged from the back.

"We're ready for you now." He took me by the hand and helped me out of my chair. "Fasten your seat belt, Miss Pearson. I'm about to make you a superstar."

CHAPTER SIX
ELLIE

ELLIE LAY HER mother's open journal facedown on her stomach. Her eyes were tired from deciphering Ashton's messy handwriting. Staring up at the paint peeling off the ceiling, she tried to process the new information she'd learned about her mother. Growing up, she'd constantly peppered her father with questions about her mother. He usually responded with a brusque "What's in the past is best left in the past." As for her last name being different from his… She didn't want to share the hall bathroom with her stepmother and two bratty half-brothers, let alone her last name.

As a nature photographer, her father was gone for weeks, sometimes months, at a time, traveling into the wild in remote parts of the world. His income afforded them a comfortable living without any extras. In the absence of a housekeeper or someone to help in the yard, her stepmother gave Ellie more than her share of the chores. On top of doing the laundry, cleaning the bathrooms, and mowing the grass, she babysat for her little brothers night after night while her stepmother went down the street to drink wine with her neighbor. Jenny barked orders at her, and she screamed at her when she left her wet towel on the floor of the bathroom or when she forgot to take out the trash, but she never had a conversation with Ellie. She never took her shopping, attended school events, or expressed an interest in any of her friends. The teenage years were the hardest, when Ellie's hormones raged inside her. She longed for a maternal figure that she could share her confusing emotions with. She'd yearned for a mother who understood her and truly cared about her. Instead, she was left with Jenny, who never taught her to use a tampon or talked to her about where babies came from. Never offered advice about boys or college or her future.

Late one night shortly after her sixteenth birthday, Ellie and her father were spooning cookie dough ice cream out of the carton at the kitchen table when she broached the subject of her mother for the umpteenth time. "Did my mother like to eat ice cream late at night like we do?"

Her father smiled into the carton. "Not ice cream, no. Ashton didn't have much of a sweet tooth. She liked to eat leftover Chinese food out of the carton at midnight."

She'd never heard him refer to her mother by name before, and the soft expression on his face gave her hope that he'd once loved Ashton. Abbott took Ellie to see a child psychiatrist once a week when she first came to live with him. But after a couple of years, when money grew tight and the therapy didn't appear to be working, they stopped going. And he stopped talking about her past altogether. In his mind, she sensed, not talking about it would make it go away.

Ellie sought therapy again during her freshman year in college when the demons that haunted her drove her to experiment with drugs. The therapist helped her to stop abusing drugs and control her alcohol usage, and she'd been seeing Patsy once a week ever since.

When Bennett Calhoun contacted her with news of her grandmother's death, Ellie phoned her father to tell him about her inheritance. He'd long since divorced Jenny and was working for *National Geographic* in Washington, DC.

"You're a grown woman, Ellie. I can't tell you what to do. But you're liable to wake up a few sleeping dogs by going down to Charleston. And I think it's best to let them lie."

"I'm going, Dad, and you can't stop me. All my life, you've refused to talk to me about my family. Are you hiding something from me? Because if there's anything you want me to know, now would be a good time to tell me before I find out on my own."

Her father had sighed heavily into the phone. "I haven't been hiding anything from you, sweetheart. I've been protecting you. You were a terrified little girl when you came to live with me. I held you at night when you cried out in your sleep. I saw with my own eyes how difficult it was for you to adjust to your new environment. I sensed that something very bad happened to you in Charleston. Whatever that *thing* is is buried so deep inside of you, your therapist couldn't reach it after years of trying. Bottom line, Ellie, I don't want to see you get hurt."

"I understand how you feel, Dad. But I'll never be able to lead a normal life until I figure out what that thing is."

*

Ellie heard a rattling engine and squeaky brakes out in front of her house. She threw back the covers and hurried over to the window. Her moving truck had arrived four hours early and was attempting to parallel park on the street. She brushed her teeth and, ignoring the rat's nest of hair at the crown of her head, changed into a pair of pink overall shorts and a white tee. She dashed down the stairs, noticing as she passed her grandmother's bedroom that the door was once again closed. No matter how many times she opened it, the door somehow managed to close itself again.

The movers were already unloading her things and placing them about the yard. She went out to greet them. The crew leader tipped his hat at her. "Morning, ma'am. If you'll tell us where to put everything, we'll get started bringing it all inside."

Shielding her eyes from the sun, she stared up at the man whose shoulders were as broad as her front porch. She stifled a smile when she imagined him lifting his moving truck with a single hand. "That's a good question." As excited as she'd been for her things to arrive, Ellie had given little consideration to where she would store the things she didn't need.

She noticed her housekeeper observing them from the porch. "Maddie, is there any room in the attic for some of this stuff?" She'd abandoned her tour of the upstairs after she'd gotten locked in her grandmother's bedroom.

"Lawd, yes! There's plenty of room. Your attic runs from one end of the house to the other. It's easy to get up there, too."

Ellie turned back to the monster mover. "Let's put the bed, mattress, and this chest"—she ran her hand across the dresser she'd used in her bedroom in San Francisco—"in the attic. The rest of the furniture will go in the sunroom at the back of the house. The wardrobes go upstairs in my room. It's the corner front bedroom, first door on the left at the top of the stairs."

With Maddie leading the way, Ellie and the movers paraded into the house and up two flights of stairs to the attic. Buckets in every shape and size were scattered about under the eaves at the front of the house. "What's all this?" Ellie asked Maddie.

"The roof leaks," Maddie said. "Didn't the roofing man tell you that when he was here?"

"He mentioned that the roof had leaks, but I never envisioned it being this bad. No wonder his proposal was so high. Did my grandmother know about this?"

"Yes'm. She made me move everything out of the way so it wouldn't get wet." Maddie gestured at the odd assortment of furniture and lamps, cardboard boxes and steamer trunks, fans, and garment racks lined with old ball gowns pushed to the back of the attic.

Ellie shook her head. "I can't believe she was too cheap to have the roof fixed."

"Your gramma was ninety-five years old, Miss Ellie. She wasn't interested in much of anything, least of all fixing things that were broke."

Instead, she left this mess for me, Ellie thought to herself.

For the rest of the morning, Ellie supervised the movers, instructing them on where to place her things throughout the house. She dug through the boxes marked *Kitchen* for her microwave, Keurig, electric corkscrew, and stemless wineglasses. She positioned her upholstered furniture—all covered in textured fabrics in shades of pale gray—to take advantage of the view of the garden, with the back of the sofa facing the hallway and the two club chairs in front of the bookcases.

Her sisal rug covered most of the floor with the exception of several feet at the end of the room where her grandmother's portrait once hung. The space was the perfect place to set up her easels. She put her Lucite desk behind the sofa and replaced the card table with her antique walnut table and four chairs, items she'd purchase years ago with proceeds from the sale of her first painting. When the monster mover brought in her computer monitor and flat-screen television, she made a mental note to call the cable and Internet provider.

Late that afternoon, as she and Maddie stood admiring her new studio, Ellie said, "I understand why a ninety-five-year-old woman wouldn't have Wi-Fi, but I'm surprised there's no TV in the house. I've been so busy, I didn't realize it until today."

"Your gramma didn't approve of television."

"Well that's gonna change, but not until Wednesday of next week. That's the earliest Verizon can come. I don't watch much TV, but I like to have at least one in the house for special news and sporting events."

"Put one in the kitchen, and I might sneak a peek at my stories while I'm doing the ironing." Maddie let out a cackle that made Ellie smile.

"Consider it done," Ellie said. "You deserve to watch your stories after all these years."

"Want me to bring a painting from one of the other rooms to cover that up?" Ellie followed her gaze to the white rectangle on the far wall where her grandmother's portrait once hung.

"Don't you dare! I have big plans for that wall."

*

First thing on Thursday morning, Ellie drove her rental car to Lowe's in West Ashley for supplies. She found a stepladder in the corner of the detached garage out back and positioned it in front of the wall. She then rolled the entire wall in dove gray and waited for that to dry. She spent the afternoon creating an abstract mural by splattering paint—in shades of charcoal and white and several hues of pink that matched the decorative pillows on her sofa—in an organized fashion all over the wall. She put her supplies away, tidied up the room, and stretched out on the sofa to admire her work. She'd transformed her grandmother's shabby Florida room into a comfortable studio that was beginning to feel the tiniest bit like home.

"One room down, Pix. A whole house full of rooms to go." Pixie looked up at her, thumping her tail on her pink doggy bed. Suddenly overwhelmed, Ellie scooped the dog up and held her tight to her body. "We're out of our league here, you know? We have enough money to live anywhere in the world we'd like. We could go someplace exotic—a city or island or countryside where I'll never run out of scenes to paint and you'll never run out of places to explore."

Her eyes came in contact with the floor-to-ceiling bookshelves. "But first I need to find the answers I'm looking for." She jumped up. "It's gotta be here somewhere." One by one, she removed the books from the shelves, studying each one carefully for clues—a newspaper clipping or photograph or pressed corsage from a long-ago dance. She found nothing, not even a church bulletin from her grandfather's funeral.

CHAPTER SEVEN
ELLIE

BENNETT'S WIFE, LUCILLE, invited Ellie to go for coffee on Friday morning. "Black Tap Coffee caters to the college crowd," Lucille had said on the phone. "But the coffee's the best in town." The quaint coffee shop was located on Beaufain Street, a seven-minute bike ride from home. Ellie had been thrilled to see her vintage bicycle complete with front basket being unloaded from the moving truck. Considering the congestion problem in Charleston, she suspected that two wheels might be the easiest and fastest way to explore downtown without having to navigate traffic or worry about finding a place to park.

Lucille was waiting for her at a table by the window. She was the picture of casual elegance with her sleek silvery-blonde bob tucked behind her ears and the tanned skin on her face pulled tight over prominent cheekbones by an expert. They went to the counter together to order. Ellie requested the latte with homemade lavender syrup and a pastry, while Lucille asked for the Guatemalan brew.

After questioning her about her work for a few minutes, Lucille asked, "How is it that a lovely young woman such as yourself never married?"

Normally Ellie would've been bothered by such a personal question, and especially from someone she'd just met. But Lucille asked in a manner of genuine interest. "I just never met the right man," Ellie said with a shrug. "My one regret is not having children."

"Have you looked around lately?" Lucille waved her bony hand at the nearly empty coffee shop. "Women your age are giving birth every day. I have a friend whose daughter recently gave birth to triplets at age fifty. That's the drawback, of course. The older you are, the more likely you'll need to resort to a fertility treatment, which increases your chances of having more than one baby. I'm sure I don't need to tell you this."

"I should probably find the daddy for my baby first," Ellie said as she sipped her latte.

"Now that I can help you with!" Lucille slid back in her chair and crossed her legs. "We'll get started right away introducing you around town. Bennett and I are attending a gallery showing tonight. You must come with us. I know nothing about the artist. I'm going as a favor to the gallery owner, who is an acquaintance of mine."

Ellie opened her mouth to decline the invitation. She was not yet ready to meet Charleston's elite, the offspring of ancestors who were among the soldiers that fired their cannons from Fort Sumter. But Lucille didn't give her a chance to speak. "We'll pick you up a few minutes before six. The gallery is on Meeting. We'll walk, of course. Finding a place to park has become such an ordeal in this town."

She could tell from the firm set of Lucille's delicate jaw

that she wouldn't take no for an answer. "That sounds lovely. Thank you for the invitation."

Ellie spent the rest of the afternoon contemplating the blank canvas on her easel and feeling overwhelmed by her choices of subject matter. This extraordinary city with its eccentric inhabitants and pungent smells enamored her, but she found it strange that everything seemed so foreign to her. After all, she'd lived here as a child. Shouldn't she at least have a vague recollection of the area—the park, the waterfront, the marketplace?

She took off on foot with her camera slung over her shoulder. She meandered through the vendors at the market until she found an old basket weaver who allowed Ellie to take her picture. In exchange, despite the high price, Ellie purchased an oval-shaped sweetgrass basket from her. Admiring its craftsmanship, she thought she got the better end of the bargain. She snapped photographs of window boxes overflowing with flowers and of horse-drawn carriages packed with tourists. She walked along the waterfront imagining the sun rising over the harbor, and she strolled through Battery Park admiring the majestic live oaks. In the end, she decided to start with her garden—more specifically the view of her garden through her studio window.

The breakup with Jake had zapped her creativity. Six weeks had passed since she last set down her brush and abandoned the piece she'd been working on—a row of houses with vividly painted front doors in Russian Hill. She needed to ease back into her work, to start with a simple project to tune up her skills. First thing in the morning, she would get to work.

*

Ellie deliberated on what to wear for nearly an hour before

finally settling on a pair of slim-fitting cropped pants, a hot-pink sleeveless silk top, and a pair of gold Tory Burch strappy sandals. Better to be underdressed than overdressed for her first social function in Charleston. At the last minute, she added a tassel necklace in shades of pink, orange, and turquoise, and a tan silk sweater that matched her pants.

"You look smashing," Bennett said when she greeted him at the door.

Lucille nodded approvingly. "I've always admired a redhead who can pull off that shade of pink."

As she locked the door, Ellie heard Pixie whimpering down the hall in her studio. Her dog seemed content in Maddie's care, but being left alone was stressful for her. Truth be told, Ellie felt the same way. Aside from the two rooms she'd marked as her own—the guest bedroom and her studio—the house felt like a mausoleum. Eleanor Pringle's tomb with her knickknacks displayed on every furniture surface, her urn of ashes in position of honor on the mantel, and her restless soul still occupying her bedroom upstairs.

As they walked up Church Street toward the gallery, she admired some of the smaller, more charming homes. If she decided to stay in Charleston, wouldn't a house like one of these be better suited for her needs? She dismissed the idea, reminding herself that staying in Charleston was a big *if.*

When Lucille's cell phone rang, she dropped back several paces to accept the call.

"You know that all eyes are closely watching this hurricane," Bennett said to Ellie.

She cut a sideways glance at him. "What hurricane? I'm afraid I'm out of the loop without a TV."

He gaped at her. "Who in this day and age doesn't own a TV?"

Ellie smiled. "Funny thing is, I didn't realize there was no Internet or cable until my flat screen arrived with the moving van on Wednesday. I've called the cable company, but they can't get to me until next week."

Bennett took hold of her elbow, steering her around a sidewalk that had buckled from tree roots. "There's no need to worry about the storm yet; just be aware of it. It's bearing down on the Caribbean as we speak. There's a cold front making its way across the country. The hope is the cold front will push the hurricane out to sea. If the cold front weakens, though, as several models are predicting it might, the storm could pose a threat to the South Carolina coast. Best thing to do now is stay tuned to the local stations for updates, which presents a problem since you don't have a TV."

She removed her phone from her small shoulder bag. "I have the weather app on my iPhone. It'll tell me what I need to know."

"The Weather Channel is useless in situations like these," Bennett said. "Do you have a transistor radio?"

Ellie thought about it, but she didn't remember seeing a radio anywhere around the house. "Not that I know of, but I'll check with Maddie."

"I'll be keeping an eye on the storm and will let you know if we need to make preparations."

They cut over a block to Meeting Street and entered the art gallery. A woman with dark cropped hair and heavily made-up eyes strode toward them like a fashion model making her way down a Paris runway. "Lucille." She kissed the air beside Lucille's cheek and then offered her hand to Bennett. "I'm so glad you both could make it."

Lucille grabbed Ellie by the elbow. "Felicia, I'd like you to meet my friend, Eleanor Pringle. Ellie is an artist as well."

Felicia gave Ellie a quick once-over. "Did you say Pringle? I don't believe I've heard of you."

Ellie flashed Felicia her most brilliant smile, the one she reserved for snooty women. "Oh, but you will. I've only just moved to town."

Bennett drew himself to his full height like a proud papa, and Lucille pressed her lips together to hide her amusement.

"Right. I'll be sure to be on the lookout." Felicia glanced around the crowded room. "I must greet my other guests. Be sure to introduce yourselves to Faye Ryan, the artist. She's floating around here somewhere."

Ellie waited until Felicia was out of earshot before asking, "What was all that about?"

"Felicia fancies herself the darling of contemporary art in this town," Bennett said in a low voice.

Ellie watched the gallery owner mingling with patrons on the other side of the room. "Leave it to me to get off on the wrong foot with the woman who can make or break my career."

Lucille patted her arm. "No need to worry, dear. You handled her well. She has a higher opinion of herself than she deserves. Felicia is best taken with a grain of salt."

Lucille and Bennett introduced her to so many of their friends, Ellie stopped trying to remember their names. She'd never been good at meeting people. She preferred socializing in more intimate gatherings. She waited until Lucille and Bennett struck up a conversation about the hurricane with a group of their peers before sneaking off to explore the exhibit. She was particularly drawn to an abstract of a tree in bloom, its branches with their waxy green leaves and dinner-plate-size, cream-color blooms. She was standing out of the way of the crowd, admiring the painting, when she felt someone's presence behind her.

In a gentle Southern drawl, a deep voice asked, "Are you a fan?"

She glanced back to see a handsome man about her age staring down at her. His unusual eyes, more golden than chocolate, the color of cognac, studied her from behind black-rimmed glasses. His lips were curled up in a soft smile that produced a dimple on his right cheek.

"Of the artist or the painting?" she asked.

He inched closer to her. "The subject. How do you feel about Southern magnolias?"

Of course. The magnolia tree. How could she have forgotten?

A memory of her five-year-old self curled up at the foot of her mother's bed rushed back to her from out of the blue. Her mother lifted a weak arm and pointed her long finger at the window. "Be a love and open the window for Mama," she said in a hoarse murmur.

Ellie slid off the bed and padded over to the window in bare feet. She struggled with the window, managing to open it enough for the cool night air to penetrate her mother's stuffy bedroom with the intoxicating aroma of magnolias in bloom.

"My grandmother has an enormous tree like that in the back corner of her garden," Ellie said to the man. "I've been trying to remember the name. Magnolias don't grow well in San Francisco where I'm from."

"I don't imagine they do. They're indigenous to the

South." He stepped in line with her and offered his hand. "I'm Julian Hagood. Welcome to Charleston. Are you in town visiting your grandmother?"

She gave his hand a quick squeeze. "Actually, I live here now, in my grandmother's house. She recently passed away. I'm Ellie Pringle."

"That would make you Eleanor Pringle's granddaughter. Our grandmothers were acquaintances. If I'm not mistaken, they were once in the same bridge club, decades ago before your grandmother became a recluse. No offense."

"None taken." She turned to face him. "I didn't know my grandmother, but she didn't have any other living relatives, so she left her house to me."

"Try not to sound so excited about it."

"You would understand if you saw the inside of the house. The roof leaks. The walls haven't been painted since before the Civil War. And the same stain is still on the sofa in the living room where I spilled my grape juice thirty-five years ago."

He tilted his head back and laughed. "You just described three-fourths of the houses on the Battery."

Ellie returned her attention to the magnolia painting. "I can't explain why, but this painting speaks to me."

"Then you should buy it. Her prices are reasonable. I've already inquired."

"About this piece?" She held her hand out to the painting. "By all means, if you have first dibs."

"Not about this particular piece." He removed a folded sheet of paper from the inside pocket of his navy sport coat and handed it to her. "Here's the price list for all the paintings. I picked it up on the table by the door when I came in."

Her eyes traveled down the price list until she reached the

painting titled *Sweet Southern Magnolia*. Ellie was willing to pay four times what the artist was asking for it. But she would keep that information to herself.

Voices grew loud and animated from a nearby conversation about the hurricane.

"This hurricane is all anyone seems to want to talk about tonight. I've never experienced a hurricane. Should I be worried about it? My grandmother's house is right off the harbor. The water can't come over the seawall, can it?"

An amused expression crossed his face. "Oh, it definitely can. I've seen it happen many times. But there's no reason for you to worry just yet. These people have nothing better to talk about. Every time a storm comes along, they work themselves into a frenzy. Nine times out of ten, the storm goes out to sea or the damage ends up being minor.

"Believe me, you'll know when you need to worry. The governor will declare a state of emergency and issue a mandatory evacuation for all low-lying areas. People will board up their houses and place sandbags at their doors. They'll load all their valuable possessions in their cars and join the standstill traffic on I-26. Ten hours later, when they arrive in Columbia, they'll check into a cheap hotel and eat fast food while watching the hurricane coverage on TV. Depending on the extent of the damage from the storm, they'll be stuck in Columbia for days. State and local authorities won't let you back into Charleston until they deem it safe. Hence the reason I never leave town during a hurricane."

"Why would anyone put themselves through that?"

"Because there are plenty of people around here who remember storms like Hurricane Hugo that hit back in 1989. Including me. With those kinds of storm surges, you're risking your life when you choose not to evacuate. People with small children would rather be safe than sorry. If that time comes, and that's a very big *if* considering we have threats like this at least once every year, you'll have to make the decision that's right for you. Hurricane preparedness is a skill learned through experience. You don't want to stay in your grandmother's big house alone if you've never been through a hurricane before."

Ellie gulped. "Thank you, Julian, for your advice. You're quite the authority on hurricanes."

"Like I said, I've lived through a few."

She surveyed the room for the Calhouns. "It's been a long day. I'm going to purchase this piece and head home. And pray I'm not driving my painting to Columbia on Monday."

He chuckled. "You'll be fine. I promise."

Ellie paid for the magnolia painting and arranged to have it delivered to her grandmother's house the following day. She bid goodnight to the Calhouns, who weren't yet ready to leave, and meandered her way back to South Battery. The sun was sinking toward the horizon, but the air was still thick with humidity. She looked for a familiar face in the people she passed who were out for an evening stroll. When she recognized no one, she reminded herself that this wasn't San Francisco. She missed the cooler weather, the familiar neighborhoods, and the small apartment where she'd lived for more than ten years. For the first time since she left California, she felt homesick for her artist friends who, after being shut up with their canvases and brushes all day, gathered most evenings for dinner or coffee.

Despite the early hour and the grumbling in her tummy, Ellie decided to go to bed early. A thought struck her as she climbed the stairs to the second floor. *That's it! Why didn't I think of it before?*

She entered her mother's bedroom for the first time since the day she'd arrived. She stomped on the random-width pine floorboards on both sides of the bed until she felt one give the tiniest bit beneath her foot. Getting down on all fours, she pounded the board loose and peeped inside. In the dark hole where her mother had once stashed her jar of cash, Ellie discovered another one of her journals. As she was replacing the board, she got a whiff of the same rotten stench she'd experienced on her first day in Charleston. Journal in hand, she hurried out of the room, careful to close the door tight behind her.

CHAPTER EIGHT
ASHTON

MY MODELING CAREER took off like a racehorse out of the starting gate. And I owe my instant success to Abbott. He took a special interest in me. Olga Porter admitted to me once that she would never have agreed to represent me if not for him. Abbott is one of the most sought-after photographers in New York. He's offered the best gigs, and he requests that I be his model for those gigs.

Three years have passed since I left home, since I last spoke with my mother. I don't expect to hear from her. In fact, I pray I won't hear from her. Regardless, I send her boxes of lavish gifts every Christmas—silk Hermès scarves and an Ultrasuede coat designed by Halston, items I know she'll never wear. They are symbols of my success, representations of my life of high fashion. I hope she gets my message—I'm living my dream, the dream I've made come true all on my own.

I won't stay on top of my game forever. Girls ten years younger than I, with bodies not yet fully developed, are making their way onto the scene. I'm considering moving out to

Hollywood and auditioning for the movies. I know nothing about acting, about as much as I knew about modeling when I first came to New York. Transitioning from modeling to acting seems like a logical career move. I can see myself starring in serious roles for mature leading ladies like Faye Dunaway.

For the past month, Abbott has been working in Hollywood on a series for *Vogue*. He speaks of warm, fragrant nights and palm trees rustling in the breeze. He wants to have a serious conversation about our future next week when he gets home. I've pressed him, but he refuses to say more until we talk in person. Neither of us is ready to make a lifetime commitment. We've talked about marriage a time or two, but we've agreed to wait. We are in our prime. We need to get as much out of our careers as we can, while we can. I'm certainly not interested in starting a family anytime soon. Pregnancy and childbirth will ruin my figure and bring my career to an abrupt halt.

A year ago, Louisa and I moved to a larger two-bedroom apartment on a safer, more prominent street in the Village. Louisa has given up on becoming a model and is focusing on her career at the ad agency. Turns out she has a talent for copywriting. She's been put up for a promotion. I hope she gets it. It would take some of the pressure off me. Louisa tries hard not to let it show, but I know she resents my success. Abbott thinks it's creepy the way she tries to emulate me, but I'm flattered by the attention. What harm is there in Louisa wearing the same shade of lipstick as me, even if the color is all wrong for her skin tone? What bothers me more is the way she constantly flirts with Abbott. He makes dreams come true for girls like us. He turns them into superstars. And I get the impression she would choose him over me in a heartbeat if given the chance.

The stomach flu or whatever it is that has been making me feel puny for a week finally caught up with me yesterday, and I had to call in sick from an important gig. I hope I feel better tomorrow.

*

Louisa pounded on the door this morning a few minutes before eight. "Nettie, are you alive in there?" She entered the room without waiting for a response. She gasped when she saw me curled into a fetal position on my queen-size bed. "Your face is as green as split pea soup."

"Please!" My hand shot out from beneath the blanket. "Don't talk about food. Especially food as gross as split pea soup. Whatever this is, I can't seem to shake it."

Louisa pressed the back of her hand against my forehead. "You don't have any fever. If I didn't know any better, I might think you're pregnant."

"But you do know better," I said without lifting my head off the pillow. "You're the one who insisted I see your gynecologist."

Louisa reminded me that diaphragms aren't foolproof and left the room. She returned a minute later with a plastic sleeve of saltines, a can of ginger ale, and the *New York Times.* "Are you going to call in sick again?"

I drew my legs even closer to my body. "I hope not. We'll see how the day goes. I don't have to be at work until this afternoon. We're doing an evening shoot in Central Park."

"Call me at work if you need anything," she said, and sashayed her ample hips out of the room. My roommate stopped caring about her weight when she abandoned her dream of becoming a model. A pity, too. She has such a pretty face.

I rolled over on my back and reached for the sleeve of crackers. When *was* the last time I had my period? Three months ago, maybe four. I stopped keeping track of my cycle a long time ago. An extra pound on the body is like ten on the camera. I starve myself to the point of malnourishment, which in turn affects my menstruation. At least I don't make myself vomit like so many of the other girls.

The more I lay there thinking about vomiting, the more it seemed like a good idea. I yanked back the covers, sending the *New York Times* scattering across the floor, and bolted to the bathroom. I threw up again and again until my stomach was empty. The tile felt cool against my face as I curled up on the bathroom floor beside the toilet. Was it possible that my diaphragm failed me? There was that one time, the night after the pre-release party for the movie *Rocky,* when Abbott and I went back to his apartment and had drunken sex. I didn't use my diaphragm that night, but Abbott... well, he implemented the old-fashioned method of birth control. That was months ago, back before Thanksgiving. And it's already March.

I knew if I was really pregnant, I would have to take care of it soon. I shuddered to think what taking care of it would involve. I staggered back to my bedroom and dropped to the floor beside the *New York Times*. As I was sweeping the sections into a pile, I spotted a photograph of Abbott on the front page of the arts section, his arm draped over the shoulders of an attractive woman I didn't recognize. The headline beneath the photograph read: New York Fashion Photographer Accepts Job with Warner Brothers Studio. I studied the grainy photograph and saw the woman's name in the caption. Lindsay Lynch. I said the name out loud to my empty room, but it didn't sound familiar. I skimmed the article but saw no mention of the woman's identity.

According to the news source, Abbott would start working for Warner Brothers at the beginning of May. I let go of the paper and watched it fall to the floor. This is what Abbott wants to talks to me about. A baby will inconvenience his new career. I can't, I won't, go to California as his pregnant wife.

I got to my feet and walked unsteadily to my closet. I changed from my nightgown into a pair of baggy corduroys and one of Abbott's old Northwestern sweatshirts. I stuffed my hair beneath a black felt hat, pulling it low to hide my face. Despite the cloudy day, I slipped on my oversize Polaroid sunglasses and grabbed my purse. I race-walked to the corner and hailed a cab to my doctor's office, where I demanded the receptionist arrange for a pregnancy test. When I left the doctor's office three hours later, I walked to the nearest subway station and hopped on the first train that came along. Stunned by the results of the test—I'm more than three months pregnant—I rode on that train for hours, with no destination in mind, ignoring the blank stares of the homeless people who inhabit the undergrounds of New York. By the time I arrived back at my apartment, I'd made my decision. I would leave New York. My suitcases were packed and waiting by the door at six o'clock when Louisa arrived home from work.

Louisa didn't seem surprised when I showed her the news clip about Abbott and the mysterious woman. "I was hoping it wasn't true. I didn't want to tell you, but I heard some of Abbott's friends talking at a party the other night. They said he's been seeing someone else."

I blew the air out of my lungs. "Why didn't you tell me?"

"Because I didn't think it was true."

I reached for my suitcases, but Louisa blocked the door. "Where will you go?"

"It's better for you not to know, in case Abbott comes looking for me."

"He's going to come looking for you, silly. He loves you. You know that. Look, Abbott told you he wants to talk to you about the future. That means he's going to ask you to marry him. I'm sure the woman in the photograph doesn't mean anything to him." She pointed at the newspaper on the kitchen counter. "Maybe this isn't what you planned for yourself, but you'll make a great mother, and you'll get to live the life of a movie producer's wife in Hollywood."

"That's just it, Louisa. I don't want to be the filmmaker's wife. I want to be the movie star. This is my one and only chance in life. I'll have the baby, put it up for adoption, and be back in front of the camera by the end of September." I gripped the handles of my suitcases. "I left an envelope for you in your bedroom. There's enough money there to cover my portion of the rent until I come back. Promise me you won't rent out my room until you hear from me."

"I promise," Louisa said.

"Can I trust you to keep my pregnancy a secret? No one can know. Not Abbott, the folks at the agency, or any of our friends."

Louisa drew an *X* across her chest with her fingertip. "I'll take it to my grave."

CHAPTER NINE
ELLIE

ASHTON'S JOURNAL LEFT Ellie desperate to know more. What happened to her mother's plans to put her up for adoption? Had she fallen in love with her baby and decided that raising her was more important than her modeling career? Or had the agency found out about her pregnancy and fired her? And who was the woman in the photograph with Abbott? Not Jenny. He didn't meet her until several years later. The father she knew didn't seem the type to cheat on his girlfriend. Maybe he hadn't loved her after all. Maybe that's why he refused to talk about her. How had her grandmother received Ashton upon her return to Charleston? Surely she hadn't welcomed her with open arms and congratulated her on her pregnancy.

Unable to sleep, Ellie returned to her mother's bedroom and searched the floor on all fours for more loose boards. When she found none, she turned the room upside down looking for more journals. Someone, probably Maddie, had removed most of her mother's belongings. Gone were the taffeta and silk party dresses she remembered hanging in the closet and the shoes lined up in rows beneath them on the floor. Gone were the assortment of perfume bottles, cosmetics, and creams from the top of the dresser.

Ellie finally grew frustrated and gave up. She went back to her room and fell into a fitful sleep plagued with dreams about a distraught young woman on a train staring out of the window into the dark night as she traveled south to a place she didn't want to be, with a child in her belly she didn't want to keep.

*

The magnolia painting arrived before ten on Saturday morning. With her grandmother's depressing art decorating the walls in the other rooms, she propped the canvas against the bookshelves in her studio for lack of a better place to hang it. When she redecorated the house, she would replace the gilded mirror in the center hallway with the painting. She had an image in her mind of the piece of furniture she hoped to find to place under it—either an oriental console or a huntboard made of mahogany or walnut with lots of inlay. She studied the brushstrokes and composition of the painting for more than an hour and then went into the back garden to look at her own magnolia tree.

She crawled beneath the thick branches and lay down on top of the dead leaves on the ground. Staring up through the branches at the peeks of blue sky beyond the top of the tree made her feel dizzy. She closed her eyes and realized with absolute certainty that this tree had played a major role in the first six years of her life. She'd felt safe with the tree's massive, curvy branches wrapped around her like the arms of the mother who lay inside the house dying, like the father she'd never met but so often dreamed of. She remembered Bella, the doll she'd found in the back of her mother's closet that had belonged to her mother as a child. She'd loved that doll, with her naked cloth body and bald plastic head, her bright blue eyes and upturned rosy lips. Bella had been her only toy, her only friend. And her grandmother had refused to let her play with it.

One morning when she was around four years old, her grandmother had caught Ellie pretending to feed Bella cereal for breakfast at the dining room table. "What on earth is that?" She'd snatched the doll away from her. "This doll is filthy dirty, not fit for a proper young lady."

Her grandmother had stuffed the doll in the kitchen trash, but Maddie had rescued her for Ellie. After that, she'd kept Bella hidden in a plastic grocery bag tied from one of the branches of the magnolia tree. She wondered what had happened to her doll. To the best of her recollection, she hadn't taken it with her to California.

Ellie stayed beneath the tree until her back began to ache. She went in the house and gathered the art supplies she needed from her studio. She preferred to work with oils, but for this project she chose watercolors. To avoid drip lines, instead of working at her easel, she sat cross-legged in the grass with her pad of watercolor paper in her lap. She created puddles of the colors she wanted to use in the pan beside her. She dipped her flat wide brush in the jar of water and wet the paper first before reaching for the brush she used the most with these types of paints—the big fat round one with the sable bristles her father had given her one Christmas when she was in high school. She worked tentatively at first and then with carefree abandon.

Some four hours later, she made her final stroke and set the pad of paper on the ground. She studied her work with a critical eye. She'd portrayed the tree not as it was now but as she remembered it from her youth—in full bloom in the springtime. The work was no masterpiece. It would appeal to no one except her because of what it represented—the pain and heartache from a time in her life so traumatic that her mind had blocked it out. The tree had opened the flood-gates. Her therapist had warned her it wouldn't be easy. She would need to remember everything. Now, more determined than ever, she would face her demons and then lock them away forever.

It was dinnertime, but her stomach was too tied up in knots to eat. With Pixie lying spread out on the bluestone terrace beside her, she snacked on almonds and sipped Chardonnay until the sun dipped below the horizon. She went up to her room and changed into her nightgown, a gauzy white one that resembled the ones she'd worn as a child. She located a flashlight in the junk drawer in the kitchen and returned to the tree.

On warm nights, for no other reason than to be rid of her, Ellie's grandmother had allowed her to stay in the garden until bedtime. Even in the dark, she'd felt safer under the tree than in the house. What had she been so afraid of? Her grandmother's menacing glare and harsh words? The sting of her wooden stick against her hands and bare legs? Of making a noise that would disturb her mother's rest? Had she been afraid her mother would never get well? Or had she been afraid of death itself—that the hand of death gripping her mother's neck would one day come for her, too?

As she'd done earlier in the day, Ellie stretched out on

the ground beneath the tree, but this time Pixie leaped onto her stomach, digging her moist little nose into her neck. The scent of magnolia blossoms in bloom, like sweet homemade lemonade, filled the air around her. Where was the fragrance coming from? The tree had long since bloomed out for the season. She closed her eyes and inhaled deeply as she remembered the fleeting moments of joy she'd experienced here as a child. The drawings she'd made with the pencils and notepaper that Maddie smuggled out of the house for her. The imaginary friends she'd fabricated to ease the loneliness. The stories she'd dreamed up to suppress the feelings of hopelessness—fantasies inspired by her picture books where her handsome prince father rode in on his white stallion, scooped her up, and carried her to another part of the world, far, far away from her grandmother. She was allowed to have picture books—she remembered that now. Eleanor Pringle had been an avid reader, as evidenced by her crowded bookcases, and reading was the one indulgence she'd allowed Ellie. The scent of magnolia blooms vanished, and the rotten smell she recognized from her mother's and grandmother's bedrooms assaulted her nose.

Her grandmother's angry voice echoed in her ears, "Reading is a leisure-time activity. It's good exercise for idle minds, but we must limit ourselves to one chapter a day."

Ellie had owned three books—worn copies of *Cinderella*, *Hansel and Gretel*, and *Snow White*. She'd memorized the stories, knew every word by heart. But how? She'd never been taught to read. She was too young. Her grandmother had certainly never read to her. Had her mother read them to her at bedtime before she became ill? There was that feeling again, the sense that she was supposed to remember something important, something too monumental to ever have forgotten. If only she could find the rest of her mother's journals. If there were more journals. There was one person who would know. Ellie planned to have a heart-to-heart talk with Maddie when she came to work on Monday morning.

CHAPTER TEN
ELLIE

Ellie STAYED UP well past midnight on Saturday tearing the house apart looking for more diaries. She searched every room except the attic and skipped that one only because the lone overhead light bulb was out. In a state of desperation, she ventured into her grandmother's bedroom, placing a small chest in front of the door to keep it from closing while she was inside. She gave up when the rot and mildew stench chased her from the room. The house had seemingly been wiped clean of all traces of her mother.

Exhausted from her efforts, she slept until nine the following morning. She slipped on a pair of jeans and a long-sleeve lightweight sweater and went to the kitchen to make breakfast. She took her coffee and oatmeal, sprinkled with brown sugar and piled high with blueberries, outside to the terrace. While she ate, she skimmed the local section of the Sunday *Post and Courier*, which included the arts. She was eager to start her day so as not to waste such glorious weather with the sun glistening in the brilliant blue sky and the air so crisp and cool. She packed the provisions she needed for her outing in her backpack—acrylic paints and brushes, several bottles of water, and a pimento cheese sandwich for her lunch. With her canvas and easel tucked under her right arm and her backpack slung over her left, she strolled across the street to Battery Park. She set up shop and commenced working on her new project: the depiction of the homes on South Battery looking out from beneath the sprawling live oak trees in the park. She sketched her first layer with thinned raw umber. Her brush flew across the canvas with confidence for what she anticipated would be her best work yet. While she maintained reservations about moving here, as an artist, Charleston inspired her in a way San Francisco never had.

Other than a fifteen-minute break to eat her sandwich around one, she worked straight through until four o'clock. When she finally lifted her head and stretched, she saw dark gray clouds moving in across the area and her neighbors along Battery Street scurrying in and out of their houses, packing their belongings into their cars and SUVs as though preparing to leave town. The hurricane, of course. The weather had been so pleasant, she'd forgotten all about the threat of a serious storm. She rummaged through her backpack and patted her pockets, realizing she must have left her cell phone on the kitchen counter.

She carried the wet canvas to the house first and then returned for the rest of her things. Her phone was not on the kitchen counter but beside the sink in her bathroom upstairs. She had four missed calls from Bennett Calhoun and one from her father. She accessed the weather app, which forecast a 20 percent chance of rain for that night increasing to 50 percent on Monday. The video segment for the hurricane showed the projected path heading out to sea.

She ignored her father's call—he had been avoiding all of hers since she told him she was moving to South Carolina—and clicked on Bennett's number.

"I've been trying to reach you," he said, omitting any pleasantries. "They're predicting the storm will make landfall in Charleston sometime late tomorrow afternoon."

She lowered herself to the edge of the bed. "I just now saw the article in the newspaper, but my weather app is forecasting for only a slight chance of rain."

She heard the note of impatience in his voice when he said, "You can't trust those weather apps. That's what I tried to tell you the other night."

"I have zero experience with hurricanes, Bennett. What do you think I should do? Are you and Lucille leaving town?"

"I guess you don't get many of these type storms in Northern California," he said in a softer tone. "We've decided to stay, as have all my children and many of our friends. You are welcome to move in here for a couple of days."

Ellie was quiet as she contemplated her dilemma. Packing her valuables in her rental car would take ten minutes and two trips—one for the magnolia painting and one for her suitcases. She had no interest in driving her rental car to Columbia and staying in a hotel alone. She was finally remembering the events from her childhood. Leaving the house now might hinder her progress. How bad could a little rain and some wind be anyway?

"Thanks for the offer, but I'll be fine here," she said after a long pause.

He let out an audible sigh. "All right then. But we're right around the corner if you change your mind. I have some supplies you might need, including a portable television I use at tailgate parties. I'll drop them off tonight before supper. In the meantime, if I were you, I'd haul buggy down to the Harris Teeter while they still have bread on the shelves. There'll be nothing left if you wait till morning. Be sure to stock up on batteries, candles, and bottled water. Fill your car up with gas on the way home. And stop by the liquor store." He snickered. "If you're anything like my family, you'll want to have plenty of booze in the house."

*

Bennett was right. The grocery store was a mob scene with people crashing carts and throwing elbows as they frantically fought over the last of the hot items on the shelves. As she wandered the aisles of the store, uncertain of what one actually needed to survive a hurricane, she took note of what the other shoppers were purchasing. She already had milk and bread, good thing, too, since little of either was left. She bought canned goods, toilet paper, matches, raw fruits and vegetables that didn't require refrigeration, the last three cases of an off-brand bottled water, an economy-size package of both C- and D-cell batteries, and several bottles of wine. She chose red because, if she lost power, she wouldn't be able to chill the white. *Congratulations, Ellie,* she thought to herself. *You're thinking like a true hurricane shopper.* She waited for thirty minutes in the long checkout line. As she approached the cashier, an employee announced a new shipment of bagged ice over the loudspeaker. The shoppers cheered, and Ellie told the cashier to add two bags to her tab.

Bennett was waiting in her driveway when she returned home. He greeted her with a peck on the cheek and grabbed an armful of groceries from the trunk of her car. "I'm glad to see you were able to get ice. They were out when I went to the store earlier."

"They'd just received a shipment," she said, following him into the house. "You can have one of my bags. I'm still not clear on why ice is such a hot commodity."

"You'll know by the time it's all over," he said with a chuckle. "Keep your ice. You'll need it." He set his bags down on the counter. "Many liken the aftermath of a hurricane to Armageddon."

As they finished unloading the groceries from her car and the supplies he'd brought from his, Bennett painted a clear picture of what she should expect. "The power will go out, and because the modern world runs on electricity, everything will be affected. Whatever you do, don't open your refrigerator or freezer until you have to. Let the cold air stay in. After a day or so, if your power hasn't come back on, you'll need the ice you bought to keep the perishable goods chilled in a cooler. I brought you one, by the way, in case you don't already have one." He removed an Igloo cooler from the back of his SUV. "Depending on the severity of the storm, trucks may not be able to get back into Charleston with supplies for several days, possibly even a week. People will need gas to fuel their generators, so gas will become scarce. Which is why I suggested you fill up."

On their last trip inside, Bennett set his canvas tote on the counter and one by one removed the items he'd brought: a portable TV, a battery pack to recharge Ellie's cell phone, and two battery-operated lanterns. "Keep all your electronic devices plugged in so that when you lose power everything will have a fresh charge." He plugged the television into the nearest wall outlet and fiddled with the antenna until he picked up the local news station. The meteorologist was reporting strong winds and high seas in Florida. He gave an overview of the timeline of the storm, pointing to a graphic that projected it would travel from northern Florida up the Georgia coast to South Carolina, making landfall in Charleston early tomorrow evening.

"Fill your bathtub with water," Bennett continued. "You may need it for washing yourself and flushing the toilet in the event we lose our water supply, which sometimes happens for a brief period of time after a storm." Bennett went to her refrigerator and lowered the settings on both sides. "There now. That'll give refrigerated and frozen foods a head start."

He turned to her. "Have I sufficiently frightened you into coming to stay with us?"

"I'm not having second thoughts about coming to stay with you. But I'm having doubts about living in Charleston." Ellie offered him a teasing smile even though she was dead serious.

He squeezed her shoulder. "You'll be fine here, Ellie; I promise. But if you decide to go, I wouldn't leave tonight. The traffic will be horrible. Get on the road first thing in the morning, before the sun comes up." He reached for the doorknob. "Call me if you get scared during the storm, and I'll send one of my boys over to pick you up. But I'll check on you beforehand." He started out and turned back around. "Did you get your roof fixed yet?"

Ellie shook her head. "They were supposed to start tomorrow."

"Call them first thing in the morning. Tell them to get over here and put a tarp on your roof. While they have their ladders up, have them close your hurricane shutters. I'll have my son drop off some sandbags at some point during the day."

Ellie stood staring at the door for a long time after he left. She was way in over her head.

CHAPTER ELEVEN
ELLIE

THE ROOFERS ARRIVED on their own at seven o'clock Monday morning. Ellie answered the door in her bathrobe. She could see the wind swaying the oak and palmetto trees in Battery Park and the white caps on the harbor beyond. The hurricane was bearing down on them.

"I was going to call you this morning," she said to the crew leader, a scraggly-looking man who reeked of cigarettes despite the early hour. "I think we should put a tarp on the roof with this storm coming."

"My men are already on it. Do you want us to close your storm shutters while we're here?"

Pulling her robe tight around her, she walked with him to the edge of the porch. They craned their necks as they looked up to see three extension ladders propped against the gutters and a crew of men wrestling a blue tarp onto her roof. "Ain't very pretty, but she'll get the job done," he said. "We'll be back as soon as the storm blows over to get started on your repairs. Won't be tomorrow, but the next day if we're lucky."

"Do you really think we'll recover from the storm that soon?" she asked.

"No way of knowing for sure, ma'am. This hurricane is only a cat three. I've seen worse in my day." He tipped his hat at her. "If that'll be all, I have a long list of customers to get to this morning."

Ellie had changed into yoga pants and a sleeveless top and was perched on the step stool in the kitchen, picking at an egg white omelet and watching the hurricane coverage on Bennett's portable TV, when Maddie arrived an hour later, her gray hair sticking straight out from her skull.

"Storm's a coming." She closed the door but remained in her spot, her handbag dangling from her arm. "You planning to weather the storm here? Missus Pringle never left town. Said she had to man her ship. If her ship went down, she was going with it."

Ellie set her fork down and wiped her mouth with a napkin. "Against my better judgment, I'm manning this ship, even though it doesn't feel like mine to man." She had a hard time falling asleep the night before from worrying about whether to stay in Charleston or go to Columbia. Around two in the morning, she told the voice warning her that staying was a bad idea to shut the hell up, and then she took a sleeping pill.

"In that case, I need to get to the grocery. Is there anything in particular you need?"

"I've already been to the grocery store, Maddie. I'm fairly well prepared aside from filling the bathtubs. Do we have any fat candles? The tapers were the only ones I could find."

"I'll get them for you. I keep them in the garage with all the other hurricane supplies." Maddie went to the pantry closet and hung her raincoat on the coat hanger she kept on the hook. She added her purse to the hook and shut the door. Smoothing down her hair, she said, "If it's okay with you, Miss Ellie, I'd like to leave early today. The traffic is bumper-to-bumper coming into town. I suspect it's gonna be worse going home. And I need to stop by the store to pick up a few things of my own."

"By all means, please leave whenever you need to." Ellie drank the last of her coffee. "I was going to tell you not to come to work today anyway, but I couldn't find your number written anywhere in this house."

"It should be in your gramma's address book, top right drawer in the desk in the library. I'll make sure it's there before I leave today."

Ellie stood and walked her plate to the sink. "So you're manning your ship as well, are you?"

"Leonard and me... well, we don't have nowhere else to go." Maddie tied a white apron around her waist. "We live inland a ways. We won't catch the brunt of the storm like you will here."

"Maybe I'll come stay with you," Ellie said absently as she scrubbed her plate and placed it in the drying rack.

"You're always welcome in my home, Miss Ellie. But there won't be much room left with all our chilrun and grandchil-run taking up space."

"I was teasing, Maddie. Relax," Ellie said, rubbing her on the back.

"I do need to relax." She fanned herself. "I'm way too worked up about this storm. Do you mind if I have a spot of tea before I get to work?" Without waiting for her response, Maddie removed an Earl Grey K-Cup and a mug from the cabinet above the Keurig and brewed herself a cup of tea. "I sure do like this fancy coffee maker, Miss Ellie."

"I do, too, Maddie. I like the convenience of brewing only one cup at a time. You'd be surprised at the variety of coffee and tea K-Cups they offer." Ellie waited until Maddie's tea was finished before making herself another cup of coffee. "Why don't you bring your tea into my studio. I need to talk to you for a minute."

An alarmed expression crossed the old woman's wrinkled face. "Oh Lawd! Did I do something wrong?"

"Not at all. This is about me, not you."

They walked to her studio together. "You been busy this weekend," Maddie said when she saw Ellie's paintings on easels at the far end of the room.

"I haven't painted in a while. It feels good to get back to work." Ellie motioned at the pine table in the corner. "Shall we?"

They sat down opposite each other. Maddie set her eyes on Ashton's journals in the center of the table. "Are those your mama's diaries?"

Ellie's eyebrows shot up. "You've seen these before?"

"Yes'm. Your mama was always writing in her diaries." Maddie ran her hand over the smooth worn leather. "Where'd you find them?"

"I found one on the top shelf over there." Ellie inclined her head at the bookcase. "And the other in her room."

Maddie's cloudy eyes peered at Ellie from beneath her brow. "Where in her room? I cleaned all her things out of there myself."

"Beneath a loose floorboard on the far side of the bed. My mother referred to the hiding place in her first journal, which is how I knew to look there. I thought maybe she was leading me on some kind of scavenger hunt, but there weren't any clues in her second journal. At least none that jumped out at me."

Maddie read the last page in each journal before sliding them back to the center of the table.

"I thought maybe you might know if any more journals exist," Ellie said.

Maddie drummed her fingers on the table as she thought about it. "No'm. I don't believe so if they ain't on the shelves. I know where most everything is in this house."

Ellie inhaled a deep breath. "I don't remember much from the time I spent here as a child. I have vague recollections of Sally Bell and Abraham and my mother. My memories of you are clearer. You were kind to me, and I want you to know I appreciate all the little things you did for me to make my life more tolerable. My memories of my grandmother are not exactly warm and fuzzy."

Her housekeeper nodded. "The Gullah call a mean old woman like Missus Pringle a 'debble ooman'—a devil woman." She cast a quick glance at the doorway as though she expected to find her old mistress standing there. "I don't mean no disrespect to the dead."

Maddie rarely said a negative word about her grandmother. She was loyal to the bone. "I'm sure my grandmother knew how devoted you were to her. Nonetheless, we'll both be relieved when her spirit vacates the premises." Ellie shook her head to clear her mind of ghosts and Gullah voodoo. "Anyway, as I was saying, I remember very little about my mother. How long was she sick?"

"Off and on from the time you were born," Maddie said as she took a sip of her tea.

"One of the few things my father told me about her is that she had an underlying heart condition that presented itself during her pregnancy. Do you know the details of that heart condition?"

Ellie remembered her father saying that when her grandmother notified him of Ashton's death, he had been too overwhelmed at the sudden appearance of his six-year-old daughter to ask Eleanor too many questions. Several months later, when he realized Ellie could be at risk for a genetic heart condition, he'd insisted she undergo an extensive battery of tests to rule out the possibility.

"No'm, your gramma never said." Maddie's eyes shifted about the room, bouncing off the walls and the ceiling but landing nowhere.

"What are you not saying, Maddie? Was there more to my mother's illness than her heart condition?"

Maddie sighed. "Her heart was weak, so weak it finally killed her, but she also suffered from bad depression. Your mama gave up a lot to keep you."

"I wondered about that." Ellie tapped the journals in front of her. "I got the impression from her diary that she'd originally planned to put me up for adoption so she could return to her modeling career."

"That's right, but she loved you too much to let you go." Maddie stared down into her tea, unable to meet her gaze.

Ellie reached for Maddie's hand and gave it a squeeze. "I know this is difficult for you to talk about with me. If it makes it any easier, pretend you're talking about someone else, that the baby wasn't me."

Maddie nodded, but she didn't look up.

"If my mother was so miserable, why didn't she leave?"

"She had nowhere to go. She couldn't very well go back to New York, to that modeling career of hers, with a bum ticker and a baby on her breast." Maddie sniffled, and Ellie realized she was crying. "Your gramma didn't approve of Miss Ashton keeping the baby. I still remember the hollering that went on in this house. Your gramma refused to let y'all leave. She kept you locked up here like prisoners. It was the damnedest thing I've ever seen."

Ellie's green eyes widened as alarm bells once again began ringing in her head. "That sounds like some kind of sick and twisted horror movie. What did her friends think and those of you who worked here?"

Maddie blew her nose into the tissue with a snort. "Her friends didn't know. Missus Pringle stopped having visitors to the house 'bout the time Miss Ashton come home from New York. As for the rest of us, we thought it was sinful the way she treated you. But we couldn't do nuthin about it. We were just the staff. Abraham died, and Sally Bell left when you were a wee little girl. I'm surprised you remember them at all."

Ellie got up and crossed the room to her easels. "This explains why I don't have any memories of skipping rope on the sidewalk in front of the house or playing in the park across the street." She ran her fingertips across her watercolor. "I remember spending a lot of time hidden at the base of this tree, in my own imaginary world."

"You camped out under that tree from the time you woke up in the morning till the time you went to bed at night. Most days, you and I ate picnic lunches under that tree." She chuckled. "That was back in my younger days, when my bones weren't too stiff to climb under them big branches. I felt so sorry for you. You was such a lonely little thing."

Ellie returned to the table and sat back down. "The day I arrived here, I had a flashback of a little girl with dark curly hair and dark eyes."

Maddie froze, a tissue pressed to her nose.

"I thought maybe she was one of my playmates, but it doesn't sound like my grandmother allowed me to have any friends."

More tears pooled in her eyes and slid down her cheeks. "No'm, you didn't have any real friends, only imaginary ones. And Bella, that raggedy doll baby of yours."

"I remember Bella," she said with a smile. "I'm surprised my grandmother allowed me to play outside. Wasn't she afraid the neighbors would see me?"

"Your gramma let the bushes grow so no one could see inside the backyard. You were better off out there anyway. You were underfoot in the house, with your mama on her sickbed."

"Did my mother ever talk about my father to you, Maddie?"

She glanced at her watch and squirmed in her chair. "I need to get to work, Miss Ellie, so I can get home before the storm. All you need to know is that your mama never regretted her decision to keep you. She loved you with her whole heart, no matter how weak it was."

"Just one last question." Ellie propped her elbows on the table and laced her fingers together. "I've spent a lot of time and money in an effort to remember my past. My therapist is convinced a traumatic event happened to me here that made me block out those memories. Do you have any idea what that might have been?"

A flash of anger crossed Maddie's face. "What good's gonna come from drudging up the past?"

Ellie forced her voice to remain calm. "A lot of good, actually. How can I face my future until I've dealt with my past?"

Bracing herself against the table, Maddie slowly rose to her feet. "You need to somehow find a way. Trust me when I tell you, you're better off not remembering those years."

Ellie jumped up, nearly knocking her chair over. "So you admit something bad happened to me here?"

"I ain't saying nothing more. Now, if you'll excuse me, I'll get on with my day." The speed with which the old housekeeper exited her studio left little doubt in Ellie's mind that Maddie knew more than she was willing to say.

CHAPTER TWELVE
ELLIE

THE LOUD CLANGING of the door knocker startled Ellie a few minutes past five. Maddie had long since left, and she'd been in her studio for most of the afternoon organizing her art supplies. *Who could that be?* she wondered. *Surely everyone crazy enough to ride out the storm in Charleston is hunkered down in their homes.*

The tiny blonde at her door reminded Ellie of the captain of their cheerleading squad in high school. She was attractive and fit. Ellie guessed her to be in her late forties or early fifties.

"I come bearing gifts." The woman held up two paper shopping bags bearing a logo Ellie didn't recognize. "I'm Midge Calhoun, Bennett's wife and daughter-in-law." The woman wrinkled her pert nose. "Wait, that didn't sound right. I'm Bennett Senior's daughter-in-law and Bennett Junior's wife. My life would've been so much easier if Lucille and Bennett Senior had chosen a different name for their third born. Or at least called him Ben. His middle name is

Sebastian, so I could see why they wouldn't call him that. I'm rambling. I do that when I'm nervous."

"That's funny. I have the opposite problem. I clam up when I meet someone new." Ellie stepped out of her way. "Please come in."

Midge hesitated at the sight of the little dog sniffing at her pink-painted toenails on display in a pair of high-heeled sandals. "I'm not much on dogs."

"Don't worry. She won't bite."

"If you say so." Midge stepped over the sandbags Bennett's oldest son had dropped off earlier and teetered right on down the hall in her three-inch heels like she'd visited the house dozens of times before. She paused at the end of the hallway, looking left and right, unsure of which way to go.

"To the right, through the dining room," Ellie called and followed Midge to the kitchen.

"My friend Georgia works at Tasty Provisions, this incredible gourmet market several blocks up on East Bay that opened last spring. The owner, Heidi Butler, is Charleston's caterer du jour. When I stopped by there earlier to pick up a few things for Lucille, they were clearing out their coolers in preparation of the storm. I told her I was going to drop a casserole by your house to welcome you to town. I know it's odd timing with the storm and all, but I thought since I was already there and you were staying alone in this house… Anyway, she sent over some goodies. Georgia, not Heidi, although Heidi would've wanted you to have them, too, if she'd been there. I'm not sure where Heidi was, come to think of it. Getting her house ready for the storm, I guess. I'm sorry, I'm babbling again."

Ellie watched while Midge unloaded the disposable containers of food into the refrigerator.

"Georgia sent some of my favorites," Midge said, inspecting the labels on the containers. "Her shrimp and grits are to die for. Her pâté's not bad, either, if you like pâté. It's an acquired taste if you ask me." She closed the refrigerator door and leaned back against it. Her sparkling blue eyes grew huge as they traveled the length of Ellie's body. "Wow. You're really tall."

Ellie laughed out loud. She'd never met anyone quite like this woman. *So this is what they mean by a flibbertigibbet*, she thought.

Midge's hand shot up, palm facing out. "I know. Don't say it. I'm really short. And no, my name has nothing to do with my height. My parents meant for me to be called Madge, short for Mary Margaret, but my baby brother had trouble pronouncing Madge, so he called me Midge."

Ellie smiled, unsure of how to respond. She never would have made the correlation between her name and her height if Midge hadn't mentioned it.

Midge glanced at the clock on the ancient wall oven. "Good Lord! It's almost five thirty. I told Bennett I'd meet him at his parents' house two hours ago. Won't you come with me? Bennett Senior said he invited you to stay at their house. Trust me, they have plenty of room. And I'd love to have an ally. Calhoun family gatherings get old really quick. I already know how the evening will play out. The men will retreat to Senior's study to smoke cigars, drink beer, and watch sports on TV. Tonight is Monday, so they'll be watching football, at least until the power goes out. My sisters-in-law are only capable of being nice for one glass of wine. After that, they'll start picking on me and then on each other. As for their children... well, them apples didn't fall far from them trees, if you know what I mean. By the end of the night, the whole family will be squabbling, except the men, who will still be watching sports, and Lucille, who will be sequestered in her bedroom. Oh well." She raised her arms and let them fall, her hands slapping her thighs. "There's always plenty to eat and drink, at least. Are you sure you won't come with me?"

Ellie had to work hard to keep a straight face. "I appreciate the offer, but I'm fine here, Midge. Really I am."

Midge produced a business card from the small shoulder bag she wore across her body. "Call me if you change your mind. I'll send my Bennett over to pick you up."

Ellie skimmed the card. "I see you're a realtor."

"Yep. Bennett and I own a small boutique firm. We handle both commercial and residential properties, if you ever find yourself in need of either."

"That's good to know," Ellie said, pocketing the card. "I'm actually thinking of selling this house. It's too much for me."

"We would certainly be interested in talking to you." Midge looked around as she wandered back through the dining room to the center hallway. "I'll be honest with you, though. You'll have to spruce it up before you can put it on the market. Houses on the Battery typically sell like hot potatoes, but no one will make an offer on this one in its current condition. This place is seriously gloomy."

"Well, yeah! Because the storm shutters are closed," Ellie said, surprised at her defensive tone. Was she growing attached to this creepy old mansion?

"Honey, no amount of daylight will make these furnishings look any better." She dragged her fingers across the top of the ornate oak sideboard. "I bet this piece was used as an altar in the first Church of England."

Once again, Ellie burst out laughing. She appreciated this woman's honesty and unique sense of humor. "You could very well be right about that. I agree that none of my grandmother's things are very attractive, but surely some of these pieces are valuable."

"How much value does an object have when it doesn't bring you pleasure?" Midge said over her shoulder as she moved down the hall toward the door.

"You make a valid point."

When she reached the door, Midge turned to face Ellie. "Let's get through the hurricane first, and then I'd be happy to help you either as a realtor or as a friend."

"I'd like that." This tiny woman with her spunky personality brought a smile to Ellie's face. She held the door open for Midge. "And thank you for bringing over the food. Stay safe."

She stood in the doorway watching Midge make her way down the sidewalk. She stumbled when a big gust of wind nearly blew her off her high heels, but she quickly righted herself.

Ellie shook her head. She thought her new friend seemed nice, but maybe she should consider drinking a little less caffeine.

CHAPTER THIRTEEN
ELLIE

THE SKY WAS heavy with moisture-laden clouds, but it had not yet begun to rain. Ellie looked down at her dog. "What say we stretch our legs before the storm sets in?" Pixie wagged her tail in response. "Let me get my raincoat, and we'll go to the park."

Ellie dashed up the stairs. She smoothed her hair back into a ponytail, pulled a Nike baseball cap over her strawberry-blonde head, and slipped her raincoat on over her cotton sweater and jeans. She grabbed Pixie's leash from her studio, and they ran across the street to the park. With her head tucked against the wind, they race-walked the length of the park twice. When Pixie begged for more, they made a third trip up and down the dirt path. They were starting back toward home when Ellie spotted a golden retriever bounding toward them and its owner jogging along beside him. As they drew near, she recognized the dog's owner as Julian Hagood, the man she'd met at the gallery opening three nights ago.

"This place is deserted," Ellie shouted over the wind as

they approached. "I was beginning to think I was the only one left in town."

He stopped jogging and bent over, hands on knees, to catch his breath. "There are plenty of people still in town—smart people hunkered down in their homes awaiting the storm. You and I are the only ones crazy enough to be out in this weather."

The dogs performed a waltz as they greeted each other. When Julian gave her cheek a peck, she caught a whiff of his manly scent—an expensive cologne she couldn't identify mixed with a hint of sweat—that made her want to bury her face in his neck.

Whoa, Ellie! Remember, you've sworn off men, warned her voice of reason.

No harm in an innocent flirtation! responded the voice that controlled the nether regions of her body.

"I was just thinking about you." He pointed across the street at her house. "I saw the tarp on your roof and was wondering if you decided to stay."

"For better or worse, here I am," she said, her arms akimbo. "I'm all set for Armageddon. I have sandbags at my doors and the hurricane shutters are closed tight. I must say, though, not being able to see out of the windows is unsettling."

"I know what you mean," he said with a nod. "But they serve a purpose. You'll be glad you have them when the wind reaches a hundred miles an hour and trees begin to fall."

His intense gaze made her squirm, and she looked away.

He leaned over and rubbed Pixie's ears. "What's your dog's name?"

"Pixie," Ellie answered. "And yours? I've never seen a golden retriever with such a white coat."

"Mills, named after the renowned architect Robert Mills."
Ellie shook her head. "Never heard of him."

"He's most famous for designing the Washington Monument. He's originally from Charleston, graduated from our very own College of Charleston." When she stared at him with her mouth agape, he added, "I'm an architect. I'm not in the same league as Mills, but I've designed a noteworthy home or two. Mostly I renovate historic homes. I have a passion for protecting the integrity of our antebellum houses while modernizing them to meet the needs of the owners' lifestyles."

Ellie cast her eyes toward the dark skies. A heavenly being had dropped this man at her doorstep. Well... if not her doorstep, then just across the street from the antebellum house she wanted to modernize to meet her needs.

"When can you start? Because, Mr. Hagood, do I ever have a project for you."

He chuckled. "What'd you have in mind?"

"A kitchen expansion for starters."

"I've studied the architecture of most of these homes, but I've never been inside yours," he said. "I'd love to see it sometime."

As the words left his lips, the skies opened up and a gust of wind forced Ellie to grab hold of her hat. "Is now too soon for a tour?"

"I think now is an ideal time," he said, pulling his hood over his head. He clapped his hands, and both dogs flew to his side. "Come here, Pip-squeak." He snatched Pixie up, tucking her inside his rain jacket, and they took off running across the street, up her sidewalk, and onto her porch. They fell against the side of the house, gasping for air. Their clothes, including their raincoats, were soaked through to their skin.

"We were tempting fate by staying out so long in this weather." He pulled his phone out of his jacket pocket. "At least my phone didn't get wet." He accessed his radar app. "I hope you're in the mood for company, because it doesn't look like I'm going anywhere anytime soon."

"You're welcome to stay as long as you like," she said, removing her key from under the mat. "But you might change your mind when you see inside."

"Are you kidding me? I'm in love already," he said, running his palm along the hand-carved columns that flanked the massive front door.

They stepped over the sandbags and stood just inside the door, dripping onto the floors.

His eyes took in everything at once as they entered the house. "Wow! And here I thought Dracula's Castle was in Transylvania."

"Is it really that bad?" she asked in a wounded voice.

"You seem like a stylish woman. I'm sure I don't need to tell you that the furnishings need updating, but the house has great bones. I'd explore if not for…" He eyed the puddle of water collecting on the floor around him.

"Don't move! I'll get some towels." Ellie ran upstairs to the linen closet and returned with an armful of towels.

They dried their dogs as best they could, but the stench of wet dog fur was already permeating the air.

She handed Julian Pixie's wadded-up towel. "The laundry room is at the end of the hall. Put your clothes in the dryer, and I'll see if I can find you some clothes to wear."

With the dogs at his side, Julian headed down the hall to the laundry room. Upstairs in her room, Ellie changed into a dry pair of jeans, a gray T-shirt, and a pale-pink hoodie. She combed and towel-dried her hair and smeared clear gloss over her lips. She grabbed her robe from the hook on the bathroom door and went downstairs to the laundry room. Julian was standing beside the dryer in his boxers, which clung to his firm rear end. Covering her eyes with one hand, she thrust the robe at him with the other. "This is the best I can do. Sorry about the color."

"Don't apologize. I personally think that pink rocks!"

She smiled, her hand still covering her eyes. Not only was the robe pink, it was hot pink. And velour. Most men she knew would refuse to wear it.

She snapped her fingers at the dogs. "Come on, you two. Let's get you some water."

She led the dogs to the kitchen, where Julian joined her a few minutes later. She bit down on her lower lip to keep from laughing at the sight of him in her robe, although she had to admit she found his muscular calves sexy.

"Go ahead, laugh. Don't hold back for my sake," he said to Ellie, and then turned to his dog, who was staring up at him with his tail wagging. "What're you looking at?"

"The dryer is one of the newer appliances in this house. Vintage 1970. If the power doesn't go out, your clothes should be ready by the time we finish our tour." Ellie opened a cabinet and retrieved two of the stemless wineglasses she'd brought from California. "Let's start with the kitchen since we're already here. Can I offer you a glass of wine? I have red and white."

"Wine would be great. I'll have whatever you're having."

She uncorked a bottle of pinot noir and poured two glasses. She handed him a glass and held hers out to him. "Cheers!"

He clinked her glass. "Here's to surviving Hurricane

Lorene." He took a gulp of wine and set his glass on the counter. "Tell me what you're thinking in terms of a renovation. This kitchen could certainly use a makeover."

"I'm thinking of adding on. You can see for yourself how tiny the space is."

He circled the small kitchen as he explored the space. He paced back and forth several times in the butler's pantry, peeked inside Maddie's closet, and stood in front of the back door for several long minutes staring through the glass panes. "If you go out the back here twenty feet, you'd have plenty of room for a nice-size work space and an eat-in area. You could incorporate the butler's pantry if you wanted, but you'd have plenty of room in the new addition without it. Personally, I find butler's pantries charming."

"Why on earth would I want to keep the butler's pantry? That space is awkward and serves no purpose except housing china, crystal, and glassware I never plan to use."

"Holding on to generations of Pringle family heirloom silver, china, and crystal may not be of interest to you, but I can promise you, you'll miss the storage space if you take it out, especially if you like to entertain. Most of my clients convert a portion of their butler's pantry to a wet bar of some sort. If you decided to keep it, I would update the cabinetry and create a pouring station with a sink and ice maker or wine cooler or both."

"Hmm." Ellie tilted her head to the side as she considered his suggestion. "On the other hand, if I tore out the butler's pantry, I could put the wet bar over there." She waved her arm at the far corner of the room.

"That works, too. The point is, you have plenty of options to modernize this space."

"Do you think it would be possible to have a banquette table and bench seats built into a wall of windows in the new area?"

Julian reached for the pen and notepad on the counter, the one she used to make out her grocery lists. The pen flew across the pad as he drew. He spun the notepad around and slid it across the counter to her. "You mean something like this?"

She picked up the notepad and studied the elevation he'd drawn. "You're very talented, Julian, as an architect and an artist. This is exactly what I had in mind."

"That's a popular configuration these days. My clients like to bring the outdoors inside as much as possible." Wineglass in hand, he walked up and down the back hallway between the kitchen and her studio. "You'll want to reconfigure this area in here. What do you call that room by the way?" He swept his hand in the direction of her studio. "I hope you don't mind, I stuck my head in there while you were upstairs. I'm guessing those furnishings are yours, since they look nothing like the rest of the house."

Ellie smiled. "That's my stuff from California. For now, I'm using it as my studio. I haven't decided what purpose it will serve going forward."

"So you *are* an artist. I noticed the easels."

Ellie felt her face flush. "I hope you didn't look too closely at the paintings on the easels. One is an image I need to get out of my head, and the other I just started."

He offered her a warm smile. "I'm sure your work is wonderful, Ellie. But I didn't go in. I didn't want to drip water all over your sisal rug."

She wasn't embarrassed about her work. She just wasn't

ready to share the magnolia watercolor yet. The painting elicited such strong emotions for her. At a glance, it was nothing more than a simple painting of a magnolia tree. And not a very good one. The observer had to look closely to see the little girl with her doll baby hiding behind the thick branches.

She followed Julian back to the butler's pantry. "This was the exterior wall in the original house," he said as he inspected the thickness of the dining room doorjamb. "Whoever added the kitchen did a crappy job."

"I'm not following you. Where was the original kitchen?"

"In a separate building out behind the house. Prior to the Civil War, slaves cooked all the meals for the homeowner and his family over an open fireplace. Outhouses were built to keep the cooking smells and heat away from the main house. Most of these homes had a whole village of outhouses. In addition to the kitchen, they had a washhouse and a carriage house that would've served as a livery and the slaves' quarters. Not to mention sheds to house the gardening equipment. Many of these kitchens and carriage houses were destroyed in the great earthquake of 1886. Of those that still exist, some have been attached to the main houses, while others have been converted into small homes." As he spoke, his amber eyes were alive with excitement over what was undoubtedly his life's passion.

"That's fascinating, Julian. You are a real expert. I have so much to learn about this area."

"I'm glad to hear your enthusiasm. So many folks today deem our cultural heritage as politically incorrect."

Ellie wrinkled her brow. "I don't understand. We can't change history. Why not learn from the mistakes our forefathers made?"

"I agree with you," he said, his face serious. "If only everyone felt that way."

She knocked on the dining room wall. "So if this was the exterior wall, where would the back door have been?"

"Where the laundry room is now. Having a center hallway with doors on either end helped circulate the air back before the invention of air-conditioning. I can almost smell the salty air flowing through the hallway off the harbor on a cool day."

Ellie closed her eyes and imagined herself descending the staircase in a hoop skirt while Julian, dressed in his three-piece suit, waited at the door to take her for a carriage ride. *Getting ahead of ourselves now, aren't we, Ellie?* She opened her eyes again and shook off her daydream.

*

Ellie refilled their wineglasses, and they toured the rest of the downstairs, stopping at each room in turn, starting with the dining room and working their way clockwise. She saw the house in a whole new light through Julian's eyes. He pointed out things she either hadn't noticed or hadn't known, like the Waterford chandelier in the dining room, the rows of crown molding, and the intricate carvings on the mantelpieces. He referred to the living room as the drawing room and the porches as piazzas. He was impressed by what he thought was cypress paneling in the library and suggested ways to lighten up the room by using neutral tones and putting an animal-print rug on the floor.

"You sound like a decorator instead of an architect," Ellie teased.

He laughed. "It's a fine line sometimes. My clients get so used to me making decisions for them, oftentimes they don't know when to stop. I saw what you did with your studio. You have great taste, Ellie. You should clear out all of Count Dracula's stuff and breathe fresh life into the other rooms."

"How would I go about doing that? I put my bedroom furniture in the attic. Everything else from my tiny apartment in San Francisco is in my studio. If I donated all my grandmother's things to Goodwill, I'd have to start over with nothing."

"Would that be such a bad thing? But I wouldn't donate it to Goodwill—not until you learn the value of your grandmother's possessions. I have a friend who owns an antique store on King Street. I'll get him over here after the storm. He'll make you an offer on anything he's interested in and make suggestions on how to get rid of the rest. If you're looking for a designer, I've worked on a couple of projects with Jackie Hart of JSH Designs. She's good at blending the old with the new. I'd be happy to introduce you."

"I'd like that." Ellie nodded her head with enthusiasm. Her luck was changing. In the course of a stormy afternoon, not only had she made two new friends, she'd located a realtor, an architect, an antiques dealer, and a decorator. Maybe she would survive in Charleston after all.

He asked to see the master bedroom and bolted up the stairs before she could stop him. "Wait! Where are you going?" She rushed to catch up with him with the dogs scrambling after her.

At the top of the stairs, he turned right and barged into her grandmother's room.

"You're wasting your time in here, Julian. It's just more of the same gloominess." She propped herself against the door to prevent it from closing on him. The dogs stood on the threshold with their fur raised in lines down their backs.

Julian circled the room and opened the door to the bathroom. "This is one of the biggest masters I've seen in a house from this era. Are you sleeping in here?"

She shook her head. "Not while my grandmother's spirit is still here."

"Now, Ellie." He cocked his head to the side, reminding her of a fish wife with his hairy arms and legs sticking out from her pink bathrobe. "Are you saying you believe in ghosts?"

A week ago, before some otherworldly force had locked her in this room, she would have thought the idea preposterous. "Look at them." She pointed at Mills and Pixie, their fur still standing to attention. Mills let out a little woof. "See! Your dog just growled at the room."

"That wasn't a growl. That was a woof." He looked down at the dogs and then up at her. "Does your grandmother's spirit have anything to do with why you're standing sentry in front of the door?"

"You can make fun of me all you want, but on my first day here, I got locked in this room." She gripped the doorknob. "Even though there's no locking mechanism on this knob.

"Every time I open this door, I come back five minutes later to find it closed." His smile grew wider, his smirk more annoying, as she continued to talk. "According to my housekeeper, the Gullah people believe a spirit can't rest until it passes into the afterworld. Maddie worked for my grandmother for forty years. She knew her better than anyone. She says my grandmother needs to know it's okay for her to pass over, or whatever it is spirits do, and that keeping the door open will help her realize that."

With a flippant shrug, he said, "Then why not just take the door off its hinges?"

"I can't do that." She shivered and drew her hoodie tighter around her. "If you remove the door, my grandmother's spirit will be free to roam the house."

"Isn't that what you want?"

"I want her spirit out of the house, not roaming around inside, floating over me while I'm sleeping." She realized how ridiculous she sounded. Besides, she'd do just about anything to get rid of her grandmother's spirit. "How hard is it to remove the door?"

"It will take less than a minute if you'll get me a flathead screwdriver and a hammer."

Ellie didn't budge. "Maybe we should wait until after the storm. Her spirit might not be able to exit the house with the hurricane shutters closed."

His arm shot out with his pointer finger aimed at the stairs. "Go."

She hung her head and did as she was told. When she returned, Julian was squatting down talking to the dogs in a soothing voice and stroking their fur. Mills and Pixie relaxed and plopped down with their bellies flat against the floor. They watched with their muzzles resting on their front paws as Julian hammered the pins out of the hinges and removed the heavy door from its frame. He wrestled the door to the empty bedroom across the hall and returned to admire his handiwork.

"Tell me the truth, Julian," she said as they stood looking into her grandmother's room. "You've lived in Charleston all your life. Do you not believe in ghosts?"

"I've experienced some strange phenomena in my day. Most of the houses in historic downtown date back to before the Civil War. We're talking generations of interesting characters and domineering figures, many from the same families, living and dying in these homes. It stands to reason that some of their spirits may linger."

"I'd be willing to bet that none of those domineering figures ruled a household like my grandmother. And now you've set her spirit free to come after me in my sleep."

CHAPTER FOURTEEN
ELLIE

WHILE THEY WAITED for his clothes to finish drying, Julian and Ellie nibbled on pâté and watched the coverage of the storm on the local news channel. The circular mob of green and yellow was rotating on the radar in a definitive path toward the South Carolina coast.

Julian explained that the worst of the storm would hit at low tide around midnight. "Which means the flooding won't be too bad."

Knowledgeable on a variety of subjects, Julian was more worldly than Jake. She'd learned everything there was to know about her former lover during their first month together. Except, of course, that he was married with children living in the next state up.

When the dryer buzzer sounded, he drained the last of the wine from his glass. "That's my signal to leave."

"So soon? I have all this food. I was hoping you'd stay for dinner. If you don't like the color"—she tugged on the sleeve of her robe—"I have a floral one upstairs you can wear instead."

He wrapped his arms around himself. "I like this one, thank you very much. It's cozy and warm. I'm a real man. I can wear pink." He stared down at Mills. "I'd love to stay for dinner, but I really need to feed this one before he starts gnawing at the pedestals on your dining room table."

Ellie scratched the golden retriever between his ears. "Pixie would be happy to share some of her food with her new friend."

"You mean kibble for pip-squeaks? He'd eat the whole bag in one go." He left the room and returned a few minutes later fully dressed. "I need to check on my house anyway."

"Of course you do." She walked with him down the hall to the front door. As he was putting on his raincoat, she risked a glance toward the stairs, expecting to see her grandmother's ghost floating toward her.

Julian pinched her chin. "Don't worry, pretty lady. There's no such thing as ghosts." He pulled his hood over his head and took off down the sidewalk with Mills at his side.

Ellie closed and locked the door. She looked down at her dog, who stared back at her with the saddest eyes she'd ever seen. "I know, little girl. I wanted them to stay, too." She picked her dog up and held her close. "After we eat dinner, we'll find a way to entertain ourselves." Without Wi-Fi, her choices were limited. She couldn't watch Netflix on her iPad or download a book to her Kindle app. "Maddie brought in plenty of wood. Maybe we'll build a fire in the library. It can't be that hard, right? We can always Google best practices for lighting a fire." Her shoulders slumped. "Or not. We'll just have to wing it on our own."

Ellie placed her casserole in the oven, preferring a slow reheat to the microwave. She was scooping penne with vodka sauce onto a plate forty-five minutes later when someone pounded on the front door.

Who in the world is out in this weather? she thought as she hurried to the door.

She was surprised to see Julian on her front porch, dressed like a sailor in head-to-toe yellow foul weather gear. Mills shivered beside him, and torrents of rain blew sideways behind them. When a gray yard-size trash can bounced down the street, she grabbed him by the arm. "Get in here," she said, and yanked him inside. She closed the door against the stormy night. "What're you doing here?"

"You forgot to give me your number." Her face scrunched up in confusion, and he added, "For the antiques dealer."

"I'm pretty sure that could've waited, Julian." She planted her fists on her hips, pretending to be cross, but secretly she was pleased, not only because she wanted to be with him but because she didn't want to be alone in the house during a hurricane with her grandmother's spirit on the loose.

"I brought a change of clothes with me," he said, holding up a black trash bag. "Although, I think my sailor suit kept these dry." He slipped off his coat and stepped out of his bibs. He felt his plaid cotton shirt and jeans. "Yep. All dry." He removed a towel from the bag, draped it across his dog, and then stuck his hand in the bag once again. "For you." He handed her a bottle of liquor. "Consider it a housewarming gift."

She read the label on the cognac bottle. "I'm impressed. You brought the good stuff."

He dropped his bag to the floor beside the door. "We're having a hurricane party. The situation calls for the best."

"I applaud your enthusiasm." She set the cognac bottle on the Church of England altar. "I was just getting dinner ready. Are you hungry?"

He patted his belly. "Starving."

"In that case, do you mind starting a fire in the library while I fix our plates?"

He rubbed his hands together like a little boy on his first camping trip with his father. "I'm on it."

*

Forty-five minutes later, Julian and Ellie abandoned their empty plates on the coffee table beside them and sank deep into the velvet cushions at opposite ends of the sofa. The dogs napped on the floor in front of the crackling fire while the wind howled outside the shuttered windows.

"You realize I'm going to have to spend the night," Julian said.

She cut her eyes at him without moving her head. "You can sleep in my grandmother's bed."

"No thanks." He closed his eyes and placed his folded hands in his lap. "I'm plenty comfortable right here."

They lounged in a food coma until Pixie stirred twenty minutes later. She stretched her front legs and wandered over to Ellie, sniffing at her right hand that was dangling off the side of the sofa.

Julian cracked an eyelid at Pixie. "Bigger dogs have bigger bladders. You should consider that the next time you shop for a pet."

Ellie swung her legs over the side of the sofa and sat up. "I can put paper down in the kitchen for Pixie. That won't work for your large dog."

"It would work, but Mills has better manners than that." Julian rolled off the sofa. "Let's open the front door for them and see what they do."

As it turned out, Pixie followed Mills's lead. They ran to the edge of the porch, squatted to do their business, and scampered back inside to the library, resuming their positions in front of the fire. Julian took their dirty plates to the kitchen while Ellie went upstairs for bedding. She gathered all the duvets, blankets, and pillows she could carry. She had no intention of sleeping upstairs alone with her grandmother's spirit floating around and the hurricane wailing like a banshee outside.

They sipped cognac and talked well into the night. Julian confided in Ellie about his ex-wife who had come home from her nursing job at MUSC three years ago and announced she was taking their daughter and moving to Spartanburg, about as far away as she could get from Charleston but still be in the state of South Carolina in order to abide by custody laws. "She totally blindsided me," he said. "I thought everything was fine in our marriage. I was happy. I assumed she was as well. She said she no longer loved me and she needed a change. I wish she'd at least given our marriage a chance, but she refused to consider seeing a marriage counselor. Weekends twice a month with a seven-year-old isn't enough. At least not for me. We used to be close. Now our relationship feels strained. I sense her mother may be feeding Katie some unflattering lies about me."

He reached for the bottle on the coffee table and poured each of them another finger of cognac. "It's your turn to share. Tell me your deepest, darkest secret."

"If only I could remember it." She spoke of her memory loss and her mother's diaries. "Something bad happened to me in this house when I was a child. I know it, like I know my name is Ellie Pringle. A have a strong hunch there are more of my mother's diaries somewhere in this house that will provide the answers I'm looking for."

"And you have no idea what that something might have been? I'm a good listener, if you want to talk about it."

Ellie smiled at him. "I sense that about you, actually." Her expression turned serious. "I'll tell you about it sometime, but not tonight. I'd hate to ruin a perfectly good hurricane party."

Tipsy from the cognac, they snuggled together under a mound of blankets with him spooning her from behind. When she opened her eyes six hours later, Julian and the dogs were gone. She heard the soft murmur of voices on Bennett's portable TV from down the hall and smelled the faint aroma of coffee brewing. She folded the bed covers into a neat pile on the sofa. She was headed toward the kitchen when Julian appeared in the doorway.

"Coffee?" He held out a steaming mug. "I took the liberty of adding cream and sugar. You seem like a super sweet girl to me."

She took the mug from him. "That's bad, Julian," she said in response to his cheesy remark.

"I guess I'm a little rusty. I haven't tried to pick up a girl since my college days."

She would let him pick her up any day, corny lines and all.

The dogs, reeking of wet fur, appeared at his side. "I take it they've been out."

"I had to drag them. Pip-squeak was too afraid to venture into the yard. This time she pooped on the porch. Lucky for you, her turd was so lightweight, the wind blew it away."

Ellie rolled her eyes at him. "I can't believe we haven't lost power yet."

"Shh!" he said, bringing his fingers to his lips. "Don't say it. Most of Charleston is without."

"Are the streets flooded?" she asked.

"Not too bad." He stepped out of her way and gestured toward the front door. "See for yourself."

They were nearing the door when the sound of dripping water coming from somewhere upstairs stopped her in her tracks. "Do you hear that?"

He narrowed his eyes and listened. "That's not good." He handed her his mug, yanked the door open, and ran barefoot out into the yard. She stood in the doorway, holding both coffee mugs, watching him. He leaned into the wind as he shielded his eyes and stared up at the house. She noticed a small river flowing down South Battery Street behind him.

"The tarp has blown back," he called to her, his voice barely audible over the roar of the wind. "Get every bucket you can find and meet me in the attic." He darted back into the house and up the stairs.

Ellie deposited the coffee mugs on the Church of England altar on her way to the laundry. She searched all the cabinets and closets in there and in the kitchen. The cooler Bennett had dropped off and the two Maddie had brought in from the garage were the only suitable containers she could find for water collecting. She dragged them up the stairs to the attic. The rain was pouring in through leaks in the roof and then seeping through the ceiling in her grandmother's bedroom. For the next hour and a half, they ran up and down the stairs, emptying and repositioning the buckets until the flow was finally under control.

Exhausted, she collapsed on a nearby steamer trunk. "I blame this on you, Julian. You unleashed my grandmother's spirit on us by removing her door."

He kneed her to move over so as to make room for him on the trunk. "Are you suggesting your grandmother is responsible for the tarp blowing off?"

Feeling herself near tears, she propped her elbows on her knees and buried her face in her hands. "I know it sounds twisted. I didn't believe in ghosts until I came here. Why'd my grandmother have to drag me into it? She should've donated this money pit to the Charleston Historical Society and called it a day."

He nudged her with his shoulder. "Are we feeling sorry for ourselves?"

"You're damn right I'm feeling sorry for myself." She swiped at her eyes with the back of her hand. "Eleanor Pringle totally disrupted my life. I moved all the way across the country to live in a house that's falling down around me and haunted by ghosts. I'm creeped out by all her possessions, and I've become obsessed with remembering my past when I'm clearly better off not knowing what happened to me here."

"Look." He rubbed circles on her back between her shoulder blades. "You've just made a drastic change in your life. It's only natural for you to feel overwhelmed. Give yourself some time to adjust. I agree, there is an enormous amount of work that needs to be done to this house, but I can help you with all that."

She sniffled. "Would you?"

He pulled her close to him. "Of course I will. You're a super sweet girl." He kissed her on the side of the head. "You need a friend, and I enjoy your company. I'm even growing attached to Pip-squeak. But don't tell anyone I admitted that."

Tears blurred her vision as she stared down at her lap. She noticed a brass plate on the top of the steamer trunk and ran her fingers across the engraved initials—A. L. P. She leaped to her feet. "Wait a minute! What are we sitting on?" She took him by the arm and hauled him off the trunk.

"An old trunk, like the one I took to camp every summer," Julian said.

"Those are my mother's initials." She pointed to the brass plate. "Maybe her diaries are in here." She knelt down in front of the trunk and fidgeted with the lock. "No telling where the key is."

Removing a pocketknife from his pocket, he knelt down beside her. "I can pry it open, but it might ruin the lock."

"The lock is the least of my concerns," she said, and moved out of his way.

Julian jimmied the lock open and lifted the lid. Ellie's heart sank when she saw the party dresses stuffed inside— elaborate frocks made of taffeta, satin, and velvet. She dug through the dresses, tossing them in a heap on the attic floor beside the trunk. When she reached the bottom, she fell back on her rear end. "Nothing."

Julian tilted his head from side to side as he scrutinized the trunk from different angles. "Maybe not. It looks like the trunk might have a false bottom." Leaning over, he reached inside and pried free the board that served as the fake bottom. "Bingo!"

Ellie peered inside the trunk. Scattered across the bottom were six leather-bound journals.

CHAPTER FIFTEEN
ASHTON

THE TRAIN RIDE south seemed endless. The other passengers were tucked away for the night in their berths, but I couldn't sleep for worrying over how Mother would react to my predicament. Pacing up and down the aisles did little to alleviate my anxiety, and the six-hour delay at Union Station in Washington only added to my angst. When we finally arrived in Charleston, I took a taxi from the train station and got home just as my mother was sitting down to dinner in the dining room.

She barely glanced in my direction when I entered the room. "Well now. Look what the cat drug in."

"It's nice to see you, too, Mother." I'd learned from years of experience that the direct approach was the best approach with her. Pulling a chair up to the table beside her, I placed my hands on the table and laced my fingers together. "I know how much you appreciate it when people are up front with you, so I'll come right out and tell you why I'm here. I'm pregnant, Mother—too far along to have an abortion, not that I would even consider it if it were an option. If you'll allow me to stay here until the baby comes, I plan to put it up for adoption and return to my life in New York. I'll be out of your hair for good."

Mother dropped her fork to her plate with a clatter so loud it made me tremble all over. Her eyes bore into mine. "So you've come running home to me with your tail between your legs and a baby in your belly. Who and where is the father?"

I told her the father is no longer a part of my life, that we had a relationship but it is over, and that is all she needs to know. I was reassured by the strength in my voice. I'd grown a backbone during my time in New York.

"Humph. If you'd married James Middleton like you were meant to, we'd be planning your baby shower, not hiding in shame. And hide you will. I won't have you out on the streets for everyone in Charleston to see your womb swelling from the bastard growing inside it. If word about this gets out, it will spread like wildfire. Flaunting your half-naked body in those raunchy fashion magazines has earned you celebrity status around here. I've had to cut down on the number of social engagements I attend because your starstruck fans are constantly approaching me. One young woman had the audacity to ask me for my autograph."

"Most mothers would be proud of my success."

"Success!" My mother brought her fist down on the table, rattling her plate. "You've made a mess of your life and brought that mess home for me to deal with. You call that a success?"

I sat up taller in my chair. "In the past three years, I've appeared on the covers of every major New York fashion magazine. Yes, Mother, I call that a success."

"I think your behavior is deplorable. You've cheapened yourself. No self-respecting man will ever marry you now." She folded her linen napkin, placed it on her plate, and rose from the table. "If you want to remain in my house, we'll discuss in the morning the rules by which you'll live here."

But Mother had already left for church by the time I woke up the next morning. Homesick for New York, I walked north to Broad Street and west until I located a newspaper stand. I purchased a *New York Times* and strolled the long way back to the Battery, enjoying the fragrant spring air. My mother was waiting for me at the front door when I arrived home, her black pillbox hat still perched on her head and her handbag dangling from her arm. "I told you not to leave this house."

Holding the paper out as evidence, I explained that I'd only gone over to Broad Street for a newspaper.

"When I said don't leave this house, I meant don't walk to the end of the sidewalk. You may go out in the back garden, and that's it."

I rolled my eyes at her. "Geez, Mother, don't you think you're overreacting?"

I did not see the blow coming when she hauled off and smacked me across the face. My hand flew to my cheek. Out of the corner of my eye, I saw Maddie, the young black maid Mother had hired in my absence, peeking at us from around the doorway to the dining room.

"Don't you roll your eyes at me, young lady," Mother said, wagging her finger in my face. "You will abide by my rules while you're living in my house, or you will leave." She grabbed my father's jogging stick from the umbrella stand in the corner of the hall and chased me to the stairs with it.

My hand still pressed to my cheek, I went to my room,

where I stayed for the rest of the day. Someone had stripped my room of every trace of my past life. Gone were the clothes from my closets and drawers. Gone were the ribbons and trophies I'd won showing horses and sailing in regattas. All my framed photographs of friends, including the only picture I owned of my father, had disappeared. The collection of black-and-white images I'd photographed and matted in my photography class in college had been taken off the walls. The white eyelet comforter and chintz skirt of lavender bouquets that had once adorned my bed had been replaced with a set of scratchy sheets and a thin cotton blanket. The only sign that my room had ever been inhabited was a flimsy cardboard box stuffed full of toys and tucked away at the back of my closet.

When I asked Mother about my things over dinner, she told me that since I'd left town without so much as a note or a goodbye she assumed I no longer wanted them and gave them away to the Salvation Army.

Mother has always been strict, but she's never hit me before. She changed while I was in New York. Her stare has grown colder and her demands more rigid. Her mistrust of the world now borders on paranoia. Things have worsened in the days, weeks, and months since I got home. Mother rules over this household with dictatorial superiority. Dead bolts have appeared on the doors downstairs, and the ones leading to the second-floor piazza have been permanently sealed. The security system she had installed is controlled by a small silver key, which she wears on a red satin ribbon around her neck. She's stopped going out altogether, preferring instead to watch over me like the warden on a jailhouse block.

The grim reality of my new existence has set in. Life crawls by for me upstairs in my spartan room, which has become my refuge. I bide my time by doing as I'm told and staying out of Mother's way as much as possible. I take my meals up here unless I'm summoned to the dining room for another one of Mother's many lectures. I yearn for my glamorous life in New York. I miss Louisa, and God help me, I miss Abbott something terrible. I keep the newspaper article announcing his job with Warner Brothers Studio hidden beneath my mattress as a reminder of his betrayal. Every time I look at it, seeing the photo of him with his arm around another woman brings on a torrent of fresh tears. To pass the time, I write letters to Abbott I'll never mail and read whatever my mother brings home from the library—nonfiction books, classics, and the occasional mystery. Romance novels are out of the question, of course. "No smut for the slut," Mother said to me one day.

The fear of being hit with my father's jogging stick, now an appendage of Mother's arm, keeps the staff in line. But sympathetic to my situation, they contribute what little they dare to make my life more tolerable. Maddie brings in fresh flowers every morning: a single stem from the rose garden in a sterling bud vase or a small bouquet of blue hydrangeas in a crystal container. And every afternoon, Sally Bell delivers my tea tray piled high with delicate sweet cakes and finger sandwiches. Abraham lugged an old chaise lounge and floor lamp down from the attic for me and positioned them in the corner by the window. I read into the wee hours of the morning with the night air, fragrant with the citrusy, sweet scent of magnolia blossoms, drifting through the open window. I'm allowed to keep my bedroom window open, because, without the aid of a ladder, I have no means of escaping. Why would I escape when I have nowhere to go?

Mother refuses to let me see a doctor. She's hired a midwife instead, who she claims is capable of getting the job done. A midwife is fine by me. I like Jeanette Lane quite a lot. She's the grandmother type with gray hair, plump cheeks, and a calm manner of speaking. Jeanette scored extra brownie points with me when she asked Mother to wait out in the hall during the examination. She declared the baby's heartbeat strong and me fit as a fiddle. She gave me a bottle of prenatal vitamins and a chocolate eclair she brought from a bakery on Broad Street.

Subsequent checkups followed a similar pattern until her fourth visit in June when I was seven months along.

"Your mother tells me you're considering giving the baby up for adoption. I can make the arrangements for you, if you're absolutely certain this is what you want." Jeanette sat down on the edge of the mattress beside me. "You know, Ashton, no one can make you give away your baby. This is something you must decide for yourself."

"When I first learned I was pregnant, adoption seemed the right choice for the baby and me. But I'm not so sure anymore." I stared down at my immense body sprawled out on the bed—swollen breasts, belly the size of Mount Everest, and thighs so fleshy they rub together when I walk. I will never again fit into any of my clothes, much less appear in any fashion magazine. I placed my hand on my abdomen and felt the baby moving around. "She's an active one."

"You're convinced it's a girl," Jeanette said.

I nodded. "It sounds stupid, I know. But I've grown attached to her. I feel like I already know her. She's part of me."

Jeanette smiled. "The bond between a mother and her offspring is strong."

My throat ached with unshed tears. "I'm honestly not sure I'll be able to give her up."

Jeanette glanced toward the door where my mother was no doubt eavesdropping on the other side. "How would your mother feel about you keeping the baby?" she said, her voice a near whisper.

"She'd throw a fit like you've never seen and ship me off to Siberia. Which is why I don't plan on telling her until the baby comes."

Jeanette stroked my arm. "Promise me you won't let her force you into making a decision while you're having these reservations."

"I promise." I drew an imaginary X across my chest, just like Louisa did when she promised not to tell anyone about my pregnancy.

So far, I've managed to change the subject every time Mother mentions adoption. But I won't be able to put her off for much longer.

Jeannette removed her stethoscope from her black medical bag and lifted my maternity blouse. The lines in her face deepened as she listened to my belly.

"What's wrong?"

Jeanette shook her head and lifted a finger to silence me. For several excruciatingly long minutes, she moved the round end of the stethoscope to different parts of my abdomen. Finally, she sat back and freed the earpieces from her ears.

"What is it, Jeanette? You're scaring me!"

"Nothing's wrong, dear." She opened my file and flipped through the pages. "This explains a lot of things, actually. The weight gain and measurements—it all makes sense."

I struggled to sit up. "What makes sense, Jeanette? Tell me now."

"I'm hearing two heartbeats today."

My mouth dropped open, and my eyes grew wide. "I don't understand. How can that be?"

"I've heard of it happening before, although it's never happened to a patient of mine. It's possible for one baby to hide behind the other, sometimes all the way through until delivery." She squeezed my knee. "I dare say your decision just got a whole lot more complicated."

The door flew open, the knob banging against the wall, and in marched Mother. Jeanette rose to face her. "Congratulations, Mrs. Pringle. Your daughter is expecting twins."

CHAPTER SIXTEEN
ELLIE

ELLIE FELT HERSELF on the verge of insanity. The power had gone out as she and Julian were coming down from the attic. Without the reassuring hum of the air conditioner, the stillness of the house tap-danced on her already-frayed nerve endings. She'd barricaded her bedroom door with a chest of drawers. With the hurricane shutters blocking the windows, there was no way out. The idea was to prevent the evil spirits that tormented her from getting in. Her voice of reason warned her she was being melodramatic, but her terrified self convinced her otherwise. She'd upset her grandmother's spirit by reading her mother's diaries. "Get mad all you want, you old bat! My mother's story needs to be heard!" she screamed to the empty room.

She couldn't see her hand in front of her face in the pitch black. She'd been reading for hours by the light of Bennett's lantern. Her mother's scribble made the reading slow. The light had eventually grown dim, and then went out completely. Ellie hadn't thought to bring more batteries upstairs with her when she came to bed around eight. Julian had long since gone home. Truth be told, she wasn't sure what time he'd even left. Early afternoon was her best guess. She'd barely raised her head from the diary to tell him goodbye. She would give anything to feel his capable arms around her again. She hadn't thought to bring her cell phone upstairs with her, either. A lot of good it was doing on the kitchen counter. She was desperate to call her father, to tell him about her twin, his other child. Boy or girl, who knew? What had happened to her sibling? Where was he or she now? Was the dark-haired girl from her flashbacks her sister? Was whatever happened to her twin the traumatic event that caused her to block out those years?

Her stomach ached from hunger. She hadn't eaten anything since breakfast. Following Bennett's instructions, she'd kept the refrigerator and freezer doors closed to preserve her food. The coolers were needed in the attic, although, over the course of the afternoon, the rain had slowed to a drizzle. She'd been too preoccupied with her mother's diaries to think about eating, anyway. And what she'd learned in those diaries had stolen her appetite until now.

Ellie succumbed to her tears. She grabbed Pixie and crawled beneath the bed. She squeezed her eyes shut and buried her face in her little dog's fur. She fell into a fitful sleep plagued with angry voices, slamming doors, and the faint sound of a child sobbing. When she woke again, a beam of sunlight cast a warm glow on the floorboards in front of her. Crawling from beneath the bed, she saw a workman waving and offering a thumbs-up from the window. She nodded her head vigorously at him. *Hell yes! I want those storm shutters open.*

Manhandling the dresser out of the way, she went downstairs and out into the yard. Much to her surprise, not a cloud lingered in the periwinkle sky. Floodwaters had receded from the streets, and hordes of workmen swarmed the yards up and down the block, picking up downed tree limbs and raking up debris.

The crew leader for the roofing team approached her. "I'm disappointed to see the tarp didn't hold. Was there much damage inside?"

"The master bedroom was flooded. But it's not your fault. My grandmother never should've let her house get in such disrepair." Shielding her eyes from the sun, she stared up at the men crawling on her roof. "How long before you get it fixed?"

"There's no rain in the forecast until the weekend. We'll have all the leaks repaired by then. The whole project should be completed by midweek next week."

"Just in time for me to put the house on the market." Ellie turned her back on him and went inside for her phone.

When she discovered her battery had died during the night, she connected the phone to the battery pack Bennett had left for her. She popped a K-Cup into her Keurig but remembered the power was out. *Ugh. No coffee, either. This is shaping up to be a truly miserable day.*

She drummed her fingertips on the counter while she waited for her phone to power up. When it came back to life five minutes later, she scrolled through the missed calls and texts. Two texts were from her father, but the missed calls were all from Julian. He'd left several voice messages, each growing more concerned as the night wore on. The most recent call had come in an hour ago. In his message, he asked if he could stop by around eleven that morning with the antiques dealer.

She clicked on his number. "Ellie, thank goodness," he said when he answered. "I've been worried about you."

She sank down to the step stool, propped her elbow on the counter, and braced her forehead with her palm. "By accident, I left my phone in the kitchen when I went to bed. I was too terrified to leave my room to come get it."

"Uh-oh! Sounds like someone had a rough night."

"I learned some unsettling things from my mother's diaries. I'll tell you about them when I see you. Eleven is fine to meet with the antiques dealer. The sooner I get my grandmother's things cleared out of this house the better."

"I hear ya," he said with a chuckle. "I also left a message for my builder friend about giving you an estimate to fix the ceiling in the master. If he's available, I'll bring him along as well."

"Thank you, Julian," she said, her voice a whisper. "I really appreciate it. I'm sorry for going on and on about my problems. How did your house survive the storm?"

"This old house is built like Fort Sumter. She came through unscathed. I even have my power back."

Ellie sighed. "Lucky you."

"The local news is reporting that most of the power in the downtown area will be restored by the end of the day."

"Oh, good, a hot shower to look forward to" she said, without any enthusiasm. "I'll see you at eleven."

For the next hour, Ellie paced the kitchen floor, drinking orange juice in the absence of coffee, while she waited for Maddie to arrive. In all the talks they'd shared since Ellie had arrived in Charleston, the housekeeper had never once mentioned her twin. And Ellie was anxious to find out why. When there was still no sign of her by ten o'clock, she began to worry she'd gotten hurt or her house had been damaged in the storm. She went to the desk in the library, but her grandmother's address book wasn't in the top right-hand drawer where Maddie said it would be. She searched the rest of the drawers in the desk and then all the ones in the kitchen and her grandmother's bedroom as well.

"I'm beginning to wonder if such an address book exists," she said to Pixie, who'd been following her around from room to room. "I've certainly never seen it."

She retrieved the coolers from upstairs and loaded them up with food from the refrigerator and freezer while she waited for Julian. He arrived with his builder friend and the antiques dealer at five minutes past eleven. After a brief round of introductions, she directed the builder to the master bedroom to assess the water damage and instructed the antiques dealer to show himself around. "Make me an offer on anything you're interested in. Everything is up for grabs."

"Everything?" Evan Luna asked, standing in front of the grandfather clock with a look of admiration on his ruddy face.

"Everything," Ellie repeated. "I didn't know my grandmother, therefore I have no sentimental attachment to her possessions. And her style doesn't suit my tastes."

"I understand where you're coming from. Gothic went out several centuries ago." His beefy hand carefully opened the clock's door. "That's not to say she didn't own some valuable pieces like this one. I'll make a fair offer on anything I can sell in my store and put you in touch with a collector whose tastes aren't quite as refined." He snickered. "In other words, he'll haul off anything you don't want and give you a reasonable sum of money in exchange."

Ellie felt the tension leave her body. "That's an offer I can't refuse. And the sooner the better."

Julian went with Ellie to the kitchen. "Are you okay? You don't look so good."

She followed his gaze to the same pair of jeans and pink hoodie she'd been wearing since they got caught in the rain in the park on Monday night. "I didn't sleep well." Once again, she reached for the Keurig, and once again she remembered she didn't have electricity.

"I'm sorry." Julian grabbed the back of her neck and drew her in for a hug. "I should've thought to bring you some coffee."

Tears welled in her eyes, and she wiped them with her hoodie sleeve.

"Why don't we take a walk," Julian suggested. "We can go to my house for coffee. You grab Pixie's leash, and I'll tell Hugh and Evan we're leaving. I'll meet you out front in five."

The salty air quieted her nerves and cleared her mind. As they strolled down Church Street toward his house, she told him what she'd discovered in her mother's journals.

He listened intently, and when she'd finished talking, he asked, "And you have no recollection of this twin?"

"Only a glimpse of a girl with dark hair, who I thought might have been my playmate. Interestingly enough, when I asked Maddie about this girl on Monday, she denied knowing anything about her. She's hiding something. I feel it in my gut."

"Do you think you scared her off, and that's why she didn't show up for work today?"

"Maybe. Or maybe her house was damaged in the storm. If there is some deep dark secret associated with my twin, what's the point in keeping it now that my grandmother is dead?"

"That's a good question. How many of the journals did you read?"

Ellie held up two fingers. "I have four more to read. I'm certain I'll find more answers. But I can take her diaries only in small doses. Am I losing my mind, Julian? I was so distraught when I finished reading last night, I slept under my bed. Of course I don't believe in ghosts. I know I'm letting my imagination get the best of me, but I don't know how to turn it off." She picked Pixie up and held her close. "My grandmother was pure evil. I can't wait to sell her house. I can't stand the thought of spending another night there." Her body started to tremble as tears slid down her cheeks.

Julian took her shoulders in his hands and gave her a gentle shake. "Listen to me, Ellie Pringle. You are *not* losing your mind. You're just under a great deal of stress. I want you and Pip-squeak to come stay with me until you figure this thing out. You shouldn't be alone while you're reading your mother's journals. My guest room is right next to my bedroom. I'll hear you if you call for me, or you can bang on the wall, and I'll come running."

Sniffling, she nodded. "I accept your offer. At least for a couple of nights. I need to tell my father about everything that's happened, but I don't want to call him until I have more answers."

"Then it's all settled." He looped his arm through hers as they walked up the sidewalk to his house. "I may even take you out to dinner."

CHAPTER SEVENTEEN
ASHTON

GIVING BIRTH TO the twins nearly killed me. My heart went out of rhythm, and I lost a dangerous amount of blood. Maddie never left my side. She told me that Jeanette begged Mother to send for the doctor or call an ambulance and even threatened at one point to drive me to the hospital herself.

Mother refused to let Jeanette leave the house. "If you can't save my daughter, then it's God's will for her to die."

That's right. Maddie heard Mother with her own ears.

I slept in a nearly unconscious state for two days after the birth. When I finally woke, I asked to see my babies. Maddie brought them in from the adjacent room, the tiny bedroom that is serving as a nursery, and placed them in the crooks of my arms. Two bundles swathed in pink blankets, twin sisters despite the striking contrast in their appearance. One so fair and the other olive skinned. One whose scrunched-up face is so much like my own and the other the spitting image of Abbott. One who takes my breath away and the other who has stolen my heart.

"Look at you, you little lovelies," I cooed. "What are we going to name you?"

Maddie sat down on the bed beside me. "Your mama done named them babies, Miss Ashton. She told Miss Jeanette y'all done agreed on what to call them."

"That is a bold-faced lie!" My sudden outburst made it difficult for me to breathe, which scared the living daylights out of me. "What's wrong with me, Maddie? Why can't I breathe?"

"You had a difficult time delivering them babies. You need to give your poor body a chance to mend."

"But she can't do this!" I said, my breath coming in gasps. "I have a long list of names I'm considering. I wanted to meet the babies first before I made my final decision."

Maddie stroked my leg beneath the blanket. "Hush now while you catch your breath."

I drew in several big lungfuls of air, all the while thinking, *So this is how it's going to be if I stay here.*

When I finally summoned the nerve to tell Mother I am keeping the babies, she threatened to throw me out on the street. After weeks of fighting, when Mother realized I wasn't going to change my mind, she finally acquiesced. But not before making me agree to her unreasonable demands. Truth is, I'll do whatever it takes to keep my babies, even life imprisonment inside this house. She's chosen their names. I can't bear to think what other decisions she will make for my daughters in the future.

I looked up at Maddie. "I'm almost afraid to ask. What did she name them?"

"This one here's Eleanor." Maddie rubbed the fair-skinned baby's head. "And the other is Amelia."

I understood why Mother named one of them after herself, narcissistic egotist that she is. I kissed the fair baby's head. "We'll call you Ellie." I kissed the tip of the olive-skinned baby's nose. "I love the name Amelia, as much as I loved my grandmother. But I don't understand why my mother chose that name. She despised her mother-in-law. What does she have against this baby and not that one?" I planted another kiss on Amelia's forehead.

"Them's the names she told Miss Jeanette to put on the birth certificates," Maddie said. "But your mama is calling them Baby X and Baby Y."

I frowned. "I don't understand. Why?"

Mother entered the room and tapped Maddie on the shoulder with her jogging stick. "You may leave us now."

"Yes'm," Maddie said and scurried out of the room.

"It should be obvious why I've nicknamed them Baby X and Y. The fair baby is the spitting image of you. The other baby looks nothing like any of our ancestors on either side. It's apparent she carries her father's genes." Mother stood beside the bed, towering over me, jogging stick in hand. "You left out an important detail about your children's father, Ashton. Why did you not tell me he's Jewish?"

My jaw dropped open. "Since when do you have anything against Jewish people, Mother? You have plenty of Jewish friends."

"That doesn't mean I want my offspring to have Jewish blood running through her veins."

I tightened my grip on the babies. "The father's ethnicity is none of your concern."

"It is when his bastard children are living under my roof, and I'm paying the bills." She raised her jogging stick. "Tell me, Ashton, is the father Jewish or not?"

For the first time ever, I saw pure hate in my mother's gray eyes. Hate mixed with something that gave me the shivers—the glint of insanity. I wondered if she was crazy enough to hit me with her jogging stick while I held innocent babies in my arms. I'll do anything, including lying, to protect my children. And so that's what I did—I lied. "No, Mother. He's not Jewish."

Mother hesitated a split second before lowering her stick. "You're lying to me, but I have no way to prove it. You can stay here for now, but when I find out the truth, and I will find out the truth, I will toss all three of you out on the street." She moved to the door. "I've allowed Maddie to tend to your children while you recovered, but she needs to get back to her other duties. These babies are your responsibility, Ashton. When you see how exhausting it is to take care of them, you'll change your mind about putting them up for adoption."

"I'm not giving them up, Mother. I'm perfectly capable of taking care of them." I forced my aching body into a sitting position and laid the babies side by side on the bed next to me. "It's obvious this living situation is not going to work out for either of us. Once I recover, I'll take my babies and leave."

"We'll see how far you get." She stamped her walking stick on the hardwood floor as she left the room.

Throwing back the covers, I swung my feet over the side of the bed and sat on the edge of the mattress until the room stopped spinning. Every muscle trembled beneath me as I carried the babies one by one to the nursery and placed them in the crib.

When I decided to keep the babies, Maddie and I scoured the attic for baby equipment. I found my old crib, a changing table, and several boxes of infant clothes. I scrubbed the furniture with hot soapy water, and Maddie laundered the yellow out of the clothes with bleach. I gave Maddie money and sent her out west of the Ashley to shop for the baby supplies I needed.

I stared down at the tiny beauties sleeping side by side as they'd done for nine months inside my uterus. "I brought you into this world, and it's my job to protect you from your wicked gramma. Don't you worry. I'll figure a way out of this mess."

I pulled the rocking chair I borrowed from the guest bedroom up close to the crib and sat for a long time admiring my babies while I contemplated my getaway. I had written Louisa two weeks before I went into labor explaining why I wouldn't be returning to New York. Unable to bear the suspense any longer, I asked if Abbott had called or come looking for me. With Maddie's permission, I used hers as the return address. Maddie mailed the letter for me and brought me Louisa's response when it arrived a week later. *I'm sorry to say, I've not heard from Abbott.* she wrote in her curlicue script. *You are better off without him, Nettie. Rumors continue to circulate about the woman he's now seeing full-time in California.*

After reading her letter, I mourned for the second time my breakup with Abbott. During all these months, I've been holding out hope that the woman in the newspaper article meant nothing to him, that it was all a big mix-up. But he'd never called or come to my apartment looking for me. I'm certain Olga told him about my mysterious departure from New York. We were in a relationship for three years. Wasn't he the least bit curious about where I went and why I left so suddenly? What a fool I was thinking he was planning to propose marriage, when all that time he was seeing someone else. If he doesn't care more for me than that, he doesn't deserve to know about the babies.

The high cost of living in New York ate up most of my modeling salary, but I nevertheless managed enough savings to pay for bus tickets to a nearby city like Columbia or Spartanburg and a few months' rent in a modest apartment until I could find a job. "We'll have to wait until the two of you are old enough to travel," I said in a soft voice to the sleeping twins. "Until I regain my strength." I let my head fall back against the chair. "If I ever regain my strength. I've never felt so tired before in my life."

When the midwife came two days later for my follow-up checkup, she confirmed that what I've been experiencing is not normal postpartum fatigue. Perched on the edge of the bed, Jeanette listened to my heart for longer than I thought normal. Standing, she crossed the room to the dresser where Mother was writing out a check to her for the delivery fee. "Your daughter needs to see a cardiologist," Jeanette said in a low voice not meant for my ears, but I heard her anyway. "I'll be honest with you, I'm concerned. I hope it's nothing, but it's better to be safe than sorry."

Mother peered at Jeanette over the wire rim of her reading spectacles. "Can't you make her better?"

"I'm not a doctor, Mrs. Pringle. Ashton needs a specialist."

"Then leave my daughter's care to me, if you can't handle it." Mother finished writing out the check and handed it to Jeanette. "I've added a generous bonus in exchange for your confidentiality. Can I trust you not to discuss my daughter's case with anyone?"

Jeanette's hazel eyes grew wide when she glanced down at the check. "Yes ma'am." She folded and pocketed the check.

"I'd be happy to treat your daughter for free if I were capable. But I'm not. If you're concerned about discretion, I can make a few inquiries."

"That won't be necessary." Mother aimed her stick at the door. "I trust you can see yourself out."

Jeanette cast a concerned glance at me. "You will find her a doctor, won't you, Mrs. Pringle? Her condition could worsen without the proper care."

"Of course, Ms. Lane. What kind of mother do you think I am?"

CHAPTER EIGHTEEN
ELLIE

JULIAN TOOK ELLIE for an early dinner at Hank's Seafood, where they shared a bottle of sauvignon blanc and gorged on raw oysters. Returning to his house afterward, he made pumpkin spice lattes, which they took to his cozy den that doubled as his home office. Julian then went to work at his drafting table, and Ellie settled into his leather chair. With Mills stretched out on his back beside the ottoman and Pixie resting her head on his belly, Ellie began to read.

Ninety minutes later, she raised her head to find Julian still bent over his work, the muscles in his arms and shoulders flexing as he redesigned some lucky homeowner's new kitchen. She dared to dream of a happily ever after with him. Countless nights spent like this one. Instead of reading her mother's journals, she imagined herself working at her easel alongside him at his drafting table, with the dogs snoring softly on the floor in front of a fire and a baby sleeping peacefully in a bassinet in the corner. She brushed her thoughts aside. She couldn't contemplate her future while her focus remained on the past. Julian had hinted that he might have feelings for her. But he was still pretty banged up over his divorce. Right now, she valued his friendship too much to confuse it with thoughts of anything more.

Julian smiled at her when he caught her staring at him.

"I'm surprised architects draw anything by hand these days," she said. "Isn't there computer software that'll do all the work for you?"

"Most architects don't draw much at all anymore. I prefer a little of both. When I start a new project, I like to create a few sketches of the elevation as I see it in my mind. Putting pencil to paper beforehand makes the work go quicker when I move to the computer phase. One day, when I retire from being an architect, I'll take up painting with you."

Ellie's ears perked up at the mention of *one day*. He was talking about their future, and she liked the sound of it. *All the more reason for you to figure out your past, Ellie, sooner rather than later.*

He set his pencil down and moved closer to her chair. "What'd you learn from the journals?"

"I have a twin sister. Am-e-lia." She let the name roll off her tongue and then shook her head. "The name doesn't summon any memories. Not even the one of the little girl I saw my first day here. It has to be her, though. My mother describes Amelia in here"—she placed her hand on the diary—"as having olive skin like my father. My grandmother was not too keen on the idea of having a Jewish granddaughter. Add anti-Semitism to Eleanor Pringle's growing list of negative character traits."

"I didn't realize you were Jewish."

Ellie heard curiosity in his tone but not distaste. She was

an expert at reading signals. Her father had taught her a long time ago that it was best to ignore the bigots.

"My father's parents were Jewish, but I don't think he practiced much of the Jewish religion growing up. He married a Christian woman, and I was raised as a Methodist. My mother lied to grandmother. She told her my father wasn't Jewish." Ellie got up and walked to the window, staring out into the dark night. "What happened to Amelia? That's what I want to know. She wasn't in the house the day my father came to claim me. I wonder if she's even still alive. What if my grandmother killed her and buried her bones in the backyard?"

Julian laughed before realizing she wasn't joking. "You're serious?"

A chill traveled her spine at the realization that she was in fact serious. She wrapped her arms around herself. "The woman was insane, Julian. She refused to let my mother see a cardiologist about her suspected heart condition."

Julian pursed his lips together. "Whoa. That is seriously sick."

"She was responsible for her own daughter's death. So yes! I think she could have harmed my sister."

He poured two fingers of bourbon from a crystal decanter into two lowball glasses and handed one to her. "Still, even if you look nothing alike, why would your grandmother harm one child and not the other when you both have Jewish blood?"

"Easier for her to forget the crime without the evidence staring her in the face."

His jaw went slack. "Wait a minute. Let me get this straight. You're saying your grandmother murdered your twin sister because she was Jewish but kept you because you didn't look the part?"

Ellie's shaky hands cupped her glass as she sipped her bourbon. "It sounds far-fetched when you say it. I don't know, Julian. I have more questions than answers right now. I'm the spitting image of my mother, and maybe deep down my grandmother loved her, although she had a funny way of showing it. At least I know my mother loved my father. I've wondered about that a lot over the years. She talks repeatedly about her love for him in her diaries."

He moved closer to her, the warmth of this body comforting hers. "Are you ready to call him?"

"Not until I've finished reading all the journals. And had a chance to talk to Maddie."

*

Ellie, feeling safe in Julian's guest bedroom, hadn't planned to read anymore that night, but her unanswered questions nagged at her, keeping her awake. She read until nearly three o'clock in the morning—two journals that covered the time frame between the birth of her and her twin sister to their third birthday. Her mother's words weighed heavily on her heart. Nothing she learned was earth-shattering, but the combination of events proved that her grandmother had been mentally ill. Taking care of two babies can be exhausting for a healthy woman, but her mother, in her weakened state, barely managed to keep up. She was too proud to ask for help. It wouldn't have done any good anyway. She'd once overheard Maddie offering to take care of the twins. "Miss Ashton looks so tired, Miss Pringle. I'm finished with my other work. Why don't I sit with the babies awhile and give her a break?"

"If I wanted a nanny for those children, I would hire a nanny for those children," Eleanor had responded in a stern voice. "If you're finished with your other work, you can clean out the fireplace in the library."

Ellie heard the sadness and fear in her mother's words when she talked about Abraham's sudden death from a heart attack. *He seemed so healthy, so vibrant, but he died in his sleep one night with no warning signs. Is that how it will be for me?*

By night, Ashton dreamed of escaping, but her brutal reality returned by the light of day. Her heart was growing weaker, her will to live along with it. She had dedicated page after page of her journals to her musings. One day she seemed optimistic about her health, and the next she fretted over her daughters' futures. She wrote about the new life she wanted to create for her small family in places like Atlanta or Raleigh or Richmond. A week later, in her next entry, realizing she lacked the resources to start that new life, she weighed the pros and cons of putting her daughters up for adoption. She worried about how they would learn if they didn't go to school. And how they would get well without antibiotics when they fell ill. She worried about how they would adapt to the real world once they were freed. She knew her mother wouldn't live forever, but neither would she. Based on how puny she felt, she would be the first to go. She kept her strength up as best she could by climbing the stairs and doing floor exercises in her room. But the time would eventually come when she could no longer take care of the girls. Wouldn't they be better off living separate lives with good families than staying together in hell?

Once, in a moment of desperation, she mentioned getting in touch with Abbott. *The girls would be better off with their father, even if they had a stepmother, than they would be stuck here with Mother after I die.* Several days later, she wrote about seeing Abbott's photograph in several of the tabloid magazines Maddie had smuggled into the house for her. *Abbott's too busy partying it up with all the movie stars to take care of two little girls.*

Ellie found her mother's revelations difficult. When she finally fell asleep near the end of the second journal, she dreamed of two little girls being held prisoner by an evil witch, dressed all in black, who poked at them with her jogging stick.

In spite of her disturbing dream, she woke feeling energized.

After stripping the linens from her bed, she smoothed her hair into a ponytail, changed into the khaki shorts and black cotton blouse she'd brought with her, and went downstairs to find Julian. He was in the kitchen folding blueberries into pancake batter. What's not to like about a sexy man who enjoyed cooking, offered a muscular shoulder to cry on, and made her feel better about herself than she'd felt in years?

He inclined his head toward the small dog bowl on the counter. "I crunched some of Mills's kibble into Pip-squeak-size pieces. I wasn't sure how much to give her."

"She'll stop eating when she gets full." She placed the bowl on the floor in front of Pixie. "Do you pamper all your houseguests like this?"

"Only the ones with four legs." He studied her face as he handed her a mug of coffee. "You look tired. You were up late reading, weren't you? Even though you promised me you'd try to get some sleep."

How was it that he knew her so well when they'd met less

than a week ago? Was she that transparent? "Busted," she said, raising her left hand. "I make no excuses. I can't help myself. I have to find out what happened to my sister. To Lia." A look of amazement crossed her face as the light bulb went off in her head. "I didn't call my sister Amelia. I called her Lia. That's why her name sounded so unfamiliar to me."

He offered up a high five. "Now that's what I call a breakthrough! With any luck, you'll remember everything you've got locked up in that pretty little noggin of yours." He tapped lightly on her skull.

Ellie leaned back against the counter. "I used to go surfing with my dad when we went on our annual vacation to Malibu. I feel like I'm riding a wave, and I'm getting ready to lose control, but my adrenaline won't let me bail."

"Then go for it. I'll be here to catch you if you wipe out."

While he ladled batter in small batches onto his griddle, she set two places at his breakfast room table. When the food was ready, they sat down across the kitchen table from each other with plates piled high with pancakes in front of them. "Did you learn anything else of importance in your reading last night?" he asked, forking off a mouthful of pancakes.

"Nothing specific." Thinking back over the pages she'd read during the night, once again she experienced that strength that stemmed from her mother's love for her. "Only that my mother was determined to keep us safe. Her heart was weak, but her will was ironclad. Her determination has empowered me to see this thing through, my grandmother's evil spirit be damned."

She felt cocooned at Julian's, safe and protected and well cared for. But her answers wouldn't find her if she was hiding out here. She needed to face them head-on.

"I have a job to do, Julian, and as much as I appreciate your hospitality, I need to be in my grandmother's house to do it."

He took a sip of his coffee. "I can understand how being there might better help you remember. If you're not comfortable being there alone, I can come stay with you. I'll even sleep in your grandmother's bed."

"Now that I'd like to see," Ellie said with a little laugh. "Lucky for you, Evan Luna is taking her bed away today." She smiled at him. "You're a good friend for offering, Julian. But I need to handle this by myself."

"You can't get rid of me that easily. I promise not to pester you, but I won't ignore you, either. You know where I am if you need me."

Ellie glanced at her watch and shoveled another bite of pancakes in her mouth. "I really should get going. I want to be at the house when Maddie arrives."

*

The power had come back on, the roofers were already at work, and the technician had arrived, a day late, to install her cable and Internet. But there was no sign of Maddie. Evan Luna showed up around eleven with Clarence Vargas, a collector he'd enlisted to take away whatever was leftover. While the movers emptied the house of furniture, Ellie packed up the rest of her grandmother's possessions—her clothing and knickknacks, the formal china, most of the silver pieces except the flatware, and a pair of ornate candelabra she found interesting. With the ceramic urn tucked under her arm, she marched through the park to the promenade. Without ceremony, she dumped her grandmother's ashes into the harbor. It dawned on her on the walk home that she should've checked to see if any laws governed the scattering of ashes. Nothing she could do about it now except pay a fine if anyone reported her. She rinsed out the urn in the kitchen sink and gave it to Clarence Vargas to haul off with the rest of the junk.

By six o'clock Ellie was exhausted, but as she wandered through the empty rooms, she felt like a thousand pounds had been lifted off her shoulders. She could breathe again without her grandmother's dreary furnishings suffocating her. She didn't care what Midge the realtor said. The house would show much better unfurnished. She poured herself a glass of wine and sat down at her desk. Her computer connected to the Wi-Fi without delay, and she spent the next hour searching the Internet for a forty-year-old woman with every variation of Lia's name she could think of. When she came up empty, she Googled Maddie Washington in the hopes of finding a phone number or an address or some way of getting in touch with her housekeeper. Again, she came up empty.

She had one more journal left to read. If she didn't find the answers she was looking for, she had no idea where else to turn.

CHAPTER NINETEEN
ASHTON

DINNERS IN THE dining room are torturous affairs for the twins and me. Mother presides over us from the head of the table like the Queen of England presiding over her court. She insists her granddaughters sit up straight in their chairs and use proper manners. They aren't allowed to be excused from the table until they've cleaned their plates of every last morsel of food. I have nothing against my daughters learning good manners. I just don't approve of Mother's method of teaching. It nearly breaks my heart to see my three-year-olds turn as green as the peas they swallow whole.

Usually when Mother invites us to join her for dinner, she has an issue to discuss. On this particular late spring evening, that issue was the girls' outdoor playtime.

"You must lower your voices when you're outside in the garden so the neighbors don't hear you." Mother glared at each girl in turn. "Lately, you've been playing too loud. I'll be forced to make you stay inside if you don't obey."

Our backyard resembles a jungle. Mother has let the

shrubs and trees grow out of control to keep the nosy neighbors out of our business.

While the girls finished eating, I talked to them about making a game out of whispering in the garden, but when they went upstairs to change into their pajamas, I turned on my mother. "The girls are three years old, Mother. Other than the garden, they've never been outside of this house. They're too young to understand that they're being kept here as prisoners."

"I beg your pardon," Mother said in an incensed tone. "No one is keeping you here against your will."

I held her gaze. "Then why are you the only one with keys to the security system and the dead bolts on the doors?"

"We have young children in the house, Ashton. The locks are there for your daughters' protection." Mother returned her attention to her Salisbury steak.

"If that's so, I'd like to see a cardiologist. I need medical care for my condition. I feel myself getting weaker and weaker."

"Go! See your cardiologist." Mother flicked her wrist as though shooing away a fly. "But take your bastard children with you, because you won't be allowed back in this house if you leave."

I glared at her. She isn't a pretty woman, at least not in my opinion. But in her younger days, she posed a striking figure dressed in the latest fashions with her dark hair coiled in an elegant chignon. She's let her hair go gray and cut it man short. She wears shapeless black dresses and matching lace-up, rubber-soled shoes. Her constant scowl has etched deep lines in her forehead and around her eyes and mouth. If I met her on a street corner, I might mistake her for the Wicked Witch of the West.

"Why are you doing this to me, Mother? Do you hate me so much you want me to die?"

She brought her fist crashing down against the table. "If death is your sentence, then so be it. God is punishing you for your sins—for running away from home, having sexual relations out of wedlock, and giving birth to your bastard children." My mother's gray eyes were wide and wild with an evil glint that made my blood run cold.

"I have a clean conscience. I loved Abbott, and I'm not ashamed of our relationship."

I got up from the table and stormed out of the room, but my mother quickly caught up with me. "Where do you think you're going? I haven't given you permission to leave the room." She grabbed me by the arm, but I jerked free. I walked faster, anxious for the safety of my room, but she matched my pace, step by step, as I climbed the stairs.

When we got to the top, my mother spun me around and smacked me hard on the cheek. "Don't you ever walk away from me, young lady!"

"I'll walk away from you anytime I damn well please. Just watch me."

When I started toward my room, she stuck her foot out and tripped me. I stumbled off-balance, and as I was reaching for the railing to break my fall, my mother shoved me down the stairs. My arms and legs and head banged against the hardwood treads as I tumbled all the way to the bottom. I tasted blood on my lips when I screamed, "You're insane! God will punish *you* for that."

I waited for her to come check on me, but she went into her bedroom and closed the door. I hurt too much to move, but I took the pain as a good sign, an indication that I wasn't paralyzed. My left wrist was bent at an awkward angle, obviously broken, but that appeared to be the worst of my injuries. I lay curled up on the floor in the front hall for what seemed like hours, until I no longer heard Mother's footsteps moving around in her bedroom over my head. Clutching my broken wrist against my body, I crawled up the stairs, one excruciating step at a time, and through my bedroom to the nursery. Much to my relief, the girls were sound asleep, their arms and legs intertwined in the twin bed they shared. I prayed they hadn't witnessed the horrific scene that had just played out in the hallway beyond their bedroom door.

I passed out from the pain and woke the following morning on the floor beside the twins' bed with two sets of eyes peeking down at me from over the edge of the mattress. Wincing, I rolled over on my side and closed my eyes against the sunlight streaming in through the windows. "Ellie, be a darling and go see if Maddie is here." Ellie is my go-to child in times of need. Somehow I know, even at such an early age, that my firstborn, if only by eight minutes, is the more trustworthy and the strongest of the two.

I heard Ellie's tiny bare feet hit the floor and pitter-patter out of the room. She returned some minutes later with Maddie in tow.

"What on earth happened to you?" Maddie gasped.

I silenced her with a shake of my head and glance toward the girls.

Maddie regained her composure. "Girls, run along downstairs to the kitchen. Sally Bell's got some fresh blueberry muffins in the oven. I'll be down in a minute."

At the mention of food, the girls scurried out of the room.

Maddie helped me up off the floor and gripped my good arm tightly while I limped to my room. "Should I get your gown?"

"No!" I shook her off. "I won't give my mother the satisfaction of knowing she sent me to my sickbed."

Maddie's brown eyes nearly popped out of her head. "You mean to tell me your mother did this to you?"

"Who else, Maddie? I may be weak, but I'm not clumsy. I didn't fall. She pushed me down the stairs." I lowered myself onto the edge of the bed. "She's gone totally insane. I've got to get my girls out of this house before she hurts one of them."

"Lawd." Maddie sat down on the bed next to me. "Let us help you, Miss Ashton. I got a little money saved, and I'm sure ole Sally will pitch in."

"You're sweet to offer, Maddie, but I wouldn't dare drag y'all into this. Neither of you can afford to lose your job. You've got your families to take care of." I glanced at my chest of drawers where I kept my money hidden. "I have some money of my own saved. I just need to figure out a plan."

"That don't look good." Maddie eyed my broken wrist. "You need to see a doctor."

"I will, when I get where I'm going." I gasped in agony as I drew my broken wrist closer to my chest. "Maddie, be a dear and get me some aspirin and an ice pack."

"Yes'm," she said and hurried out of the room.

While she was gone, I managed to change out of my clothes and was struggling with the button on a fresh sleeveless blouse when she returned ten minutes later.

"This just ain't right, Miss Ashton," Maddie said as she finished buttoning the buttons. "I done told Sally what happened. We think you should call the police."

"We can't do that! They'll take my children away from

me! I appreciate your concern, but this is not your problem to worry about. I'll figure out a solution."

Maddie wrapped my broken wrist in an ACE bandage and tied it around my neck using a makeshift sling she fashioned out of an old bedsheet. She produced a prescription bottle of pills from her apron pocket. "I found these at the back of your mother's medicine cabinet." She pointed at the label. "Says here to take as needed for pain. The doctor gave them to her last year when she strained her back. She won't miss them."

"I don't care if she does miss them," I said, popping one of the painkillers into my mouth.

I heard happy squeals coming from the backyard and wobbled toward the door. "I need to get to the girls before my mother does. She warned them about making too much noise."

I leaned on Maddie for support on the way down the stairs and out into the garden. I shushed the girls, reminding them to play quietly, and stretched out on the chaise lounge on the terrace so I could keep an eye on them while they played under the magnolia tree.

The late spring sun warmed my face, and the medicine eased the pain. I dozed off and on while I formulated my plan. Putting one of Mother's sleeping powders in her tea at dinner seemed too risky. I racked my brain until another idea presented itself to me.

Sally Bell served grilled cheese sandwiches and tomato soup on the terrace. She didn't say a word but sat close to me while we ate. The silent camaraderie gave me strength. After lunch, I took the girls upstairs for their nap. I tucked them in and read them a quick story before going to my room. I emptied the clothes from the drawer where I kept my money. As best I could manage with one hand, I pulled the drawer all the way out and set it down, bottom facing up, on the bed. Before the twins were born, I had secured my savings account passbook to the bottom of the drawer with packing tape. But when I peeled back the tape, the passbook was gone and in its place was a note written in my mother's tidy handwriting. *You didn't expect to live here for free, now did you?*

Anger pulsed through my veins, causing the room to spin around me and my heart to flutter. I sank to the bed and lowered my head between my legs, taking deep breaths until the dizziness subsided and my heart rate steadied. I slowly rose and dragged myself down the stairs to the library, where I found Mother paying bills behind my father's desk. I slapped the note down on the desk. "Where's my money, Mother?"

She looked up at me from her checkbook. "Long gone." She got up from her chair and came around the desk. "It was simple, really, to have your money wired from your account to mine. All I needed was your birthdate and social security number. I'm surprised it's taken you this long to discover it missing. Seriously, Ashton, you should be ashamed of yourself for allowing yourself to be bullied. Then again, you always were weak like your father. Does it hurt much?"

I took a step back as her fingers grazed my broken wrist. "Don't touch me ever again, you crazy bitch! You won't get away with this!"

The sound of Mother's maniacal laughter echoed throughout the house as I fled the room. Trudging up the stairs, I felt the energy draining from my body as my heart grew weaker and weaker. My situation is a lost cause. My mother has gotten away with stealing my savings, and she will undoubtedly get away with so much more before it's all over. There is no way out of this prison for me. But I will die trying to find a way out for my girls.

CHAPTER TWENTY
ELLIE

ELLIE NEVER CLOSED her eyes on Thursday night. She couldn't find a light bulb to replace the burned-out one in the attic in any of the obvious places in the house. So by the light of Bennett's battery-powered lanterns, she spent the early hours of the morning scouring the attic for more journals. Her energy was fueled by her rage at her grandmother, frustration at her mother, and bewilderment at Maddie for her mysterious disappearance. She left no box unsealed and no trunk unopened. There were no more journals in the house.

Eight o'clock Friday morning came and went with no sign of or word from Maddie. She spoke for an hour with her therapist, Patsy, in California, who warned her the worst was yet to come. "You've dislodged a stone in the wall that protects your memories. Prepare yourself for that wall to come crumbling down."

She felt the urge to work, but the canvas she'd started before the hurricane—the image of the row of houses on

South Battery as seen from the park—no longer inspired her. She needed to get something off her mind, although she wasn't sure what. Drawn once again to the magnolia in the backyard and lacking the patience for the slow process of painting, she took her sketchbook and drawing supplies out to the terrace. She settled herself in a chaise lounge and sharpened her graphite pencil to a fine point. As her sketch progressed, the tip of her pencil became fat and dull, perfect for the amount of shading her subject required.

It was midafternoon when she lifted her head again. The scene staring back at her from her sketch pad was one from her memory, the one she'd been so anxious to get out of her mind. Two little girls were huddled together in the dark, not under the magnolia tree but cowering behind their mother's bedroom door as they watched the scene unfold in the hallway. *I was there that night with my sister. I saw—we both saw—our grandmother push our mother down the stairs.*

She got up and strolled around the perimeter of the garden. She felt drained from her sleepless night and her drawing efforts, but she experienced a great sense of accomplishment as well. Witnessing her grandmother shove her mother down the stairs had indeed been a traumatic event. But was it *the* traumatic event? She didn't think so.

Ellie's stomach growled, reminding her she hadn't eaten since dinner last night. She peeled back a banana and wandered through the empty house while she ate it. Horrific memories waited for her at every turn and in every corner. Her grandmother's shrill voice reprimanding her for the grape juice stain and for disturbing her mother while she rested. Her grandmother had beaten Ellie with the jogging stick for acts as benign as leaving the bathroom light on. Never on the face where anyone could see, but on her bottom and her thighs. Her memory of Lia was the strongest in the nursery they'd shared, her twin's tangled mass of dark hair and her eyes so full of fear. How had she blocked her twin from her memory for all these years?

"We're not staying here another night." She picked up her dog. "I don't know where we'll go, but anywhere is better than here." She carried Pixie downstairs to her studio where she'd left her phone. She located Midge Calhoun's business card in the top drawer of her desk and dialed the number. The realtor answered on the second ring, and they exchanged pleasantries.

"I know this is last minute," Ellie said. "But is there any chance you could stop by this afternoon? I'm ready to move forward with putting the house on the market."

"I'm meeting a client at four," Midge said. "But I could swing by afterward, around five, if that's not too late for you."

"Five would be fine," Ellie said, and ended the call.

She lay down on the sofa for a quick rest and was awakened by the pounding of the door knocker at five thirty.

"I'm the first to admit when I'm wrong. This place looks a hundred times better with no furniture." Midge teetered around the downstairs on stiletto heels, her long, gauzy, gray sweater flowing behind her. "I can't imagine the expense of painting a house like this, but I assure you, you'll get your money back."

"I don't want to wait, Midge. I want to put this house on the market today. This minute. Right now." Hard as she tried, she couldn't prevent her voice from trembling.

Midge stopped in her tracks and spun around to face her. She looked into Ellie's eyes. "What's wrong, honey?"

Ellie choked back the tears. "Everything."

Midge placed a hand on Ellie's shoulder. Even in three-inch heels, she didn't reach Ellie's breasts. "You need a break from all this. I live just down the road in a waterfront condo. Why don't we go there and have a glass of wine out on my balcony terrace?"

The idea appealed to her. "I wouldn't want to intrude."

"Are you kidding me? I'd welcome the company. Bennett is working late tonight, anyway. I've had a long week, and I'm ready to kick up my heels." Midge stared down at her shoes. "I'm actually ready to kick *off* these heels." Walking toward the door, she waved her on. "Bring your little dog. I'll drive."

*

Midge's condo offered views overlooking the harbor, but the modern interior lacked the kind of charm that Ellie had grown to appreciate—the random-width floorboards and heavy moldings as in her house and Julian's.

Midge showed her to her generous balcony. "Chardonnay okay?"

"Anything is fine with me. Don't go to any trouble." Ellie settled in one of two lounge chairs. Feeling the nip in the air, she drew her lightweight sweater tight around her shoulders.

Midge returned a minute later with two glasses, a bottle of chilled Chardonnay, and a small bowl of almonds. She sat down in the lounge chair beside Ellie and kicked off her shoes. "Ah, that's much better," she said, rubbing her feet. "I don't know why I torture myself by wearing those shoes."

"Because you have the legs to pull it off."

Midge's eyes traveled the length of Ellie's legs from the bottom of her Bermuda shorts to the tops of her walking shoes. "What're you talking about? You've got great legs."

"Not for walking," Ellie said. "I'm a total klutz. I'd break my ankle wearing shoes like those." She gestured at the Christian Louboutin black patent leather pumps. She knew the brand well. She'd salivated over them often enough at Neiman Marcus.

"Lucky for you, you're tall enough you don't have to wear them." Midge poured each of them a glass of wine and relaxed back against her chair. "Now, tell me what's gotten you so down in the dumps."

Ellie hesitated, trying to decide how much to tell her. She barely knew Midge, but she sensed she could trust her. And she desperately needed someone to talk to. While Julian had proved to be a patient and sympathetic listener, she needed a woman's perspective.

"When I first came to Charleston, I remembered very little about my time spent here as a child. But certain things have sparked those memories."

Midge listened intently as Ellie walked her through the events of the past two weeks, leaving nothing out but the part about her grandmother's lingering presence. No sense scaring her new friend away by sounding like a nutcase.

Neither of them touched their wine while she was talking, but when she finished, they both took a big gulp.

"So can you see why I want to get rid of the house?" Ellie said, setting down her wineglass.

"I can certainly understand why you're upset. But houses like yours don't come around very often. You need to make your decision to sell based on logic, not emotion."

"You don't understand." Ellie lowered her head. "I need to feel at peace in my home. I don't see that ever happening for me in a house where my evil grandmother once lived."

Where her presence might still remain, she thought to herself, although she'd seen no signs of Eleanor Pringle's ghost since Julian removed her bedroom door.

"But where will you go?"

"Not back to California, that's for sure. My life there is over. I considered moving to DC to be near my father, but I'm not a big-city gal at heart. I'm thinking about staying in Charleston. I like what I've seen so far, but I've been too preoccupied with the house to explore much. There are many scenes here I'm inspired to paint. One of the smaller houses off the Battery, on Church Street or Meeting, might better suit my needs."

Midge's blue eyes were full of warmth when she asked, "I don't mean to pry into your finances, but are you in a position to make a down payment on another property without selling your grandmother's house first?"

She nodded, thinking how she had inherited enough money to buy three houses in downtown Charleston. "I don't understand why my grandmother left her estate to me when she obviously hated me so much," she said, her eyes filled with tears. "I guess there was no one else for her to leave it to. Living in her house, spending her money, feels so dirty to me, like it's blood money."

Midge shifted in her chair to face her. "You listen to me, Ellie Pringle. Your grandmother owes you that money." She ticked the points off on her fingers. "She robbed you of a happy childhood. She robbed you of the chance to grow up with your sister, wherever she may be. She robbed your mother of the chance to grow old. If she'd received proper medical care, your mother might still be alive today."

Ellie stared across the water as she considered what

it would be like to have a mother, not just as a child and teenager but now, as an adult. "That's true. She may not have poisoned her or drowned her in the bathtub, but my grandmother is responsible for my mother's death just the same."

Midge sunk her fingers into the bowl of almonds. "The way I see it, your inheritance from your grandmother is payment for the mental and physical abuse you endured under her roof. That money would have rightfully gone to your mother. And since she's not alive, it belongs to you." She popped a handful of almonds into her mouth.

"It belongs to my sister and me. She has a right to half the money," Ellie said, verbalizing for the first time what she'd been thinking since she learned she had a twin. "That is, if she's still alive. I'm worried that maybe my grandmother killed Lia."

Midge sucked in her breath. "It's hard to imagine, but it's not out of the question when you consider what you already know about your grandmother. She pushed your mother, her own daughter, down the stairs. Maybe she killed Lia by accident. Find your housekeeper. She has the answers you need."

"Of course she does. Why else would she disappear when I started pressing her for information? But who's she covering for? My mother and grandmother are both dead."

"Maybe she's covering for herself. I'm not saying she's the one who harmed your sister, but she may have helped with the cover-up. And what about the cook? How does she fit into the picture?"

"Who knows? Maybe Sally Bell had something to do with Lia's disappearance."

"Do you have any idea where she is now?" Midge asked.

"I'm sure she's dead," Ellie said. "She was an old woman even back then."

"Which brings us back to the housekeeper." Midge looked at the table and picked up her phone. "I might be able to help you find her. I have a couple of online resources I can check. What's her last name?"

"Washington. Maddie Washington," Ellie said as Midge keyed the name into her phone.

"Have you asked Bennett Senior? He may know how to find her. I'm sure I'll see him at some point over the weekend. I'm happy to mention it to him."

"That's fine. Just don't make a big deal out of it. If my grandmother turns out to be a murderer, I don't want the whole town to know about it. I trust Bennett, but the fewer people who know about my situation the better. So far, I've told only you and Julian."

A wicked grin spread across her lips. "Julian, huh? Is he someone special? The only Julian I know is Julian Hagood."

"He's the only Julian I know as well."

She nudged Ellie's arm playfully. "He's a catch, girlfriend. Half the single women in town are lusting after him."

Ellie smiled. "Sorry to disappoint you, but Julian and I are just friends."

"Then why is your face as red as your hair?" Midge said, tugging a lock of Ellie's hair. "He's a good man. That's all I'm saying. He didn't deserve his wife walking out on him like that."

They sat in silence while they sipped their wine and watched the blue sky fade to yellow.

"I'm curious," Midge said, breaking the silence at last. "When your father came to Charleston for you after your mother died, did your grandmother mention anything about him having another child?"

Ellie jerked her head back. Was it possible her father knew about her twin sister? Surely he would've told her if he did. "As far as I know, she never mentioned my twin, but my past is not my father's favorite topic of conversation."

"I didn't mean to hit a sore nerve," Midge said.

"It's a legitimate question, Midge, the first one I plan to ask my father when I talk to him." Ellie finished her wine. "But there's another possibility that makes the most sense to me. My mother mentions putting us up for adoption several times in her journals. My guess is, she either put Lia up for adoption or found someone to take care of her."

"If that's true, why Lia and not you?"

"Because my grandmother hated Lia more, if that's even possible. My twin was the spitting image of our Jewish father. I'm embarrassed to admit, my grandmother was a bigot."

Lines creased Midge's forehead. "You may be on to something, Ellie. I'm sure your mother was terrified for your lives after your grandmother pushed her down the stairs. If she had the choice of getting only one of you to safety..."

"She would have chosen the one most at risk."

CHAPTER TWENTY-ONE

ELLIE

ELLIE DECLINED MIDGE'S offer to drive her home. "Thanks, but I'd rather walk." Energized by the crisp salty air, she race-walked down the waterfront to East Bay Street. She was determined to find out what happened to her sister and locate her if she was still alive. She'd been so intent on finding her answers, she hadn't considered what these revelations could mean for her. Maybe she and Lia would become friends, long-lost twin sisters with decades of making up to do.

She called Julian when she was a block away from home. "I need a favor."

"So now you need my help," he said in a teasing tone. "You've been avoiding my texts all day."

"I'll explain when you come over." When she heard Mills barking in the background, she slowed her pace. Had she been presumptuous in thinking he'd make himself available to her whenever she summoned him? "Unless, of course, you're in the middle of something."

"Actually, I'm in the middle of making shrimp ceviche. If you can give me forty-five minutes, I'll bring dinner."

Relief swept over her. Her feelings for him were deepening. "You're on. I can never say no to ceviche." *Or to you,* she thought.

Ellie took her first shower in two days and dressed in a gray knit tunic, black leggings, and ankle booties. She smeared on some makeup and blow-dried her strawberry-blonde mane. She was descending the stairs when Julian arrived with Mills by his side, a sketchbook tucked under his arm, and a tote bag stuffed with edible goodies. She took the tote bag from him and led the way to the kitchen.

"I love what you've done with the place," he said about the empty rooms. "One can actually hear themselves think in here now."

"I know, right?" she said over her shoulder. "Makes me want to go out and buy a pair of roller skates."

He was unloading the food containers and bottle of wine from the tote bag when she reached for his sketch pad. "Are you planning to work while you're here?"

He smacked her hand away. "I have some drawings I want to show you, but they'll have to wait until after dinner. Let's get the work out of the way first. I'm guessing you don't need my help moving furniture since there's none left."

"Ha-ha. Aren't you the comedian?"

When she told him what she wanted, he dropped his smile and studied her face. "Have you been drinking?"

"I may have had a glass of wine with Midge earlier. But that has nothing to do with this." She took him by the hand and dragged him through the house and up the stairs to the second floor. She handed him the tools he needed as he rehung her grandmother's bedroom door.

"There. Now." He stepped back to admire his work. "Are we going to stand here and wait to see if the door closes?"

She slapped his arm with the back of her hand. "You'll understand my paranoia when I tell you what my grandmother did to my mother."

Back in the kitchen, Julian uncorked the bottle of rosé he'd brought over while Ellie filled two bowls with ceviche topped off with the pita triangles he'd toasted. They took their dinner to the table on the terrace.

"The air is so fresh." Ellie inhaled deeply. "I know the tree isn't in bloom right now, but I can almost smell the fragrant magnolia blossoms."

"The spring and autumn months are by far the most enjoyable in Charleston. You have an unpleasant surprise in store for you come summer. The humidity here is almost unbearable."

Ellie thought about it a minute. "Now that you mention it, I remember how hot and humid the weather could get in the summer. We used to keep our windows open all the time with the ceiling fans rotating on full blast. We must not have had air-conditioning back then. Or my grandmother was too cheap to turn it on."

With their arms occasionally touching, they nibbled at their ceviche and sipped wine while she filled him in on what she'd learned in her mother's final journals.

"What did your father have to say about all this?" he asked when she finished talking.

She stared down at her empty plate.

"Please tell me you called your father."

"Not yet. But I'm going to on Sunday." She tucked a strand of hair behind her ear as she looked up from her plate. "It's been a long couple of weeks, and I need the weekend to myself to process everything."

"I can understand that." Propping his elbows on the table, he leaned closer to her. "Do your plans for the weekend include me?"

"Only if you're interested in helping me buy a car. I figured it was time I returned my rental to the airport."

He puffed out his chest. "As it happens, I'm an expert at negotiating good deals on cars. What kind of car are you looking for? I know salespeople at most of the dealerships."

"I was thinking about a MINI Cooper. The small size is perfect for navigating this awful traffic."

"And for chauffeuring Pip-squeak around town." When Pixie's ears perked up, Julian reached down and petted her on the head. "Good girl. You're learning your new name."

Ellie laughed and tossed her wadded paper napkin at him.

They took their empty plates to the kitchen, rinsed and stored them in the dish rack, and refilled their wineglasses. "Can I look at these now?" she asked, her hand on his sketchbook.

He nodded. "You may."

She flipped through the elevation drawings he'd done of her kitchen. Several of the drawings showed walls of cabinets with built-in, commercial-grade appliances. One of the two she liked the best featured a table and banquette incorporated into a wall of windows, while the other was an illustration of the wet bar area with wine storage they'd discussed.

"These are stunning, Julian. I hate to disappoint you when you've given my renovation so much thought, but I talked to Midge about putting the house on the market today."

"Do you really want to make that decision now with so many unanswered questions looming over you?" She started to interrupt, but he silenced her with a fingertip to her lips. "This house has been filled with too much sadness for way too long. She has strong bones and an honest soul. Why not breathe a little life back into her by giving her a face-lift?" His face softened as he spoke of the house as one might a loved one. She realized then the depth of his commitment to the historic buildings in the area.

"I'm not sure how much life a forty-year-old unmarried woman and her pip-squeak dog can breathe into a centuries-old mansion."

She flipped to the next page of his sketchbook, a drawing of her reclined in the leather chair in his den, her hands gripping her mother's journal and her face pinched in pain. She ran her fingers across the drawing. "Whoa. I look so…"

"Fixated? You didn't even realize I was sketching you."

"I was going to say desperate." She let the cover on the sketchbook fall shut and backed away from him. "Is that what I am to you, Julian? A lost soul you feel the need to rescue like one of your beloved old buildings?"

"Hold on a minute. I'm sorry you got the wrong impression. Yes, your emotions are raw in the sketch, but desperate? Never. Pained? For sure, and understandably so considering what you're going through. But that's what I admire so much about you. You're not afraid to show your emotions. You're one of the few women I've met in a very long time who has real honest-to-goodness feelings." Closing the gap between them, he cupped her face in his hands. "What are you to me? Right now, you're my friend, but I'd like for you to be a whole lot more than that one day, once you've sorted out your life."

She kissed him softly on the lips. "I've been trying to figure out my past for a very long time, Julian. I stopped putting my life on hold for it years ago. At least I thought I had. Until I came here. I've become obsessed with reading my mother's journals, and in the process, I've let an important part of myself slip away from me. I had an aha moment today about what happened in the past."

"What's that?" he asked, his voice a hoarse whisper.

"It's not my past."

Confusion crossed his face.

"That didn't come out right. Of course it's my past. I was here. I lived it. But I was merely a child. What happened to me here happened because of the decisions other people made for me, not because of the decisions I made for myself. I'm not to blame for any of it. And being angry at my grandmother is giving her the power to control me all over again. I refuse to let that happen. I'm taking my life back. Next week, I will solve this mystery of my missing sister once and for all. In the meantime, I plan to enjoy my weekend. If I want to spend it having sex with you, then by golly, I'm going to do just that."

A naughty-boy grin spread across his face, bringing a sparkle to his golden eyes. "Do you?"

"Do I what?"

"Want to spend the weekend having sex with me?"

Again, she kissed him on the lips, this time with more passion. "Damn right I do."

He kissed her back with increasing urgency. He pressed his body against hers, pinning her against the refrigerator. When they came up for air several minutes later, they noticed two sets of brown eyes looking up at them.

Ellie laughed. "Why do I feel like we're the teenagers and

they're the parents, and they just caught us making out on the family room sofa?"

"Because it's not far from the truth." He nibbled at her lip. "Are you sure this is what you want?"

She let out a soft moan. "Positive."

"What do we do about them?" He tipped his head at the dogs.

"Give them a treat and lock them in my studio," she said as she reached for the box of Greenies.

*

Ellie had never known a man who made love with such tenderness and skill. Not that she considered herself an experienced lover, but she'd been in several long-term relationships. They finally dozed off around three, and she woke an hour later to the sound of the wind howling in the eaves. She slid out of bed, slipped on her robe, and tiptoed down the hall to her grandmother's room, relieved to find the door still open. She moved to the window and stared out over the trees swaying in the park to the full moon glowing off the harbor. This bedroom offered the best views of the waterfront in the house. She imagined sipping coffee on the piazza in the mornings and making love by the light of the moon at night. Maybe Julian was right. Maybe it was time to breathe new life into this house. If she wasn't the right person to do it, then maybe her sister would be. Did her sister have a husband and children? She was suddenly curious to know about her potential extended family—her nieces, nephews, and brother-in-law.

She sensed Julian behind her before she felt his breath tickle her neck. "I take it your grandmother's spirit has exited the premises."

"Mm-hmm." She leaned into him. "Apparently so. I told you I don't believe in ghosts. But I do believe, like the Gullah people believe, that the souls of the recently departed may sometimes have a difficult time moving on to wherever they're supposed to be. In my grandmother's case, I shudder to think about where that somewhere might be. I don't care where she is as long as she's no longer in this house. With any luck, she's made atonement for her sins."

The room filled with the citrusy fragrance of magnolia blooms.

Julian tugged on her arm. "Come back to bed, sweetheart. We have several more hours before dawn."

CHAPTER TWENTY-TWO
ELLIE

E LLIE AND JULIAN spent their weekend like a newly married couple, tackling their to-do list while sneaking kisses and gropes every chance they got. He followed her out to the airport to drop off her rental car and then drove her around to the various dealerships while she shopped brands and models. After much debate, she finally decided on the MINI Countryman. She was torn between Island Blue and Moonwalk Gray, but he convinced her to go with the more subtle color. On the way back to town, they stopped at Hominy Grill for a late lunch on the terrace before returning to the house on South Battery. They appeased the dogs by taking them for a long walk, and then, at Julian's suggestion, they lugged her bedroom furniture down from the attic to her grandmother's room.

"Stop thinking of it as your grandmother's room," Julian said, as they wrestled her box spring onto her bed frame. "You'll feel right at home in here, surrounded by all your things. Your father will need somewhere to sleep when he comes. This way he can have the guest room."

"If he even comes," she said as she stretched her aching back. "He wasn't exactly thrilled about me moving to Charleston."

"Surely he'll come when he finds out what you've been going through."

"Maybe," Ellie said with a shrug. "And maybe not. My father is a wonderful man, and we have a close relationship, but he doesn't think drudging up the past is in my best interest."

"As a parent, I can see his point. As someone who cares about you, I think you deserve some answers."

Finding out about her sister was the only answer she needed. She hoped it was the only answer she got.

Ellie was pleased at the results of their efforts. Her furnishings from California wiped away all traces of her grandmother. The patterned rug was a tad too small, but it covered enough of the floor to warm the room and soften the echo. Crystal lamps adorned matching side tables while a Kate Spade striped comforter—with its splashes of navy, orange, and several shades of pink—brightened her gray lattice headboard. Her pine armoire occupied most of one wall, and her dresser and two side chairs filled the other. The builder's drywall installers repaired the damage caused by the leak. The painters would take care of the rest. She thought about making a dramatic show on the walls by choosing a bold color in a high-gloss paint. Maybe she would hire a decorator after all.

For dinner, they ordered takeout sandwiches and salads from Bull Street Gourmet and Market and picnicked in the park while the dogs chased each other and frolicked in the grass.

After they'd finished eating, Julian stretched out on the

blanket and placed his head in her lap. "Have you planned what you're going to say to your father when you call him tomorrow?"

"I'll just wing it. When it comes to my father, I never plan anything. That's his job." Ellie ran her fingers through Julian's dark hair. "My father is very levelheaded. I'm the one prone to hysteria in the family." She smiled down at him. "Does that surprise you?"

Wrapping his arm around her neck, he pulled her face to his and gave her an upside-down kiss on the lips. "I'm all for the kind of hysteria you exhibited in the bedroom last night."

She touched the tip of her nose to his. "There's more where that came from. Sleep with me in my grandmother's room tonight, and I promise to show you how hysterical I can be." As much as she wanted more of what they'd shared the night before, she wanted company on her first night sleeping in her grandmother's room.

He sat bolt upright. "Let's go."

Placing her hands on his shoulders, she pushed him back down. "Calm down, cowboy. It's still daylight outside."

"Fine. But once it gets dark, you'd better watch out. My fangs will begin to show." He returned his head to her lap. "Composed as your father may be, learning he has another forty-year-old daughter might come as a shock."

The burden of her responsibility weighed heavily on her. "I have no idea how I'm going to break that news. I guess I'll start by telling him about my mother's journals."

*

Julian made certain her first night in her new bedroom was magical. They made love until well past midnight with the full moon streaming through the bare windows. When the dogs woke them a few minutes before seven, Julian hurried downstairs to let them out and feed them. He returned with a tray of coffee, two bowls of oatmeal, and the Sunday paper. They made love again and lounged in bed until after ten.

She waited as long as she could, but at eleven o'clock, she and Julian headed downstairs to her studio for her to place the dreaded call to her father. He answered on the second ring and listened patiently while she explained the situation. When she was finished talking, he told her he'd call her back in a few minutes.

Julian raised an eyebrow when she drew the phone away from her ear. "Did he hang up on you?"

"He's going to call me back. That's the way my father operates. He never raises his voice. When he gets angry, he walks away from the situation until he calms down."

Julian rubbed the stubble on his chin. "That's impressive. We could all learn a lesson from his playbook."

"It's a coping mechanism he acquired from working with temperamental models and movie stars."

He furrowed his brow. "He's not still a fashion photographer, is he?"

She shook her head. "He's worked for *National Geographic* for years. As Dad likes to say, he prefers wild animals to wild women. When I was growing up, he was gone for weeks at a time, sometimes months, on long expeditions to remote parts of the world." She told Julian about how her stepmother took advantage of her, making her do more than her share of the chores and babysit every night for her stepbrothers while she was down the street drinking wine with her neighbor. "Jenny made it sound like her drinking buddy was one of her girlfriends. Turns out she was a he, and Jenny was sleeping with him. I found them in bed together when I came home sick early from school one day. My father was in Antarctica at the time. This was before we had cell phones. I had to wait ten days for him to come home. Longest ten days of my life. Jenny begged me not to tell him about her affair. She laid the guilt on thick, making me feel like I was the one to blame for breaking up their marriage."

Julian shook his head in disgust. "How old were you when this happened?"

"Sixteen," Ellie said, looking at him over the rim of her coffee mug.

"How did he respond when you broke the news? I imagine that was one time he lost his cool."

She snickered. "As a matter of fact, he didn't even raise his voice when he told her to pack her bags and get out. If you want to know the truth, I think he was relieved to be rid of her. Their marriage had been on the rocks for some time." Ellie stared down at the phone in her hand. "He's never taken this long to call me back."

But when her father finally called back five minutes later, his tone was one of concern. "I owe you an apology, honey. I should've never let you go to Charleston alone. How are you holding up?"

"I'm okay, Dad. I've made a new friend." She winked at Julian. "He's been very sympathetic."

"That explains the cheerful tone in your voice," Abbott said. "I hope I get a chance to meet him."

Julian nibbled at her neck, and she pushed his head away. "Does that mean you're coming to Charleston?"

"That's why it took me so long to call you back. I just booked myself on the six o'clock flight tonight."

Ellie got up and moved to the window. "Thanks for coming, Dad. I know this is a shock for you, but I really need you here with me right now."

"I wish you'd called me sooner, sweetheart. I have a lot of questions as to how and why forty years have gone by without me knowing I have another daughter."

She had so much she wanted to tell him, but she thought it best to wait until she saw him in person. "I don't have much furniture in the house, but I have an extra bedroom if you'd like to stay here. Otherwise, there's an inn several blocks down."

"We have a lot to talk about. If it's not too much trouble, I'd like to stay with you."

"I'd like that." She offered to pick him up at the airport, but when he insisted on getting an Uber, she promised to have a late dinner waiting for him.

"That sounds perfect. I should be there by nine at the latest."

She told him she loved him before ending the call.

Within seconds of hanging up with her dad, Ellie's phone rang again, and Midge's name flashed across her screen. Midge talked for a minute straight without pausing to breathe. "I've exhausted all my resources, honey, and I came up absolutely zero on Maddie Washington. I'm over at my in-laws' house. I haven't mentioned anything to Bennett yet, because I wanted to clear it with you first. But you really should talk to them. They knew your mother and grandmother. They may be able to tell you something that might help. We're just finishing with brunch. Can you come over now?"

Ellie glanced at Julian, who was sitting close enough to hear Midge's voice over the phone. He pointed at himself and shook his head. "Can you give me forty-five minutes?"

*

When Ellie arrived at the Calhouns' an hour later, Bennett Junior and Midge had just departed for an open house they were hosting that afternoon. The housekeeper showed Ellie to the piazza where Bennett Senior and Lucille were finishing dessert. "Can I offer you coffee or lemonade, perhaps a slice of Key lime pie?" Lucille asked.

"I'm fine, but thank you."

Lucille quizzed Ellie about how she'd survived the hurricane and how she was settling into the house on South Battery before excusing herself to see to her staff in the kitchen.

Ellie was careful about what she said to Bennett. She didn't want to give too much away about her knowledge of all that had happened in her grandmother's house in the past. "I was wondering, Bennett, if you have any idea how I might get in touch with Maddie. She hasn't come to work since the day of the hurricane. I'm worried she's fallen ill or that her house was damaged badly in the storm."

He knitted his bushy gray eyebrows into one. "Hmm, that's odd. I understand why you're concerned. Unfortunately, I don't have a phone number for Maddie. Whenever I needed to speak to her about Eleanor's affairs, I phoned her at your grandmother's house. I'll double-check my files when I get to the office in the morning, but as far as I know, we don't have any contact information for her."

Ellie lowered her voice and leaned across the table. "How much did you know about my mother?"

"Well, let's see." He tugged at his chin as he stared out across the adjacent garden. "Not that much, when I think about it. I knew *of* your mother. She was a celebrity around here during her brief career as a fashion model. She appeared on the covers of all the popular magazines. But she was much younger than me. I can't say we ever actually met. You can imagine the rumors when she suddenly dropped out of sight. I asked your grandmother about her once, early on in our professional relationship. Your grandmother shut me up with a look that nearly stopped my heart. I never asked too many personal questions after that."

Pushing back from the table, he stood up, and she followed his lead. "I need to stretch my legs. Shall we stroll around the garden?" He held his arm out and waved for her to go ahead of him.

As they walked through the gravel paths, Bennett pointed out the various plantings, showing off his expertise as a gardener. They arrived at a gazebo and sat down side by side on the teak bench.

"Do you know anything about my mother's death, like where she might be buried?"

Bennett shook his head. "I never even knew Ashton had passed away until your grandmother asked me to draw up a new will leaving everything to you."

"Do you remember when that was?" Ellie asked.

His gaze shifted skyward as he considered her question. "Sometime in the late nineties, if I'm not mistaken. Her will is the original will. She never made any changes."

"How did you know how to find me after my grandmother died? Did she leave contact information for me?"

He chuckled. "That would certainly have made my job a lot easier. But your grandmother knew nothing about you, aside from your name and your father's name. Your father was easy enough to find with his impressive résumé."

Ellie had long since stopped caring whether her mean old

grandmother had ever loved her. But hearing she'd known nothing about Ellie's life aside from her name cut her to the quick.

"I sense there's something you're not telling me, Ellie. If there is anything I can help you with, you can speak to me confidentially."

"I appreciate that, Bennett. It's nice to have someone I can trust. I'm trying to figure a few things out on my own. If I reach a dead end, you'll be the first to know."

CHAPTER TWENTY-THREE
ELLIE

HER FATHER HADN'T changed since Ellie last saw him at Thanksgiving. Then again, Abbott Cohen hadn't changed much as long as she'd known him. He was trim and fit with the healthy glow of a man who spent a lot of time outdoors. His hawkish nose prevented him from being considered handsome, but with soulful dark eyes and determination etched in his expression, his face commanded attention.

He gave her a warm embrace before reaching for Pixie. He nuzzled his nose in the dog's fur and cooed about how much he'd missed her. Ellie smiled at his affection for her little dog. She thought of Julian and Mills. What was it about men and dogs?

Clutching Pixie to his torso, Abbott took in the empty hall and living room. "You weren't kidding when you said you didn't have much furniture. Do you have *any* furniture?"

"Ha-ha, yes. A few of the rooms are furnished. If you'd witnessed my grandmother's taste, you'd understand why I got rid of everything."

A serious look crossed his face. "I was here for five minutes once. I never made it past the front hall, but I remember the interior being rather dismal."

"Dismal is an understatement." She dragged her fingers across the damask wallpaper. "This god-awful wallpaper is the next to go. When Julian first saw the house, he likened it to Dracula's Castle."

"Julian, huh? I'd like to meet him. I hope he's coming for dinner."

Ellie shook her head. "I invited him, but he insisted you and I needed time alone. He's eager to meet you, too, though. Maybe tomorrow night, if we haven't taken off on a road trip to find my sister."

Abbott's body stilled. "Do we even know where to look?"

"Not yet. I'm hoping we'll come up with a clue once we put our heads together." Ellie glanced down at her father's suitcase resting upright on the floor beside him. "Believe it or not, I have two completely furnished bedrooms upstairs. Would you like a few minutes to get settled, or are you ready to eat?"

"I don't need to freshen up. Let's eat." He rolled his suitcase to the bottom of the stairs and then followed her down the hall to the kitchen.

While her father uncorked a bottle of pinot noir, Ellie ladled chili into two bowls and drizzled vinaigrette dressing onto the arugula salad. "Julian's an architect," she said when she saw him thumbing through Julian's sketchbook. "I'm thinking of expanding the kitchen, adding more work space and an eat-in area out back." She motioned toward the door.

"That would be nice." Moving to the back door, he squinted his eyes as he peered out through the darkness. "Renovating a house like this is a big step for someone who's never owned a home."

"That's why I'm dating an architect." Her attempt at making a joke fell short. "I haven't made any final decisions about anything, Dad. I may sell this house and buy a smaller one in Charleston, or I may decide to move to Paris and live out my days painting the Arc de Triomphe and the Eiffel Tower. A lot depends on what happens with Lia."

"If you move to Paris, I'll come visit you." He returned to the sketchbook and flipped through to Julian's drawing of Ellie. "It's obvious how much Julian cares about you. The emotion he captured on your face is so intense. What were you reading when he drew this?"

"One of Mom's journals."

She sprinkled cheddar cheese on the chili and added a sleeve of Saltines to the tray. When she started to lift the food tray, Abbott bumped her out of the way. "Here, let me get that." She grabbed the wine and two glasses and led him down the hall to her studio.

"Thank goodness," he said, setting the tray down on the table. "I was worried we were going to have to eat on the floor."

She tilted her head to the side as she studied her father's face. "What's with you, Daddy? You're in an awfully good mood considering the circumstances. Do you have a new girlfriend?"

Pink spots appeared on his tan cheeks. "I wouldn't call Tracey my girlfriend. We haven't been seeing each other long enough for labels. But yes, I like her quite a bit."

"Good for you!" She clapped him on the shoulder. "Does Tracey have a last name?"

"Tribble," he said, coughing into his hand.

"Tracey Tribble?" she mouthed, and he nodded. "I'd be hard-pressed to repeat her name ten times in a row sober, and definitely not after I've had a glass of wine."

"Good thing you won't ever need to." Abbott chucked her chin. "And before you ask, she's a lobbyist, originally from Montana, and she likes to watch birds as much as I do."

She rolled her eyes. "Sounds like a real match made in heaven. When do I get to meet her?"

"Soon, I hope. But you're right. This situation with your sister is serious. We need to put our love lives aside for the time being and focus on finding Amelia." He moved to the windows, the light from the terrace sconces enabling him to see into the garden. As he wandered around, getting acquainted with the room, the sketch displayed on her easel caught his eye. "Is that Amelia with you?" he asked of the sketch.

She joined him in front of the easels. "We called her Lia. And yes, that's her."

"The two of you look so terrified. What are you hiding behind?"

"Our mother's bedroom door, watching as our grandmother pushed her down the stairs." Ellie felt a chill and rubbed her bare arms.

"Good Lord, Ellie!" He placed his arm around her and drew her close. "Are you sure it wasn't an accident?"

"I'm positive. Mom confirmed it in her journal. She broke her left wrist in the fall. My grandmother wouldn't let her see a doctor about it, just like she wouldn't let her see a cardiologist about her heart condition."

He shook his head in dismay. "I'm so sorry, sweetheart. I underestimated the trauma you experienced while living here. The good news is, you appear to have experienced some sort of breakthrough. The memories you suppressed are coming back to you."

"I hope this traumatic event is the worst one," she said

about the sketch. "But I have no way of knowing for sure unless I find more journals or Maddie resurfaces." Ellie took her father by the arm and led him back to the table. "I'm starving. Let's eat while we talk. I have a lot to tell you."

While they ate, Ellie filled her father in on everything that she'd remembered and all she'd learned from her mother's journals. "You're welcome to read them yourself." She eyed the journals stacked neatly on her desk. "But I'll warn you, my grandmother was openly prejudiced against Jewish people. Mom was concerned that she would hurt Lia in some way because she resembled you. I'm sorry if that offends you, Dad. She was an evil woman. From what I've learned about her, I'd go so far as to label her a psychopath."

"People like that don't offend me. You know that about me. Maybe your mother sensed Lia was in danger and managed to somehow get her out of here."

Ellie said, "There's always the chance that something bad happened to Lia, even if it was an accident."

He eyed the leather-bound journals as one might an unfriendly dog. "I should probably read them. I don't care what your grandmother thought of me. It's your mother. I'm not sure I can handle what she said about me."

"She loved you, Dad. I've often wondered about that myself, but she is very clear about her feelings for you."

"Then why didn't she come to me when she learned she was pregnant instead of running away?"

Ellie wiped her mouth and dropped her wadded-up napkin into her empty bowl. She retrieved the top journal from the stack and fanned the pages until she found a yellowed newspaper clipping. She slid the clipping across the table to him. "On the day she found out she was pregnant, she saw this in the *New York Times*."

The clipping was worn thin from years of being handled, but the photograph was clear enough to see Abbott with his arm draped around a woman's shoulders.

Abbott glanced at the article. "I don't understand. What does this have to do with anything?"

"Who's the woman, Dad?"

He scrutinized the photograph. "I have no idea. I must've known her at the time, but that was forty years ago."

"Mom thought you were having an affair with this woman." Ellie tapped her finger on the newspaper clipping. "According to Mom's journal, her roommate, Louisa, claimed that rumors were circulating among your friends that you were seeing someone out in California."

"That's ridiculous. I was very much in love with your mother. I was planning to ask her to marry me and move with me out to California. I'd even gotten an audition for her in my next movie."

Ellie folded her arms over her abdomen. "How did you find out she'd left New York?"

"I went to her apartment looking for her the minute I got off the plane from California. I had a diamond engagement ring in my pocket and everything."

"Louisa wrote to Mom that she never heard from you, that you never called or came looking for her after she left New York."

He banged his fist on the table in a rare show of emotion. "That's a damn lie!"

She understood her father was upset, but she wouldn't

get her answers if she didn't press. "Why would she lie about something so important?"

"I have no idea." His eyes were dark with anger. "None of this makes any sense to me."

"You're right about that." Ellie left the table and returned to her easels. "Dad, there's something I need to ask you, and you need to tell me the truth."

"I have never lied to you, sweetheart."

"You've been a wonderful father to me. And I'm grateful for that. I can't imagine how hard it was for you to discover you had a six-year-old daughter. But every time I've tried to talk to you about Mom, you shut me out." She turned to face him. "Is that because you're hiding something from me? Did you know I have a twin sister?"

"Honey, no!" Abbott stood up and crossed the room to her. "Of course not." He fingered a stray lock of hair out of her face. "I would never have kept your sister from you."

"Then why have you been so against me remembering the past?"

He sighed. "Because, right or wrong, I was doing what I thought was best for you. You were such a scared little thing when you first came to live with me in California. I suspected you were abused in some way. And I was terrified that those memories, if they ever resurfaced, would cause you to have a mental breakdown."

"Is that why you were so angry at me when I decided to move to Charleston?"

"I wasn't angry about you moving here. I was worried. Turns out my concerns were justified."

For several minutes, they stood in silence staring at each other.

"I survived what happened to me here once, Daddy. Because of you, I went on to lead a happy life. With your help, I'll survive it a second time. I'm almost there. But I can't rest until I find my sister, if she's even still alive. Will you help me?"

"Of course I'll help you." He squeezed her arm. "She's my daughter. I have my own reasons for wanting to find her."

"The only way we're going to solve this mystery is if you tell me everything you remember. You may remember a detail that you don't even realize is important."

His shoulders slumped as he lowered his head. "We better make some coffee. It's going to be a long night."

CHAPTER TWENTY-FOUR
ABBOTT

T HEY TOOK THEIR coffee out to the lounge chairs on the terrace. Abbott found it easier to tell his daughter his story through the darkness.

"I had the engagement ring in my pocket. I was going to ask your mother to marry me. How different things might have been for all of us."

He closed his eyes as his mind drifted back forty years.

*

Abbott took a taxi straight from the airport to Nettie's apartment in Greenwich Village. He could hardly wait to ask Nettie to marry him. Fancy proposals weren't his style. When she opened the door, he planned to drop to one knee and slide the ring on her finger. He was confident she'd say yes. She loved him as much as he loved her. They had a bright future together in California as Hollywood's new golden couple—a glamorous model turned movie star and her brilliant film producer husband.

He was disappointed to discover no one home when he arrived at her apartment. Sliding down the wall to the floor, he rested his head against his suitcase. Jet-lagged from his trip, he promptly fell asleep.

Sometime later, Louisa nudged him awake by digging the toe of her black leather pump into his ribs. He climbed back up the wall. "Do you know when Nettie will be home? I've tried to call several times in the past few days, but no one ever answers. Have you girls been out partying every night?" he asked in a teasing voice.

Louisa unlocked the door and held it open for him. "You'd better come in."

Nettie's empty bedroom served as proof that she was gone. He was angry and confused, and he all but bullied Louisa for information. But he left the apartment two hours later convinced she had no clue as to Nettie's whereabouts.

Other than the first day they met, when she mentioned during her interview with Olga that she was from the South, Nettie had never spoken about her life before New York. He'd asked her repeatedly about her family and where she was from, but she refused to talk about her past. He'd never thought to press her, never dreamed the day would come he would need to find her. The South encompassed at least a dozen states, an area way too large to search for her.

Every day for the next week, on the off chance she was still in New York, he roamed the streets of the Village hoping for a glimpse of her. He went to her favorite coffee shops and restaurants. He stopped by the corner market, her dry cleaner's, and the pharmacy where she got her prescriptions filled. He called all her friends and work associates, but no one had seen or heard from her. Left with no choice, and with production on his new film starting in a week, he boarded a plane back to Los Angeles.

Abbott realized almost immediately that he'd made a mistake, that cinematography wasn't for him. He was good at directing films. One of his movies was even nominated for an Academy Award. He just wasn't inspired by motion pictures. One autumn, he spent several days on a photo safari while on location in Africa. During this time, Abbott realized his true passion lay in photographing magnificent wild animals and their unspoiled habitats. As soon as he wrapped up that movie, Abbott resigned from Warner Brothers Studio and moved to San Francisco. For the next two years, he traveled to remote parts of the world as he built his portfolio. When his savings ran out, he paid the rent and supported his new addiction by freelancing for wildlife magazines, one of which was *National Geographic*.

He met Jenny in a neighborhood bar late one night. They dated a few months, and in a moment of lust, he asked her to marry him. By the time he realized *that* mistake, his first son was on the way.

Fifteen months later, Abbott was in his darkroom late one rainy Sunday afternoon when he heard the phone ring in a remote part of the house, followed by the shuffle of his wife's bedroom slippers on the linoleum floor in the outside hallway. She knocked on the door. "Phone's for you."

He glanced at the stack of film rolls that needed processing. "Tell whoever it is I'll call them back."

"I tried. It's some lady. She says it's urgent."

Abbott went to the kitchen to take the call. Jenny, with the baby propped on one hip, leaned back against the counter, taking deep drags off a cigarette while she eavesdropped on his conversation.

In a dignified Southern drawl, the woman introduced herself as Eleanor Pringle, mother to Ashton Pringle.

Having never heard of either, he asked, "I'm sorry, who?"

"My daughter, Ashton Pringle. I believe you knew her as Nettie Pearson."

Nettie? After all this time. He collapsed against the refrigerator. "Of course. I know Nettie. What can I do for you?"

"Knew, Mr. Cohen, as in the past tense. My daughter passed away this morning. She asked me to call you in the event of her death. She's been in ill health for some time. Giving birth to your daughter weakened her heart beyond repair."

The hairs on the back of his neck stood to attention like soldiers. "Excuse me, did you say daughter?"

"Yes, Mr. Cohen, that's what I said. Your six-year-old daughter is here with me now. But she won't be this time tomorrow if you don't come get her. I'm an old woman. I don't have the energy for raising a child."

Abbott swallowed hard, his mouth and throat suddenly as dry as the Sahara. "Where do you live, Mrs. Pringle?"

"In Charleston, South Carolina," Eleanor Pringle said in a clipped tone. "If you catch the red-eye flight, you will get here in time."

Abbott was a seasoned traveler. He understood the logistical challenges of getting to South Carolina in a hurry. "In time for what, Mrs. Pringle? I'd have to leave my house in thirty minutes to make the flight. I'm not sure I can do that."

"If you're not here by noon tomorrow, I will drop your

daughter off at the front steps of the local orphanage." She spat out the address, and the line went dead.

Feeling his wife's steely gaze on him, he turned his back on her while he jotted the address on the notepad they kept beneath the phone. He replaced the telephone receiver and rested his forehead against the upper cabinet while he collected his thoughts. Six years old. He did the math in his head. The timing was spot-on. Nettie had run away to South Carolina to have his baby. Why hadn't she come to him? He was planning to ask her to marry him anyway.

"Well?" Jenny stubbed out her cigarette. "Are you going to tell me what's going on?"

"I have to go to South Carolina on a family emergency," he said as he brushed past his wife. "I don't have time to explain."

Abbott didn't realize until months later that Eleanor Pringle had been bluffing. She had no intention of taking Ellie to an orphanage. She'd given him her name. He would have gone straight to the authorities. They would've helped him track down his child, and when they saw how traumatized she was, they would've brought charges against Eleanor Pringle for child abuse.

He rang the doorbell at the address written on the notepaper in his hand. When no one answered, he clanged the heavy knocker. A woman, dressed head to toe in black, with cropped gray hair and irises as dark as her pupils, answered the door. "Mrs. Pringle, I'm Abbott Cohen. I'm terribly sorry for your loss. I'm at a disadvantage here. Nettie... I mean Ashton never told me she was pregnant. I would've done right by her. I loved your daughter very much."

Her fingers, gnarled like a bird's claws with long pointy

nails, gripped his arm, yanked him inside, and closed the door behind him. "This is not a social call, Mr. Cohen. We have business to conduct, which we will keep brief, and then you will leave."

He raked his hands through his dark hair. "I'd like to pay my respects to, um, Ashton. I brought clothes for the funeral."

"A private funeral will be held in a few days. You are not invited."

Abbott saw her then, the spitting image of her mother, hiding behind a wing chair in the adjacent living room. His heart danced across his chest the same way it had when he'd first seen her mother in that modeling agency in New York. Sensing her fear, he approached her with caution. "Hey there. What's your name?"

She removed her thumb from her mouth. "Ellie."

"That's a very pretty name, Ellie. You must miss your mommy."

She lowered her head and nodded.

"You don't know me, but I'm your daddy. I'd like very much for you to come live with me in California."

Eleanor Pringle appeared beside him. "Please dispense with the goo-goo talk, Mr. Cohen. I have other business to attend to." She pressed a folded document into his hand. "This is her birth certificate. You are listed as the father. Your daughter's bag is waiting by the door. You may take her now and leave."

Unsure of how Ellie would react to being separated from her grandmother or being forced to leave the only home she'd ever known, Abbott wanted nothing more than to flee this haunted house and the witch who owned it. He snatched up his daughter and her suitcase and bolted out the front door.

He felt Ellie's body trembling in his arms and her face pressed against his chest, but much to his surprise, she didn't cry. She sat in the passenger seat beside him on the way to the airport. She shivered so much her teeth chattered, but her eyes were wide with excitement as they crossed the Ashley River Bridge. A month would pass before she spoke, a year before she smiled, and eighteen months before she laughed. Her grandmother had taught her that bad things came to little girls who showed emotion.

Ellie never offered specifics about the treatment she'd received at the hands of her grandmother. Much of it he pieced together when it came out in bits. His daughter had been abused—mostly verbally but probably a bit physically as well. She'd never been allowed out of her grandmother's house except to play in the garden. She couldn't count to ten or recite her alphabet. She recoiled from any form of touch and called out from nightmares in her sleep. Over time, she grew comfortable in her new home. Even Jenny, the least maternal woman Abbott had ever known, was a fairy godmother to Ellie compared to her grandmother.

What surprised Abbott the most was his overwhelming love for his daughter. God had blessed him with this beautiful, fragile creature, and he vowed to protect her at all costs. The world outside her grandmother's home mystified her. The airplane that flew her to San Francisco. The crowded streets and cable cars. The supermarket and skyscrapers and ocean. Cats and dogs and babies in strollers. The playground and school. Every day offered a new experience for Ellie, and he delighted in watching her embrace them. To be near her, he worked from home that first year, selling his work to eager collectors. He read stacks of books to her at bedtime and walked her to school every day. She was a quick learner, and with him tutoring her, she caught up with the rest of her class in no time. Ellie was the only one he allowed in his darkroom while he was working. Perched on a stool in the corner, using his photographs as her inspiration, she painted six-year-old masterpieces with the watercolors and sketchbook he bought for her.

By the time Abbott understood the depths of his daughter's trauma, and comforted by the twenty-five hundred miles that separated them from Charleston, he decided to focus his attention on getting his daughter help rather than getting revenge against her grandmother. Instead of calling the authorities, he paid for years of counseling—some of which helped, most of which didn't—and he ignored her questions about her mother. He hoped she would forget, and when she did, he prayed she would never remember.

CHAPTER TWENTY-FIVE
ELLIE

ELLIE WAS MAD as hell at her father when she went to bed that night. She'd been angry with him for a long time for not supporting her need to remember the past. To find out he'd known more about her time spent in this house as a child than he'd ever let on was like adding gasoline to the fire. Although she didn't agree with his reasoning for keeping it from her, she understood he was trying to protect her. What he knew about her past could've helped her have a break-through, but it could just as easily have caused a breakdown.

She dreamed that night of her early years in California, of the patience and kindness her father had shown her when she first went to live with him. She'd forgotten about the time they'd spent together in his darkroom, how happy she'd been with her little paintbrush in hand. She'd inherited his creative gene, and he'd shown her early on how to appreciate it. She woke feeling at peace for the first time in many years, real-izing that Abbott was the best father a girl could ask for. He'd always put her needs before everyone else's, including Jenny and her stepbrothers. She understood now that his love for her was a direct reflection of the love he'd felt for her mother.

When he returned from his morning run, she greeted him on the piazza with a cup of coffee and a hug despite his sweaty clothes.

"What's that for?" he asked.

"For being you." She kissed his cheek. "And for being honest with me last night. You helped me see things in a different light."

Abbott hung his head. "Unfortunately, we're no closer to finding your sister."

With Pixie bouncing at their heels, they took their coffee across the street to Battery Park. They sat down on a park bench and took turns tossing a rubber ball for Pixie.

"Why did you never have my name changed to yours, Dad? I've always wondered about that."

"I gave it a lot of thought during our first years together, but in the end, I decided not to take away from you the one link you had to your mother."

They sat for a while lost in their own thoughts. "More and more, I'm thinking maybe Mom put Lia up for adoption," Ellie said finally.

Abbott considered the possibility before responding. "I don't think so, Ellie. Given the circumstances, I can't see Ashton contacting an adoption agency. She was a well-bred woman from a well-to-do family. What reasonable explanation could she have provided for wanting to put her child up for adoption? I doubt your grandmother would have given Ashton permission to leave the house. And even if she had, from what you've told me, Ashton was too weak to carry this out on her own."

"You're right, it would've aroused too much suspicion. Eleanor Pringle would never have allowed it." Pixie dropped the ball at her feet, and Ellie kicked it away.

"I noticed the windows in my room are painted shut and the door leading to the porch, the piazza as you call it, isn't really a door. If what you say is true, and Eleanor was the only one with a key to the dead bolts and the security system, I don't know how your mother could've snuck your sister out of the house."

"Which leaves only one other option."

"If Eleanor pushed your mother down the stairs, I would think her capable of worse. It could've been an accident as you suggested last night. Lia may have fallen down the stairs or drowned in the bathtub. I'm beginning to think we should call the police."

"I've considered calling the police," Ellie said. "But what are they going to do, excavate the backyard looking for her remains?"

"Do you have a better idea?"

"Actually, I do. I think we should start by contacting a private investigator. If nothing else, he may be able to help us locate Maddie."

Abbott shrugged. "I guess we can give it a shot."

Ellie patted her pockets. "Darn, I forgot to bring my phone again. Julian knows everyone. I'll call him when we get home and see if he can recommend one."

But when they got back to the house thirty minutes later, Maddie was waiting for them in the kitchen. Ellie was so happy to see her, she threw herself into Maddie's arms. "I've been worried sick about you. Why haven't you called me? Have you been ill?"

"I'm fine, Miss Ellie. Truth is, you scared me the other day with all your questions about your mother." Tears welled up in Maddie's eyes. "I'm too old to go to jail."

"Why would anyone send you to jail?" Ellie asked, alarmed.

The housekeeper darted a nervous glance at Abbott.

Ellie made the introductions. "Maddie, this is my father, Abbott Cohen. He came down from DC to help me find Lia."

"Oh Lawd." Beads of sweat broke out on Maddie's forehead as her trembling hands gripped the counter for support. "I was afraid of that. You remembered Lia."

Ellie's relief at seeing her housekeeper vanished, and she was suddenly furious. "You knew I would. You just said so yourself. That's why you disappeared."

Abbott cleared his throat. "Why don't we go talk on the terrace where we can enjoy this nice weather."

Ellie walked out of the room, leaving her father and Maddie to follow her. Once they were seated around the table outside, Ellie said, "I found more of my mother's journals in an old trunk in the attic during the storm. Either Mom stopped writing after my grandmother pushed her down the stairs or someone destroyed the rest of her journals, because they are not in this house. I have a lot of questions, Maddie. And I expect you to answer them all. The most important one is, do you know what happened to my sister?"

Maddie closed her eyes and shook her head. "I don't, Miss Ellie. I swear to you, I don't know." She dabbed at her eyes with a tissue. "The flu was going around something terrible that winter. Sally Bell and I were scared to death your mama would catch it. She was so sick by then, the flu would've killed her. It nearly killed me. I was out sick for ten days. When I came back, Miss Lia was gone. And so was Sally Bell."

Ellie felt lightheaded. "Are you saying they disappeared together?"

"I don't know." Maddie closed her eyes. Ellie thought she'd fallen asleep when suddenly she opened them again. "Miss Ashton told me your gramma fired Sally Bell for stealing her jewelry. But I know ole Sally wouldn't have taken her belongings. She wasn't that kind of person."

"Did Ashton tell you what happened to Lia?" Abbott asked.

"Nah. Miss Ashton refused to talk about Miss Lia. But she was all tore up, same as you, Miss Ellie. You both cried for months. You asked me the other day if something traumatic happened to you in this house. Many things happened to you here, but having your sister taken away from you was the worst."

An idea struck Ellie that made goose bumps appear on her skin. "Do you think it's possible that I hurt my sister?"

"Goodness no. Nothing bad happened to Miss Lia. At least I don't think so. I suspect your mama found a way to sneak your sister outta here. Maybe Sally Bell helped her. Maybe she didn't. Miss Ashton was upset because she missed her baby, but she didn't seem all that worried about her whereabouts. I asked Miss Ashton if she wanted me to call the police, and she said it wasn't a good idea to get them involved."

"Did you try to find Sally Bell, to ask her what had happened?" Ellie asked.

"Yes'm. I went to her house that very evening when I got off work. But she was long gone. The neighbors said she took her chilrun and went to live with family in Savannah."

"How did Mrs. Pringle reacted to Lia's disappearance?" Abbott asked.

"She never mentioned the child's name again. But she was mad as fire at Sally Bell. Missus Pringle said she'd fire me, too, if I stepped out of line."

Ellie propped her elbows on the table. "Let's assume, for a minute, that Sally Bell wasn't involved in Lia's disappearance, and Mom was able to sneak Lia out of the house. She couldn't have done it without help from the outside. Do you have any idea who might have helped her?"

"If not Sally Bell, then it could've been only one person: Miss Louisa Whitehead, One Fifty-nine West Ninth Street Apartment Three B, Greenwich Village, Manhattan. I can still remember her address from the letters I mailed to her."

Abbott cursed under his breath. "Louisa swore to me she didn't know how to find Ashton."

Ellie gripped her father's arm, signaling him to remain calm. "You said letters, Maddie, as in more than one? In her journal, Mom mentioned the letter she wrote notifying Louisa that she wouldn't be returning to New York. If I'm not mistaken, you mailed that letter to Louisa using your return address."

"That's right," Maddie said. "But your mama wrote more letters to Miss Louisa after your gramma pushed her down the stairs. They wrote back and forth a few times each."

"Bingo!" Ellie clapped her hands together. "There's the missing link."

"Let's not get ahead of ourselves, sweetheart." Abbot turned to Maddie. "Ashton was having you mail the letters and using your return address. Surely she gave you some clue about what was in the letters?"

"I was happy to deliver her mail, Mistah Abbott, but she never told me what was in the letters. She said it was best for me not to know. Miss Ashton was always worried about me like that. She didn't want me to get in trouble with her mama."

"Is there any chance Ashton kept the letters?" Abbott asked.

"No sir. After she read them, Miss Ashton had me burn them in the fireplace in the library." Maddie stared down at her lap. "Miss Ellie, I understand if you don't want me working here after I disappeared on you the way I did."

"Don't be silly, Maddie. I'm thrilled to have you back." Ellie got out of her chair, walked around the table, and wrapped her arms around Maddie's neck from behind. "But don't you dare leave this house today without giving me your phone number."

Maddie cackled. "No'm. I won't."

Ellie knelt down beside Maddie's chair. "I have one more question for you before you get to work. You mentioned a little while ago that you were worried about going to jail. Why would anyone send you to jail when you clearly don't know anything about my sister's disappearance?"

"Because I knew about all the other bad stuff happening in this house, and I didn't do anything to stop it. I should've called the police at the first sign of trouble, Miss Ellie, and gotten you, your mama, and your sister to safety. But my mama was sick around that time, and I desperately needed my job to pay her doctor bills."

Ellie gave the housekeeper's hand a squeeze. "I understand, Maddie. We all make sacrifices for the ones we love. My grandmother was an evil woman. Calling the police might have backfired, and so much worse could've happened. While you had no way to get us to safety, you took care of us as best you could. I told you the other day how much I appreciated your kindness. You helped me survive my time here." Ellie smiled over at her father. "My ending was happy. I found my way to my father. And I'm hopeful we'll find Lia alive and well. So you stop worrying about anyone sending you to jail. It's not going to happen."

She grinned, revealing a mouth full of dentures. "Yes'm, I understand." She rose from the table. "If you'll excuse me, I got a lot of work to do to make up for last week. By the way, Miss Ellie, did someone rob the house while I was gone?"

Ellie laughed out loud, remembering her second day there when Maddie thought someone had stolen Eleanor Pringle's portrait. "You'll be happy to know, Maddie, that an antiques dealer paid good money for my grandmother's portrait. Little did he know I would've given it to him for free."

*

They spent the rest of the morning searching the Internet for information on Louisa Whitehead. Abbott never went anywhere without his camera bag and his laptop. Having two computers enabled them to cover more ground in less time. By lunchtime, when Julian showed up with containers of tomato basil soup and Cobb salads from Five Loaves Cafe, they'd compiled a list of possible matches for Louisa Whitehead.

Julian and her father hit it off right away as Ellie suspected they might. They peppered each other with questions regarding their respective careers during lunch on the terrace. They went back to work once they'd finished eating and the trash was put away. Julian jumped in to help. He turned out to be a whiz at locating phone numbers for the Louisa Whiteheads listed on their legal pad. Abbott was the obvious choice to place the calls, since he and Louisa had once been friends. He began working his way down the list. His face registered recognition when the sixth Louisa Whitehead answered the call.

"Louisa, it's Abbott Cohen. We need to talk."

Turning his back on Julian and Ellie, he took his call outside for privacy. For fifteen minutes, he paced back and forth on the brick terrace with shoulders slumped and an intense look on his face. When he finally came back inside, his expression was dismal. "She claims she doesn't know anything about Lia."

"And you believe her?" Ellie asked.

"Not at all. There was something in her voice. I can't explain it, but I get the feeling she's holding something back." He sat down beside her on the sofa and flipped open his laptop. His fingers flew across the keyboard. "She lives in Urbanna, Virginia, a small town off the Rappahannock River. According to Google Maps, Urbanna is a seven-hour drive from here. If we spent the night in Richmond, we could drive the rest of the way in the morning." He looked up at his daughter. "I say we pay Louisa a visit in person. It won't be as easy for her to lie to our faces."

"Let's do it!" Ellie said, already on her feet. "Would you like to come with us, Julian?"

"Thanks for asking, but the two of you should make this trip alone. Leave Pip-squeak here with me. I'll move Command Central to my house in case you need anything researched."

CHAPTER TWENTY-SIX
ELLIE

ABBOTT OFFERED TO drive the first part of the trip, although he complained for a solid ten minutes about the size of her MINI Cooper. Her father wasn't a tall man, but he was broad shouldered and muscular. Ellie suppressed a laugh. He looked like a giant driving a toy car.

Once they got on I-26 heading toward Columbia, he shared with Ellie the details of his conversation with Louisa. "I pressed her hard, to the point I made her cry. But I have a right to be angry with her. She lied to me, and she lied to your mother. She should've told me Ashton was pregnant with my baby."

"But Mom made her promise not to tell you."

He nodded. "And that was Louisa's defense."

A wave of sorrow washed over Ellie. "How different things would've been for all of us if she'd told the truth. You and Mom would've gotten married. And Mom might still be alive."

"I said that very thing to Louisa. I blamed her for a lot of things, all of which she's guilty of. And I asked her why she told Ashton that rumors were going around about me cheating on her. That's when she started crying."

Ellie said, "I still don't understand why she would've lied about that."

"I always thought Louisa was a little off." Abbott tapped his head. "She was obsessed with your mother. Ashton would buy a new dress, and Louisa would go out and purchase the very same dress. Your mother could never see it. She always made excuses for her." He took his eyes off the road and looked over at Ellie. "But listen, sweetheart. I've had my say with Louisa. We're not going to bring any of this up again when we see her tomorrow. Harping on it won't help us find your sister."

"I agree, Dad. I'm fine with letting you take the lead." Ellie didn't trust herself to keep her emotions in check. She'd never felt such animosity toward someone she'd never met. "What did Louisa say about the letters?"

"She admitted to receiving a letter from your mother a few months after she left New York, when she wrote to say she wouldn't be returning and for Louisa to find a new roommate. But she claims to know nothing of the other letters."

"Did you explain who Maddie was and that she'd witnessed the exchange of letters?"

Keeping his eyes on the road, he said, "I told her your mother had used Maddie's as the return address."

"I don't get it," Ellie said, tossing her hands in the air. "Why not just say they were exchanging recipes or birthday cards instead of denying the correspondence altogether?"

He lifted his hand off the steering wheel in a your-guess-is-as-good-as-mine gesture. "I caught her off guard. Maybe she didn't know how else to respond."

Ellie shifted in her seat toward him. "Tell me what else you remember about Louisa."

He thought for a minute before responding. "She had a pretty face, but she was too chubby to ever be a model. Once she gave up on that dream, she focused all her attention on advertising. She was driven and talented. She was hired as an administrative assistant, but when she got the opportunity to write copy, her career took off. She was made partner in just a couple of years and was put in charge of the whole creative team."

"From what I've read and what you told me, it sounds like she and Mom were pretty good friends."

"I think Louisa was the first true friend your mother ever had," Abbott said. "The only true friend she ever had."

Ellie pulled her sunglasses down and looked at him over the rim. "I doubt that's true, Dad. Mom went to an all-girl college."

"You're probably right. We may never know for sure. Ashton always gave me the impression she didn't have many friends." He stopped talking while he passed a tractor trailer. "If you want to know the truth, I think Louisa was jealous of your mother. Ashton was living Louisa's dream. But she was careful never to let that green-eyed monster show. Most of the women I knew back then were always catfighting with their roommates. But not Louisa and Ashton. They were considerate of each other. And loyal to each other."

Ellie held her tongue. Why had her mother chosen an obsessive pathological liar like Louisa as her best friend? She'd add that to the list of questions she'd never get to ask her.

Abbott stroked the stubble on his chin, a faraway look on his face. "Your mother refused to go out and leave Louisa home alone. Not that that happened very often. Louisa always had plenty of dates. I wonder if she ever married. If she did, she never changed her name."

"Or reclaimed her maiden name when she divorced," Ellie added.

Abbott merged onto I-95 and exited at the next truck stop for gas. When they got back onto the highway, he adjusted his seat and drove with one hand resting casually on the steering wheel. He spoke about her mother as though desperate to express his feelings. He'd kept his love for Ashton suppressed for way too long. The more he talked, the more it became clear that he'd never stopped loving her.

"I worked with a lot of models back in my day, but your mother was the one true beauty I ever met. And I'm not just talking about the way the light bounced off the golden streaks in her strawberry-blonde hair, or her milky complexion, or classic facial features. Her real beauty came from within. She had an innocence about her that was as mysterious as it was mischievous. The camera absolutely loved her. I seldom had to retouch my photos. She was more in tune with the camera than any model I ever worked with."

"She mentioned in her journal that she'd never modeled before. Was it possible for someone to become an overnight sensation back in those days?"

He chuckled. "You mean back in the ice age? In the grand scheme of things, it wasn't that long ago. People became stars overnight with far less talent than your mother. Your mother was a natural. She was shy at first, for about five minutes."

"Was she that way with all photographers or just with you because of the chemistry you shared?"

"I can't answer that. I never attended any of her other

shoots. We worked together most of the time, but we were by no means exclusive." He checked the rearview mirror before easing into the right-hand lane. "Your mother loved being the star attraction. We went out nearly every night to trendy restaurants, nightclubs, and parties at tiny apartments crammed with creative people smoking marijuana and snorting lines of cocaine off any flat surface they could find." He winked at her. "Don't get me wrong. We were never into illegal drugs, although plenty of our friends were. Your mother's drug of choice was attention."

"The person you describe doesn't sound at all like the same person who wrote these journals." She placed a hand on the tote bag on the floorboard that contained her mother's journals. "You talk about her as though she was so full of life. This seemingly helpless person"—she patted the bag—"fell easily into the role of victim."

He risked a glance at the tote bag. "But remember that person had a heart condition. And I've only scratched the surface of your mother's complex personality. She also had a dark side that I sensed stemmed from her past. She once told me that her past was a closed chapter in her life and told me not to mention it again. That's when I stopped asking."

"I guess we know why now. She adopted a fake name for a reason." Ellie knitted her brow and pursed her lips. "What did Mom do when you went home for the holidays? Did she go with you?"

Abbott shook his head. "I never went home for the holidays. I wasn't that close with my family, even back then."

Ellie had met her paternal grandparents only a couple of times when they were passing through San Francisco on one of their many trips around the world.

"Your mother and I spent the holidays together. Thanksgivings were Friendsgivings for us. We invited anyone over who wanted to cook a turkey dinner and watch football. On Christmas Eve, we dragged a small tree home from the corner lot, decorated it with strings of popcorn and cranberries, and camped out in front of the fire for two days."

"At whose apartment, yours or hers?"

"Mostly mine, because I lived alone. Unless, of course, we were entertaining Louisa. We lived in the same neighborhood. We went back and forth a lot."

Ellie rested her head against the headrest. "None of this makes sense to me, Dad. You were already living like a married couple. The engagement ring was in your pocket, and you were flying back to New York to pop the question. When she suspected you were having an affair, why wouldn't she at least have given you a chance to explain?"

His expression grew serious. "Because she was stubborn as hell. If your mother got it in her mind that the world was flat, then the world was flat, and there was no convincing her otherwise."

Ellie smiled. "She inherited that particular trait from my grandmother. I may be hardheaded, but I'm not unreasonable. At least I don't think I am."

"You may see your mother when you look in the mirror, Ellie, but that's where the similarities end." Taking his hand off the steering wheel, he reached across the console and pinched her cheek. "You have her spirited personality, to a manageable degree, but you're also creative and pragmatic like me. There is no point in trying to figure out why your mother made the choices she made. What's done is done. We need to focus on the matter at hand."

They didn't talk for the next hour. Turning up the volume on the classic rock music, Abbott focused on driving while Ellie sat back in her seat, closed her eyes, and shed silent tears for all her family had lost. They used the drive-through at the Char-Grill in Benson and ate their burgers in the car on the road. Instead of bypassing the city and spending the night in a seedy roadside motel, they took the longer route through Richmond and splurged on rooms at the Jefferson Hotel. The ambiance at the historic hotel and a scrumptious dinner at Lemaire whetted Ellie's appetite for more, and she vowed to return to Richmond when she had more time to explore. After a quick breakfast at TJ's in the lobby of the hotel, they checked out and got back on the interstate heading east toward the Chesapeake Bay.

CHAPTER TWENTY-SEVEN
ABBOTT

THEY'D BEEN ON the highway for about an hour when Ellie pointed at her built-in navigation system. "Where are we exactly? It seems like we're out in the middle of the country somewhere, but we're surrounded by water."

"Welcome to rural Virginia, honey. The bodies of water you see are rivers that flow from the Chesapeake Bay."

A surprised look crossed her face. "How do you know so much about the area?"

"A friend of mine owns a house near Matthews, off the Piankatank River. I've been down here a couple of times with him bird-watching."

She rolled her eyes. "Bird-watching. I should've guessed," she said in a teasing tone.

Exiting off Highway 33 toward Urbanna, they drove through the small charming town on Virginia Street, took a left onto Cross Street, and continued five minutes outside of town until they reached a row of houses that fronted the Rappahannock River. He turned into the gravel driveway of a renovated farmhouse and parked beside a late-model 4Runner. He turned off the engine and handed the keys to his daughter. "I'll say this again. I know you're upset with her, but antagonizing Louisa won't get us any closer to finding Lia."

"I know, Dad," Ellie said as she opened her car door. "That's why I'm going to let you do all the talking."

When she saw them standing in her doorway, Louisa's large body slumped, like the air deflating out of a balloon. She'd gained at least a hundred pounds since he'd last seen her. She wore a sleeveless tent that exposed more of her flesh than Abbott cared to see.

Louisa gasped, and her hand flew to her mouth when she caught sight of Ellie. "You look just like her."

"That's what they tell me," Ellie said. "She died so young, I don't remember much about her."

Abbott heard the accusatory tone in his daughter's voice and elbowed a warning jab to her side.

Louisa turned back to Abbott. "You've wasted your time in coming here. I told you everything I know yesterday."

"What a spectacular view." Ellie pushed past Louisa and marched through the small foyer to the living room. Abbott pressed his lips together to hide his amusement. His daughter wasn't interested in the view of the river. She was interested in the family photographs arranged on the mantel above the fireplace.

Louisa hurried after Ellie as fast as her bulky body allowed, leaving Abbott to close the door behind them.

Ellie removed a framed photograph of a teenage girl who looked so much like Abbott it could only have been Lia. "Look, Daddy." She held the photograph out for him to see.

"Louisa has a photograph of Lia. Didn't she tell you yesterday she'd never met my sister?"

Sweat broke out on Louisa's brow, and her ample bosom heaved as she inhaled several deep breaths.

Abbott sunk a hand into the flesh on her back. "Are you all right? Maybe you should sit down."

"I just need a minute to collect myself. Make yourselves comfortable"—she waved a flabby arm at the sitting area—"while I get us some refreshments."

Ellie returned the photograph to the mantel and took a seat on the sofa. "Be nice!" Abbott said as he sat down next to her.

She curled her upper lip and bared her fangs at him with a little hiss. He chuckled in response. His daughter was out for blood.

"The view is amazing," Ellie said, staring out the sliding glass doors at the colorful sailboats racing up and down the river. "I wonder if this is where Lia grew up?"

Louisa was gone so long Abbott was beginning to think she'd sneaked out of the back door when the aroma of coffee wafted in from the adjoining kitchen. She waddled into the room and dropped the tray of cups and saucers on the coffee table with a rattle. She flopped down into a nearby armchair. "I didn't know there were two of you until I spoke to your father yesterday. You look nothing like your sister."

"Funny thing about fraternal twins," Ellie said.

Abbott laced his fingers together and propped his elbows on his knees. "Start talking, Louisa, and don't leave anything out."

She sat up straighter in her chair and placed her hands in her lap. "Nettie wrote to me a few years after she left and told me she was ill, that she had a heart condition that was worsened by her pregnancy. We exchanged several letters."

Ellie's hands were clasped so tight her knuckles were white. "What did you talk about in these letters?"

Louisa exhaled a deep breath. "After Nettie left New York, I married the first guy that came along. Out of loneliness or boredom, maybe a combination of both. We were having marital problems at the time, and I'd recently discovered that I was infertile. It was comforting to have a friend to pour my heart out to."

Abbott had a difficult time summoning any sympathy for this woman. "I'm sorry for your troubles. Can we move on with the story?"

"I'm getting to it." Louisa took her time dumping three spoonfuls of sugar in one of the mugs. "Late one night the following January, I received a call from a woman claiming to be a friend of Net—. I mean Ashton's. She told me Ashton had passed away. According to this woman, Ashton made a deathbed request that I raise her daughter as my own. She said Ashton was broke and had no other family to look out for the child."

Ellie's mouth fell open. "But Mom didn't die until years later."

Louisa lifted a beefy shoulder. "I had no way of knowing that. In hindsight, I was so desperate for a child, I didn't ask too many questions. And I was distraught over losing my friend, especially at such a young age." She locked eyes with Abbott. "I would've done anything for Nettie. You know that."

"Me, too, Louisa. I wish I'd been given the chance."

The room fell silent for an awkward moment. "Do you remember this woman's name?" Ellie asked finally.

"She never told me her name, not even when I flew to Charleston to get Lia. We met at the airport. We hardly spoke. She was visibly upset about parting with Lia."

"What did the woman look like?" Abbott asked.

Louisa paused before answering. "Heavyset, black, probably in her early sixties."

Abbott exchanged a look with his daughter. *Sally Bell.*

"Tell me about Lia's emotional state." Abbott thought back to the day he came to pick Ellie up from Charleston. "Did she seem afraid?"

Louisa sipped her coffee. "She might have been a little frightened. She was going off to live with a stranger. But overall she seemed like a perfectly well-adjusted three-year-old."

"I find that hard to believe," Abbott said. "Ellie was a mess when she came to live with me, and understandably so considering she'd never been outside the house before."

"Are you calling me a liar?" Louisa's blue eyes darted back and forth between them. "I didn't know any of that at the time, otherwise I might have been more concerned about her emotional state. I'd never been a parent before. Maybe I missed some of the signs. But I provided for Lia the best way I knew how."

"No need to get upset, Louisa. No one's calling you a liar." Abbott got that same old sense that Louisa's brain was not firing on all cylinders. He needed to find out as much information from her as he could, while he had the chance. He'd piece it all together later. "Where were you living at the time?"

"I was still living in New York. I hired a nanny to look after her while I was at work. When the weather was nice, Bridget took Lia to the neighborhood park. They often had playdates with other nannies and their charges, but for the most part, Lia led a sheltered life." Louisa popped a cheese biscuit in her mouth and swallowed it whole with coffee. "New York, back in those days, was no place to raise children. It's not much better now, if you ask me, although the city is much cleaner and the schools are more competitive.

"When the time came for Lia to start kindergarten, I decided I needed to make a change. I'd grown tired of the long hours and cutthroat environment in the advertising industry. I sold my share of the partnership and moved down here. I wanted somewhere quiet to live near the water where I could write. I'm a romance writer."

"I've read my share of romance novels. How come I've never heard of you?" Ellie asked in a suspicious tone.

Abbott applauded his daughter her frank manner of questioning. She'd make a good detective if she ever decided to give up painting.

"I write under the pen name Holly Knoll."

Abbott had never read a romance novel in his life, but even he'd heard of the reclusive Holly Knoll who never showed her face even though she topped the charts with every new release.

"You've made quite a name for yourself," Abbott said. "Did you ever remarry?"

Louisa turned up her pert nose. "No, I never did. I haven't been in a relationship since Lia came into my life." She drained the rest of her coffee. "I know what you're thinking, Abbott. You're not the first to ask me that question. An author doesn't have to be experienced to write about love. Every woman dreams of romance despite her age and relationship status."

"I'm sure Lia's very proud of your success." Ellie's tone was now sarcastic. "Did you ever consider trying to find my father, to let him know about his daughter?"

Louisa stared out the window at the sailboats zigzagging back and forth across the river. "I thought about it for about a second in the beginning. Then I realized Lia was my only chance to have a child of my own. After that… well, I loved her too much to give her up."

"How much does my sister know about her past?" Ellie asked.

With a trembling hand, she set her coffee cup down on the table. "She knows her biological mother was a friend of mine who passed away and left her in my care. Whenever she asked about her father, I told her I knew nothing about him."

Abbott wasn't surprised. He'd anticipated such an answer.

"I realize my sister was only three, but do you think she remembers anything from when she lived in the house? I'm curious if Lia has been plagued with suppressed memories like me."

Louisa paused a minute to think before responding. "As far as I know, she doesn't remember anything from that time in her life. She's struggled with depression off and on over the years, but I don't see how her past could possibly have anything to do with it."

Ellie glared at Louisa. "Are you kidding me? It's common knowledge that abused children are prone to adulthood depression."

"Is she mentally stable now?" Abbott asked.

"She was never mentally unstable," Louisa snapped. "So she got a little depressed. Don't you get depressed sometimes, too? She's perfectly fine now, happily married with two beautiful children."

"How long has it been since you've seen her?" Abbott asked.

"Several months. They came here last summer for the Fourth of July holiday. We don't get to see each other as much as we'd like with them living so far away in—" Louisa clammed up.

Ellie moved to the edge of the sofa. "Living where, Louisa? Where is my sister?"

Her turkey neck wobbled when she shook her head. "I can't tell you that."

Abbott peered at her from under his brow. "You can, Louisa, and you will. Otherwise I'll be forced to go to the authorities."

Tears welled up in Louisa's blue eyes and she stood up with surprising speed. "Excuse me for a minute," she said and fled the room.

"Do we really have grounds to go to the authorities?" Ellie asked once they were alone.

"Who knows?" He threw his hands in the air and fell back against the sofa cushions. "If we don't pressure her, we'll never get what we need."

"Forget about Louisa. I'll find what we need on my own." Ellie leaped up off the sofa and crossed the room to Louisa's desk by the window.

"What're you doing?" he asked in a hushed tone when she began rifling through the drawers. "You can't go through Louisa's desk without her permission."

"Watch me." She rummaged through the drawers one at a time until she found Louisa's address book. Abbott moved to her side and looked over her shoulder while she thumbed through the gold tabs. When she didn't find Lia's contact information under *P*, she flipped back to *L*. The top entry was Lia's. "Here she is. Lia Bertram. She lives on Cherry Blossom Lane in Decatur, Georgia." Ellie set the book on the desk and snapped a photograph of the contact information with her phone.

Louisa appeared in the doorway. "What're you doing?"

"Getting my sister's address. You can't stop me from seeing her." With fists clenched at her side, Ellie marched across the room to face her. Abbott feared his daughter might strike the poor woman.

Louisa took a step backward and pressed herself against the doorjamb. "What're you planning to do?"

"I'm going to Georgia to see my sister." Ellie glanced over her shoulder at her father. "How long do you think it'll take us to get there?"

"Nine or ten hours." Abbott looked down at his watch. "We won't get there until late tonight."

She turned back to Louisa. "Then you have until morning to provide an introduction for us. I don't know what kind of relationship you have with Lia, but I imagine it'll make it easier on her if you explain the situation." Ellie stopped at the door. With her back to the woman, she said, "And, Louisa, be sure to tell the whole truth this time."

CHAPTER TWENTY-EIGHT
ELLIE

ELLIE AND ABBOTT hit the road again, this time heading in the opposite direction. Her father insisted on driving. She sensed he didn't trust her driving skills, but he would never admit it.

"What's bothering you?" Abbott asked when he saw her staring blindly out of the window at the cars passing by.

"Did you get the feeling Louisa was holding something back?"

"That's vintage Louisa. She likes to play games. She'll tell you part of the story while leaving out a few key details. Maybe that's why she's made a successful career as a novelist. She likes to have control."

"She seems shady to me," Ellie said. "I don't trust her one bit."

"There's a lot that doesn't make sense to me about this situation. Maybe once we meet Lia we'll understand more."

Ellie called Julian with the latest developments and then spent the next sixty miles stalking her sister on social media.

Using Lia's married name, she located profiles on Instagram and Facebook, but she seemed to spend most of her time posting images of white sandy beaches and tropical alcoholic beverages to her Pinterest boards. Lia used the same profile picture for every account. With dark hair and eyes and a dainty version of his nose, she appeared to be a female clone of their father. The photographs in her stream of posts on Facebook showed two little girls about the age of four with doe-brown eyes and hair to match. They weren't identical, but there was no doubt they were twins.

"Looks like you're a grandfather. Twin girls, judging from the pictures." His face beamed, and she felt a pang of jealousy. "I'm sorry I never gave you grandchildren."

"I'm sorry, too, Ellie, for you and for me. You would make a wonderful mother. Women are having babies well into their forties these days. Maybe it's not too late for you, if things work out with Julian."

She shrugged it off. "You're getting a little ahead of yourself. We've been seeing each other for less than two weeks."

"I know a good match when I see one," Abbott said with a twinkle in his eye.

"He already has a daughter. I don't even know if he wants more children. We haven't talked about it."

"You'll get to be an aunt, if that's any consolation," he said in a soft voice.

"I hadn't thought of that." She wondered if, once they got to know each other, her sister would allow her daughters to visit her for a few days in Charleston. "Maybe I'll teach them to paint."

He threw his head back and laughed. "Good thing there are two of them. You can teach one of them to paint. I'm going to show the other our magnificent planet through the camera lens."

"They might not be interested in either if they didn't inherit your creative gene." Ellie returned to her stalking. "Based on her Pinterest boards, Lia likes to travel. I wonder who keeps her daughters while she's gone on all these trips. They don't look like family-type vacations to me."

"Don't judge a Pinterest board by its cover. Maybe she's planning an anniversary trip."

"Maybe." Ellie dropped her phone in her bag. "We didn't think to ask Louisa if Lia has a career. Which means we'll have to be at her house bright and early tomorrow morning to catch her before she leaves for work if she does."

The drive to Atlanta seemed to last forever. They were exhausted by the time they checked into the Marriott Courtyard in Decatur at ten o'clock that night. They booked two nights at the hotel in the hopes their reunion with Lia would go well and she'd invite them to stay in town for a few days to get better acquainted. They rose before daybreak the next morning and left the hotel without eating breakfast. Ellie's Google Maps app directed them to Lia's house, a medium-size new-construction home identical to the others on the cul-de-sac. At seven thirty, parents were departing their houses for work and a group of young children were lined up near the stop sign waiting for the approaching school bus.

Abbott parked by the curb in front of Lia's house and turned off the engine. "There aren't any cars in the driveway. I hope we haven't missed her already."

"I don't know about you, but I have butterflies in my stomach," she said as she smeared her nude lipstick across her lips.

"I'll admit to feeling a little queasy." He took a deep breath. When they got to the front door, Ellie rang the doorbell and took a step back. A couple of minutes passed with no answer, and she tried the bell again, adding a clang from the brass knocker for good measure. Still no answer. She peeked through the side window and saw light streaming from a pair of lamps on a long table in the center hallway. Pressing her ear to the door, she heard faint voices coming from a television in a distant part of the house. She rapped on the door several times before finally giving up.

"Maybe she's in the shower," Abbott suggested.

"Or maybe she ran out for some milk, which would explain the empty driveway."

"Why don't we go get some coffee and come back in a few minutes," Abbott said, and she agreed.

They located a Starbucks about a mile away. They fiddled with their phones while they drank coffee and nibbled on egg bites. Having been in the car together for two days, neither had much to say.

An hour later they returned to Lia's house. The driveway was still empty, but when Ellie looked through the window, the inside of the house was dark and silent. "This is strange."

"Maybe her car's in the garage." Abbott started around the side of the house, and Ellie followed him. He had to stand on his tiptoes to see inside the garage window. "I see a minivan—a mommy car for sure."

"Maybe Louisa scared her off and she's avoiding us."

They returned to the front door, but this time Abbott did the pounding. Cupping his hands around his mouth, he called through the window, "Lia, we know you're in there, and we're not leaving until we talk to you. We've come a long way to see you. Will you please give us a few minutes?"

They heard the pitter-patter of feet and the sound of tiny voices. The door opened a crack, enough for them to see Lia balancing one little girl on her right hip and the other hiding behind her left leg.

"What's this about?" Lia asked, a note of impatience in her voice.

"A family matter." Ellie took a step forward, forcing Lia to open the door wider.

Her sister's appearance caught Ellie off guard. Lia wore jeans and a black turtleneck despite the warm day. She was hollow cheeked and bone thin, the kind of skinny that resulted from an eating disorder. Her haunted eyes gave them the once-over and then traveled up and down the street behind them. Ellie turned around, but there was nothing of interest aside from her MINI Cooper on the curb and a tricycle on the sidewalk at the neighbor's house next door.

"We met with Louisa yesterday at her house in Virginia," Ellie continued. "She was supposed to call and tell you we were coming."

Lia set her glassy eyes on Ellie. "I've been ignoring the phone. I haven't been feeling well."

When the child Lia was holding squirmed, her turtleneck stretched down far enough for Ellie to see a burn scar, faded and puckered, that traveled up her neck and crept onto the bottom part of her face along her jawline. Every nerve ending in Ellie's body stood to attention. Was that scar connected to some event she had yet to remember?

"May we come in?" Abbott asked in a gentle voice. Ellie

sensed, without having to look at her father, that he, too, had noticed the scar.

Lia's eyes darted to the end of the street and back. "I don't think that's a good idea."

"Please, it's important." Ellie cringed inwardly at the begging tone in her voice. "I promise we'll take only a few minutes of your time. We've traveled all the way from South Carolina to Virginia to here, tracking you down."

Lia shifted the child to her other hip. "You mentioned a family matter. You'll need to be more specific."

"It's about your biological mother," Ellie said.

Lia's thin body grew rigid. "You knew my mother?"

"And your father," Abbott added.

She hesitated for only a second. "In that case, come in." She stepped out of the way so they could enter and then closed and locked the door behind them. "I'll turn on a movie for the girls, and we can talk in the kitchen."

Ellie took that as a signal to follow Lia to the rear of the house. The rooms were immaculate, not what she'd expect in a home where little children lived. Aside from the small pile of toys on the family room floor, everything appeared in its place. There were no breakfast dishes in the sink or coffee mugs on the counter. No baskets of unfolded laundry on the floor or finger smudges on the glass doors leading to the back deck. Once the girls were settled in front of the TV, Lia led Abbott and Ellie to the round dining table in the kitchen and waited for them to sit down. She did not offer them coffee or tea or even a glass of water.

Louisa's words echoed in Ellie's head. *She's perfectly fine now, happily married with two beautiful children.* The woman sitting in front of her was neither fine nor happy. *They came*

*here last summer for the Fourth of July holiday. We don't get to
see each other as much as we'd like with them living so far away.*
"How long has it been since you've seen Louisa?"

Lia lifted a bony shoulder and said, "A year or so ago, I
guess. We're not that close." She glanced at the clock on the
stove. "I need to leave for work soon."

"Do you mind if I ask what you do?" Abbott said.

Lia glared at him. They were mirror images sitting across
the table from each other. How could her sister not notice
the resemblance? "That's really none of your business. Either
tell me why you're here or I'll have to ask you to leave. I'm
not in the habit of inviting strangers into my home when my
husband's not here."

"Do you remember anything from your childhood before
you came to live with Louisa?" Ellie asked.

"Of course not. I was too young."

Ellie moved to the edge of her chair. "This may come as
a shock to you, Lia, but we share the same biological mother.
You and I are fraternal twins."

She gave Ellie's face a quick once-over. "I don't see the
resemblance." She fell back in her chair. "This can't be happening to me right now. I'm seriously not in the mood for
long-lost twin sisters today."

Ellie held back her frustration. This was not the reception
she'd hoped for. "I don't mean you any harm, Lia. I learned
of your existence only a few days ago. But I came as soon as I
could. I wanted to meet my sister."

"You're thirty-seven years too late," Lia said, her attention focused on an object outside the window behind Ellie.
"Louisa is the only family I've ever known. Lord knows, I
don't need any more of that kind of headache."

Ellie shot her father a look. *Should we stay or should we go?*

Abbott tapped the table beside Lia's arm to distract her from whatever invisible being held her attention in the backyard. "If you could give us a little time, Lia. We just wanted the opportunity to get to know you, no strings attached."

Lia jerked her head toward him. "We?" Her eyes traveled his face, from his square chin to his hooked nose to his M-shaped forehead. She aimed a thumb at Ellie. "If she's my twin, who the hell does that make you?"

Ellie noticed a slight quivering of his chin when he said, "I'm your father, Lia."

Lia let out a high-pitched laugh. "This is great. A twin sister who looks like Annie and Daddy Dearest."

The twins peered over the back of the sofa in the adjoining room when their mother laughed.

Lia planted her elbows on the table and her face in her hands. Ellie's eyes gravitated to the angry red scars peeking out from beneath her sleeves. A suicide attempt? Louisa had made light of Lia's depression, but they knew she'd been holding back. This woman in front of her was a mess. Ellie didn't need Lia's kind of problems. She observed the tender faces watching her from the sofa. These little angels were her nieces, her own flesh and blood, and she didn't even know their names. She shuddered to think what kind of life they led with a mother like Lia.

Her sister sprang out of her seat. "You've come at a really bad time. It's best if you just go away, and we'll pretend none of this ever happened."

Ellie noticed the little girls duck down behind the cushions in fear.

Abbott stood to face her. "We didn't mean to upset you, Lia."

"Once upon a time, I dreamed of finding my family. But that was a really long time ago. I don't feel any less empty now than I did thirty minutes ago when you barged your way into my home. I heard you out. Now you need to go."

She started for the door, leaving them no choice but to follow. Ellie removed the hotel notepad—with their names and numbers scrawled across the top page—from her handbag and dropped it on the kitchen counter on her way out.

CHAPTER TWENTY-NINE
ABBOTT

ABBOTT AND ELLIE drove back to the hotel in silence. He parked the car in a space out front, but he kept the engine running. "Something's wrong about this situation. What is it that we're missing?"

"There are a lot of things wrong about this situation, starting with the scars on her wrists," Ellie said. "Did you notice them?"

His stomach rolled and he tasted coffee. How had he missed that? "You mean like suicide scars? I saw the one on her face, obviously, but not on her wrists."

"I'm no expert, but Lia said, and I quote, 'I don't feel any less empty now than I did thirty minutes ago.' That sounds like a suicidal thought to me."

Despite her rudeness toward them, he felt an unexpected tenderness for Lia. He'd sensed her distraction. Maybe she was having marital problems or experiencing depression. He wouldn't cast judgment until he understood what was going on in her life.

He noticed the sky darkening to the west as the predicted storm system moved into the area. But he wasn't ready to return to his dismal hotel room.

"I'm calling Louisa. Let's use your phone so we can talk to her on speaker." He held his hand out to Ellie, and she dropped the phone in his palm. He dialed the number. The phone connected to Bluetooth, and the line began to ring. Louisa's screechy voice answered the call. "Louisa, it's Abbott. I have Ellie on speakerphone with me."

"Thank the good Lord. I've been worried sick," she said, sounding slightly out of breath. "Lia won't answer her phone. I've called at least a hundred times. Is she okay? Did you have a chance to talk to her? What about my grandchildren? Did you see them?"

Abbott felt his temperature rise. Technically speaking, they were *his* grandchildren, not hers. This woman had deprived him of precious time he could've spent with his daughter and his grandchildren.

"We saw Lia and the twins," Ellie said. "She was less than thrilled to find out she has a father and a twin sister."

"Oh dear," Louisa said. "I was afraid of that. Lia can be sorta difficult at times."

"You failed to mention that yesterday," Abbott said. "And why didn't you call us if you were so worried?"

"I don't have your number."

"Yes, you do, from when I called you on Monday." Had it been only two days since all this craziness began? It felt like two years.

"Oh, silly me. I didn't think about that."

Abbott rolled his eyes at his daughter. *This woman is a total flake.*

"How'd she get the scars on her wrists, Louisa?" Ellie asked. "You mentioned she suffered depression. You never said anything about a suicide attempt."

"What suicide attempt? You must be mistaken. Lia would never do anything to hurt herself. Maybe she burned her arms getting a hot pan out of the oven."

Ellie locked eyes with him and mouthed, "She's delusional."

Abbott asked, "How about the other scar, the one on her face and neck?"

A long moment of crackly silence filled the line. "She already had that scar when she came to live with me. Based on what I now know about her grandmother, I guess she's the one who hurt that innocent child. What did Lia tell you about how she got the scar?"

"That's hardly the thing you ask someone you've just met," Ellie said. "The bigger question is, what has Lia told you about the scar? You're the one who raised her."

"When she was little, she was too traumatized to talk about it," Louisa said. "I'm not sure she remembers how it happened now. She never mentions the scar. She acts as though it doesn't exist."

Then why was she wearing a turtleneck on a warm day like today? Abbot thought to himself. "Wait a minute! You just said Lia was traumatized when she came to live with you. I specifically asked you yesterday about her emotional state, and you told us that she seemed like a perfectly well-adjusted three-year-old."

"I said *overall* she was well-adjusted. I also said she seemed a little frightened. Frightened, traumatized, what's the difference?"

"You're an author, Louisa. You should know." Abbott felt

his frustration growing. "A child is frightened by a nightmare. When those nightmares happen every night, she's traumatized."

Louisa let out an audible sigh. "Then she was traumatized."

"Did you take her to see a child psychiatrist?" Abbott asked.

"Humph. There was never any need for a child psychiatrist. She wasn't *that* bad off. Lia adjusted to her new environment over time, and she stopped having nightmares."

"Did she ever see a therapist for her depression?" Ellie asked.

"For a few years while she was in high school. Waste of time and money if you ask me." Abbott heard a bitterness that had been absent in her voice the day before.

"How long has it been since you've seen Lia?" Ellie asked.

They heard a muffled sound as though Louisa had dropped the phone or was changing her seating position. "Sometime last spring. I'm not exactly sure when. I flew to Atlanta to see them."

Ellie gaped at the lie, and Abbott shook his head, warning her not to press.

"Lia seemed distracted today," Abbott said. "Is there any chance she could be having problems in her marriage? Her husband wasn't at the house when we were there."

"He doesn't treat Lia right, and I don't care for him very much," Louisa said.

"How'd she meet him?" Ellie asked.

Louisa slurped noisily from a cup of liquid, coffee if Abbott had to guess. "Growing up, Lia never had much experience with men. She attended an all girls' boarding school near here and then Hollins, a private single-sex college in Roanoke. When she graduated, she was eager to see the world. She took a job in the marketing department at Delta Airlines in Atlanta. She was making a good salary that included free air travel, mostly domestic but she went on a couple of international trips as well. She seemed happy, which is why I was surprised when she quit Delta and went to work as an administrative assistant at a residential construction firm. Turns out she was sleeping with the owner of that construction firm, who happened to be a married man. Fortunately, he didn't have children, but when his wife found out about Lia, his marriage ended in divorce. He whisked Lia off to Las Vegas for a quickie wedding before the ink was dry on his divorce papers."

Abbott couldn't trust anything she said. He dragged his finger across his neck, signaling to Ellie he was ready to end the call. "I think that's all we have for now, Louisa. We'll be in touch."

Ellie grabbed his arm before he could end the call. "Wait, Louisa. One more thing before you go. What're the twins' names? Lia never said."

"Bella and Mya. Sweetest little things you ever did see."

*

It had begun to sprinkle a few minutes earlier, but as he was ending the call, it started to pour.

Ellie sat in the passenger seat, a dazed expression on her face as she stared out at the rain. "What is it, honey?"

She slowly turned her head toward him. "Bella and Mya were the names of our dolls when we were little. Lia remembers, Daddy. No wonder she didn't seem surprised when I told her I was her twin sister."

Abbott let his head fall back against the seat. "I'm not sure what to think about any of this."

"I don't get it. Yesterday Louisa told me she saw Lia over the Fourth of July. Today she said she saw her sometime last spring. And Lia said she hasn't seen Louisa in a year. Was the last time they were together so unmemorable they can't recall the occasion?"

"Or so painful they are trying to forget."

"What do we do now?" Ellie asked, referring to the rain pelting down on the windshield. "Since our rooms are already booked until tomorrow, we should probably stay the night in case Lia decides to call one of us. Although I have a sneaking suspicion she won't."

"Maybe she'll surprise us," he said, without much conviction. He turned the wipers to full speed. "It's supposed to rain all afternoon. What say we find a decent restaurant and have a three-martini lunch?"

Ellie glanced at her watch. "But it's only eleven o'clock."

"Then we'll start out with a Bloody Mary." He accessed the Yelp app on his phone and searched for restaurants in the area. "The reviews are good at Leon's Full Service. Let's go there." He put the car in reverse and backed out of the parking space.

Ellie said nothing on the way over nor while they waited for their Bloody Marys at the bar in Leon's fifteen minutes later.

Abbott nudged her with his elbow. "What's on your mind?"

"I can't get over the fact that Lia named her daughters Mya and Bella. I'm anxious to talk to her and find out what else she remembers."

"I wouldn't count on her remembering much. She was only three."

The bartender, a woman in her late twenties with dark curls springing out all over her head, arrived with their drinks, and they thanked her.

Ellie dragged the stirrer around in her drink. "This whole thing is getting weirder by the minute. Aside from meeting Julian, I wish none of this had ever happened. I'd gladly give up my inheritance to be back in my tiny apartment in San Francisco." Ellie removed the stirrer from her drink and took a sip. "I suggest we don't call Louisa anymore for help. She lies so much, I'm not sure she even knows what the truth is anymore."

"Agreed. Do you think she's lying about the scar?"

"Definitely! Although I don't know why she would, unless she's somehow responsible for causing the scar and she's too ashamed to tell us. I have no recollection of Lia getting burned when we were little. That's not to say it didn't happen, considering my unreliable memory."

Abbott took a sip of his Bloody Mary and licked his lips. "What about the scars on Lia's wrists? How could Louisa not know about a suicide attempt?"

"Those scars look fresh. She may legitimately not know about them."

A large crowd of people entered the restaurant, taking the noise level up several notches. The bartender slid menus across the wooden counter to them, and for the next few minutes they studied the offerings. When the bartender returned, they both ordered the arugula salad with grilled shrimp.

Ellie stared into her half-empty glass. "If it wasn't for my inheritance, I'd drive back to Charleston this afternoon." She lifted her glass to her lips and drained the rest of her Bloody Mary. "You know, I felt guilty when I first found out about my inheritance, like somehow I didn't deserve it. But then I started remembering all the pain and suffering my grandmother put me through. Put *us* through. The money is restitution for that pain and suffering. But half of it belongs to Lia. Mom would want her to have it. I'm tempted to let my grandmother's attorney figure out the best way to give it to her. I really don't want to get mixed up in my sister's problems. Is that wrong of me?"

He placed his hand over hers. "You're overwhelmed, honey, and rightly so. You've been dealing with a lot for a long time. But she's family. If she needs our help, we should give it to her."

CHAPTER THIRTY
ABBOTT

ELLIE ORDERED ANOTHER Bloody Mary before their salads arrived and then drank two glasses of wine during lunch. She was too interested in drowning her sorrows to notice Abbott had switched to sweet tea. Her alcoholic buzz played right into his plans. She was struggling with the situation. And he respected that. She needed a break from the turmoil that had taken over her life. But he wasn't ready to give up on Lia. Call it a parent's intuition; even though he'd met his daughter for the first time only that morning, he had a gut feeling that all was not right in her world. When she'd finally answered the door for them earlier, he'd noticed her scanning the street behind them as though expecting to see someone else. And she'd been too anxious to get rid of them for someone who'd just been reunited with her long-lost family.

After he paid the tab, he drove Ellie back to the hotel, walked her to her room, and pulled the bedspread over her fully clad body. He heard the soft sound of her snores before he exited the room.

The heavy rain had subsided, and a fine mist fell over the area as he returned to Lia's neighborhood. He circled the cul-de-sac and backed into the driveway of a house that was for sale catty-corner to Lia's. Satisfied with his unobstructed view of her house, he removed his Canon from its bag and chose a 100-400 mm lens, which gave him sufficient zoom to focus on Lia's front door. Nobody stirred on the street for the next thirty minutes. The mailman was nowhere in sight, and the occupants of the houses were either at work or at school.

Abbott was feeling drowsy and had closed his eyes for a wink of sleep when he heard the loud muffler of an approaching car. He sat up straight in his seat and positioned his camera. A black Honda Civic Coupe with oversize tires sped down the street and whipped into Lia's driveway. Two average-size men, dressed in black with their dark hair slicked back into man buns, got out of the car and strutted across the lawn. The taller of the two rang the bell. When no one answered, both men began pounding on the door. The door opened a crack, and the two men forced their way in. Abbott abandoned his camera and darted across the street. He approached the house with caution. The door was open just wide enough for him to see inside. The men appeared to be unarmed, but one of them held Lia's arm in a tight grip. Abbott overheard the man say, "We won't hurt you. We just want to know where your husband is."

"Afternoon, gentlemen," Abbott said, kicking the door open the rest of the way. "Is there something I can help you with?"

All three heads jerked toward him in surprise.

Abbott placed his hand on his hip, drawing his raincoat back to reveal the revolver stuffed in his waistband. He'd gotten in the habit of carrying a weapon during his years of exploring the wild. He had a permit to carry a concealed weapon, but so far, he'd never been in a situation where he needed to use it.

One of the men spotted the revolver. "Hey, dude," he said, his hands in the air. "We don't want no trouble. We're just looking for this lady's husband. He owes our boss a lot of money."

The brawnier of the two men stepped toward Abbott. "And just who the hell are you?"

Abbott removed his pistol from its holster and held it pointed at the ground. "Not that it's any of your business, but I'm her father," he said, nodding his head at Lia.

"Chill, Pops." His hands shot up. "Like my friend said, we're just looking for her husband."

"Is your husband here?" Abbott asked Lia, who shook her head vehemently. "There. You have your answer. He's not here. Why don't you leave your business card with us, and we'll be sure to tell him you stopped by when he returns."

The brawny man said, "That won't be necessary. He knows we're looking for him."

The two men backed out of the door and then turned and jogged to their car. Abbott squinted as the Honda sped off down the street, but he couldn't make out any of the license plate.

He slammed the door shut and returned the pistol to its holster. "Where are the girls? Are they safe?"

She nodded. "They're taking a nap."

"Clearly, your husband's in some kind of danger. Tell me

everything you know. And be quick about it before they come back." She studied his face as though trying to decide whether to trust him. "If you'd rather call a friend to help you, then call them. But you need to protect your children."

Lia collapsed against the wall. "When my husband came home from work on Monday night, he told me he was in financial trouble. He'd used his construction company as collateral for a bank loan to pay back some gambling debts. I didn't know he'd been gambling. Apparently, he has an addiction. When he lost even more money gambling, he borrowed from their boss to pay the bank. Ricky, that's my husband, wanted me to borrow money from Louisa. When I refused to call her, we had an argument, and he left. I haven't seen or heard from him since."

"Have you called your husband's office?"

She looked at him as if he were the most ignorant man on the planet. "They haven't seen him since Monday, either. He's hiding out somewhere. Those goons wouldn't be harassing me if they knew where he was."

Abbott checked out the side window to make certain they hadn't come back. "How long have they been harassing you?"

Lia pressed a trembling hand against her temple. "The phone calls started on Tuesday morning; just hang-ups at first and then a man with a deep voice asking to speak to Ricky. That Honda has been driving up and down the street all day and night since Tuesday. It was even parked in front of my house this morning when I woke up."

"You're lucky I showed up when I did. These men will use you and the girls to draw your husband out of wherever he's hiding. You realize that, don't you?"

"Of course I realize that. But I have nowhere to go." She

began pacing up and down the hall. "I checked our joint bank account. Ricky withdrew all our cash. The bastard left me only thirty dollars."

"Then, like it or not, you're going to have to come with me. We need to get the girls out of here before they come back. Go pack your things. I'll get my car and pull around back."

He retrieved his car from across the street and then poked around the backyard while he waited for Lia to finish packing. When he discovered the door on the side of the garage unlocked, he went inside and moved the children's car seats from her van to Ellie's MINI. He was leaning against the hood of the car when Lia emerged a few minutes later with a sleepy twin on each hip and three small suitcases lined up on the floor behind her.

"Why can't I follow you in my van?" she asked when she saw the car seats in the MINI.

"These men have been staked out in front of your house for two days. They know what kind of toothpaste you brush your teeth with. Trust me, they have the make, model, shade of gray, and license plate number of your van memorized."

He placed their suitcases in the back of the MINI and helped Lia fasten his granddaughters into their car seats. He started the car and then sped away. "Until we sort this situation out, you need to be careful of every move you make."

*

Ellie seemed surprised, and not pleasantly so, to see her sister standing in her doorway. "What's going on?" she asked, rubbing the sleep from her eyes.

"Lia and the girls are in trouble." He brushed past her, and all four of them piled into her small hotel room.

"What kind of trouble?" Ellie pulled the door shut behind them.

Abbott explained the situation, and when he finished, she turned to face Lia. "Have you called the police?"

"No police!" Lia said, her voice raised in alarm.

"Why not? Calling the police might save your husband's life."

Lia bore her cold eyes into Ellie. "My husband brought this on himself."

Ellie noticed the two little girls looking up at their mother with terrified brown eyes. She knelt down in front of them. "This is boring grown-up talk. Would the two of you like to color?" They nodded their heads in unison. She walked them to the table in the corner of the room and set them up with her sketch pad and colored pencils.

Once the girls were settled, she corralled her father and Lia to the entryway outside the bathroom near the door. "It's not safe for you to stay in Atlanta," she said in a loud whisper.

"I can't just leave town," Lia snapped. "My husband will have no way of getting in touch with me."

"You have a cell phone, don't you?" Ellie asked.

Lia rolled her eyes. "Who doesn't own a cell phone? But if something happens to Ricky, I'll have no way of knowing."

"A minute ago, you said your husband deserves whatever he gets for dragging you into his mess," Ellie said. "Which is it? Are you concerned about him or not?"

Lia's eyes shone with unshed tears. "He's my husband. Of course I'm concerned about him."

"Have you called the area hospitals?" Ellie asked. "Considering the circumstances, something may already have happened to him."

Abbott placed a hand on Ellie's shoulder. "I don't think these goons would be looking for him if that were the case."

Ellie shrugged. "I guess that's true."

He turned to Lia. "I agree with Ellie that you need to talk to the police. I'll go with you to the local station to file a report. If nothing else, that will put the police on alert to the situation. I'll explain that I'm taking you someplace safe. We'll give them both our numbers in the event they need to get in touch with you."

"I told you I don't want to get the police involved," Lia said through clenched teeth.

Ellie glared at Lia. "Why not, unless you're hiding something?"

The air in the entryway crackled with tension. Abbott needed to make a fast move before a fight broke out between these two long-lost sisters. "Lia, if you want our help, I insist you file a report with the police. If you have other friends you can stay with, I'll be happy to take you to them."

Her face flushed red with anger. "Fine."

"Good, then it's settled." He opened the door. "Ellie, you stay here with the girls while we're gone," he said, and ushered Lia out of the room before she could change her mind.

CHAPTER THIRTY-ONE
ELLIE

ELLIE TOOK THE little girls down to the lobby and bought them each a soft vanilla ice cream cone from the cafe. She asked them about themselves while they licked greedily at the ice cream. She learned more than she wanted to know. The girls could count to twenty and sing the alphabet song. They loved Clifford the Big Red Dog and Winnie the Pooh. They shared a bedroom and slept with a nightlight on. They were not identical twins, but hardly anyone could tell them apart. Bella pointed at a small birthmark on her upper lip, and Mya explained that her face was rounder than her sister's. Sometimes, but not very often, their mother took them to the playground at the end of the street. They had a babysitter named Rosa who came in once a week. Rosa smelled funny and got mad at them when they made too much noise. The girls told Ellie that their mommy was always on the computer and that she cried a lot. They didn't see their daddy much. Whenever he came home for dinner, he cooked on the grill and they ate outside on the deck. They often heard him yelling at their mommy late at night. One time their mommy had a black eye and another she had to go to the hospital in an ambulance.

"That must have been scary for you," Ellie said. "Did you visit your mommy while she was in the hospital?"

"We weren't allowed," Bella said. "Grandma Weezie came to stay with us for a really long time."

"She cooked yummy food and played lots of games with us," Mya said. "But she got mad at Daddy, and he made her leave."

So Louisa did know Lia had tried to kill herself, assuming her hospital stay was a result of her suicide attempt. What was wrong with this woman that she couldn't tell the truth?

After they finished their ice cream, Ellie took the girls back upstairs and washed off their sticky faces and hands. She found *Sesame Street* on TV, and all three of them stretched across the bed on their bellies to watch.

The things the girls had said about their mother made Ellie soften toward her sister. So much so that she held her tongue when Lia returned from the police station complaining about how long they'd had to wait and the incompetence of the officer they spoke with. Her father seemed frazzled. Ellie could understand why if Lia had acted at the police station the way she was acting now. Like a spoiled brat.

"Lia thinks the girls will travel best if we leave now and stop along the way for dinner," Abbott said to Ellie. "How long will it take you to pack?"

"Ten minutes tops." She turned and headed to the bathroom to gather her toiletries.

Ellie didn't think to ask about the driving logistics until twenty minutes later when she and her father were cramming their bags in the back with the others. "Do you think maybe we should rent another car?"

"Nah. We'll be fine," Abbott said, slamming the hatch shut. "A five-hour drive to Charleston with five people in a MINI Cooper. I can't think of a better way to get to know one another."

"Never mind that two of those people require car seats, which take up so much more room. I'll let you sit in the back," she said as she headed toward the driver's side.

"Fine by me."

Her father was smitten with his granddaughters, and they seemed enamored with him as well. Even Lia laughed at the sight of him sandwiched between the car seats with his knees up to his chin.

Navigating the Atlanta five o'clock traffic took concentration, but once they were on the open highway, Ellie sat back in her seat and turned on the cruise control. For the next fifteen miles, an awkward silence filled the front of the car while her father spoke softly to the girls in the back. From what Ellie could hear of the conversation, she concluded that he was showing them his wild animal photographs on his iPad.

"You named them Bella and Mya after our dolls," Ellie said to her sister when she could no longer stand the tension. "How much do you remember?"

"Enough that I don't care to remember anymore," Lia said, her gaze fixed on the stream of cars in front of them.

Ellie smiled. "I know what you mean. I suppressed most of my memories from that time. You didn't seem surprised this morning when I told you I was your twin sister. Do you remember me?"

Lia shrugged. "I remember a little girl with orange

pigtails. I thought maybe you were my sister. Because of the difference in our coloring, I never suspected we were twins until Bella and Mya were born and I found out fraternal twins run in families."

Ellie risked a glance at her sister. "How'd you get the scar?"

Lia tugged her shirt sleeves down over her hands.

"I'm talking about this one," Ellie said, raising her fingers to the side of her face. "We spoke with Louisa earlier. She told us you already had that scar when you came to live with her."

"You can't believe anything Louisa says." Lia pulled her turtleneck down so Ellie could see. The oval-shaped scar wasn't nearly as large as she'd originally thought. "I pulled a pot of boiling water off the stove when I was eight."

Ellie winced. "That must've been painful. Why would Louisa lie about it?"

"Because that's what pathological liars do. They get off on lying. She probably didn't want you to know the scar happened on her watch."

Ellie returned her attention to the road. "I'm not surprised to hear you say that about her. She gave me two different answers when I asked her when she last saw you. When was the last time you saw Louisa?"

"A year ago, when I was in the hospital. She came to help out with the girls." Once again, Lia tugged on her sleeves. "She and my husband got in a fight, and he made her go home."

Ellie wondered what the fight was about, but she decided it best not to pursue the subject of her sister's attempted suicide until they'd gotten to know each other better. "What do you know about how you came to live with Louisa?"

"Only what Louisa told me—that our mother died and she wanted Louisa to raise me. If that's even true."

"It's true that our mother died. But not until three years after she sent you to live with Louisa. She was afraid for you. She wanted to get you to safety. Our grandmother was abusive. She was holding us captive in her house. Did you know any of this?"

"Not for sure, no. I have a recurring nightmare of a screaming woman tumbling down a flight of stairs. The dreams seem so real, I've often wondered if it actually happened."

Ellie nodded. "You and I witnessed our grandmother push our mother down the stairs. I think, although I'm not certain of the time, that you went to live with Louisa shortly after that."

"Why me and not you?"

"Mom was worried our grandmother would try to harm you because you look so much like Dad. She had a thing against Jewish people."

Lia pulled her visor down and studied herself in the mirror. "Lucky you. You got the ginger genes. How long did you stay with Mom?"

"Until she died."

"And you got to live with Daddy Dearest?" she said in a bitter tone.

"I lived through three more years of hell after you left, but I'll admit I was probably better off in the long run." Ellie didn't blame her sister for being bitter. She would've felt the same way if the situation were reversed. "No one seems to know exactly how Mom got you out of the house. Do you remember anything about that time?"

Lia's face grew dark. "I remember being really sick and an old black woman taking care of me. I may have even been staying in her home."

The pieces of the puzzle fit together at once. "That's it!" Ellie said, palming the steering wheel. "Maddie, who was our housekeeper, said there was a bad flu epidemic that year. Does the name Sally Bell sound familiar?"

"Maybe. I can't say for sure."

"She was our cook. She must have taken you out of the house when you got sick, either with or without our grandmother's permission. I guess we'll never know."

An accident on the highway up ahead slowed traffic to a crawl. Lia scowled and began drumming her fingers against the door panel.

"I found our mother's journals when I was going through our grandmother's things," Ellie said. "You might want to read them. Our mother loved both of us equally, Lia. The journals will help you see that."

Lia stopped drumming her fingers. "Wait a minute. Why were you going through our grandmother's things? Did she leave you some kind of inheritance or something?"

Alarm bells sounded so loud in Ellie's head she was tempted to cover her ears. Thus far, her sister hadn't asked Ellie what she did for a living or whether she had a husband and children or if she'd lived in Charleston her whole life. Which, considering their past, would've been Ellie's first questions to Lia if their roles were reversed. "She left me everything she owned. I recently moved back to Charleston from San Francisco, where I've lived since I was six. I had mixed emotions about the inheritance at first, but after reading Mom's diaries, I'm convinced the money is our birthright. Both of ours, Lia."

Her dark eyes glinted with anger. "How generous of you. Mom will make certain you receive a place in heaven for giving me what's rightfully mine. Just give me my share, and I'll be on my way."

Ellie's feelings for her sister were rapidly transitioning from mistrust to dislike. "It's not that simple. I can't just write you a check for your share of the money. The attorney is still finalizing the estate. It might take some time. If you're considering paying off your husband's gambling debts, I would advise against it."

She realized the back seat had grown quiet, and she snuck a peek in the rearview mirror. Her father, with his brow furrowed in concern, was eavesdropping on their conversation. She had no way of knowing how much he'd heard.

"I realize you're my twin sister, Eleanor. But we've only just met. You know nothing about my life. My problems are mine to solve however I see fit."

She cocked an eyebrow at her sister. *Eleanor?* She reminded herself that she was giving Lia half of her inheritance for no other reason than it was the right thing to do. She didn't have to love her or even like her. At this point, she didn't care if she ever saw her again. She would be able to sleep at night knowing she'd done right by her. "You may do with your money however you see fit. We'll make the transaction as soon as possible. In the meantime, I prefer to be called Ellie."

*

"How much of our conversation did you hear?" Ellie asked her father an hour later when they were finishing dinner at McDonald's. Lia had gone to the restroom, and the girls were happily playing in the indoor PlayPlace.

"Enough," he said, popping his last fry into his mouth.

"I'm sorry, Dad, for your sake. But she's not a nice person.

She's a chip off the old block. Our evil grandmother's block. I have no interest in getting to know her better."

"Now, honey, let's try to give her the benefit of the doubt. She's under a lot of pressure. Her husband has disappeared, and he owes some bad men a lot of money. If she wants to bail him out, it's her business. She's the mother of my grand-children. Wouldn't you like to get to know *them* better?"

Ellie watched her nieces tossing a ball back and forth to each other. "Of course I would. Bella and Mya are angels. But you heard Lia. Once she gets her money, she'll take them and leave, and we'll never see them again."

He wadded up his sandwich wrapper. "That's why you need to take your time arranging her, um… gift."

Ellie slumped back in her chair. "I don't know how these things work. It'll probably take some time anyway, regardless of whether I want it to or not."

Lia returned from the restroom, but her phone rang the minute she sat down. "Keep an eye on the girls, will ya?" she said and left the table.

Ellie watched her sister exit the side door of the building. "Louisa forgot to teach her to say please."

"Think positive thoughts." He gathered their trash on a tray and emptied it in a nearby trash can.

Lia returned five minutes later. "That was the detective we spoke with earlier. Someone broke into my house and ran-sacked the place. Nothing obvious is missing, but they have no way of knowing if anything was stolen without me there to take inventory."

Ellie's stomach lurched, and she thought she might be sick. What had she gotten herself into? Her sister's house was ransacked by goons who were looking for her husband because he owed them a lot of money. And Ellie was taking this man's wife and his children to her home in Charleston where they would all be sitting ducks.

Take a deep breath, Ellie, she said to herself. *No one will know to trace Lia to you. Even you didn't know about your connection to her until a few days ago.*

"It's a good thing you and the girls weren't there at the time." He patted the empty seat beside him, signaling Lia to sit down. "You mentioned earlier that your husband had pressured you into asking Louisa for a loan. Is there any chance he would have contacted Louisa himself about borrowing the money, or perhaps driven to Virginia to see her?"

"Wait a minute," Ellie said, straightening. "I didn't know any of that. Have you told Louisa this? If whoever broke into your house found anything with Louisa's address on it, a birthday card or old letter, her life could be in danger."

Lia leaned across the table toward Ellie. "First of all, Ricky would never contact Louisa on his own. The two of them hated each other."

"Still, I think you should warn her just in case," Ellie said.

"And that's the second thing. Louisa can take care of herself. She's a big girl. A very big girl." Lia laughed at her own joke while the rest of the table remained silent.

CHAPTER THIRTY-TWO
ELLIE

HER FATHER DROVE the remainder of the trip. Lia sat in the back between the girls. Full from dinner and exhausted from the excitement of the day, the twins fell fast asleep within five minutes. Lia spent the two hours texting with someone on her iPhone.

As they crossed the Ashley River on the way into town, Ellie said, "I'll stay at Julian's tonight so Lia and the girls can have my room."

"Are you sure?" Abbott asked. "I hate to run you out of your own home."

Lia snorted, and Ellie knew she was thinking that half of that home belonged to her.

"It's fine, Dad. I can hardly wait to see my dog. Julian says she's been moping around, missing me."

When they arrived home, Abbott carried one sleeping child and Ellie the other. Lia trailed them, dragging their suitcases up the stairs, showing no apparent interest in the house that had once served as her prison.

Ellie waited for everyone to get situated before leaving for Julian's. She texted him on her way over: *Are you still awake?*

He responded right away. *I've been waiting for you to get home. Can you come over?*

I'm at your back door.

Julian greeted her with a hug, but when he tried to kiss her, she pushed him away. "Not before I see my dog."

He placed his hand over his heart. "I'm hurt," he said, but his smile lit up his whole face.

He looped his arm through hers as they walked down the hall to his den. "Make no mistake, Pip-squeak clearly missed you, but she and Mills had a big time together. I took them to the park twice a day."

The dogs were curled up in front of the fire, but when Pixie saw Ellie standing in the doorway, she bounded over to her, tinkling on Julian's Oriental rug along the way.

"What on earth? She hasn't done that since she was a puppy." Ellie picked up the little dog and nuzzled her neck. "You know better than that, you naughty girl. I'm so sorry, Julian."

He waved off her concern. "She's excited to see you. I'll get a towel to clean that up."

"Thank you. I'll take them outside to make sure that doesn't happen again."

After the dogs did their business, they returned to the den, and Ellie spent a few minutes on the floor playing with Pixie. Julian seemed to sense that she wasn't ready to talk about Lia, and she was grateful to him for giving her a chance to relax. Finally, she kissed her dog good night and wrapped her arms around Julian's neck. "Now it's your turn."

He swept her off her feet and carried her to his bedroom.

"Pip-squeak's not the only one who missed you." He kissed her neck as he unbuttoned her white cotton blouse. "I realize we haven't known each other for very long. But I'm gaga over you."

They fell into bed and for the next few hours made crazy love to each other. They went to sleep with their bodies tangled together and woke early the following morning. After making love yet again, with her head resting on his shoulder, she finally described everything that'd happened with Lia.

"Dad is right. We should give Lia the benefit of the doubt until she's sorted this mess out with her husband. But when it comes to my sister, that's easier said than done. She pushes all my wrong buttons. Every word that comes out of her mouth makes my skin crawl. What's wrong with me, Julian? Shouldn't I be thrilled to be reunited with my twin sister?"

"That's the way it goes sometimes with siblings. Your personalities might have clashed no matter what, even if you hadn't been separated for all these years. Give it some time."

"I will, for the sake of my nieces. They're adorable, Julian. I can't wait for you to meet them."

Ellie felt so revived after a night in Julian's arms that she nearly skipped the few blocks to South Battery. She found her father talking on the phone at her desk in her study. When he spotted her in the doorway, he pressed the phone to his gut. "I'm on the phone with the wholesale mattress store. I can't have my daughter living in sin. I've ordered two queen-size mattresses for the other bedrooms upstairs. They're delivering them this afternoon."

Ellie tilted her head back and laughed. "You're one step ahead of me." She dug her credit card out of her wallet and slapped it down on the desk in front of him.

She went to the kitchen and was making waffle batter

when Maddie arrived thirty minutes later. She shared with her the details of her trip, including her visit with Louisa, the reunion with her sister, and Lia's predicament relating to her husband's gambling problem.

Maddie clasped her hands together and pressed them against her bosom. "Sweet Lia's done come home. I can hardly wait to see her."

"Brace yourself, Maddie. She's not as sweet as you remember. But I'll let you form your own opinion." Ellie shook the excess batter off her whisk and set it down in the spoon rest. "Lia has a burn scar on the side of her neck and face. She claims it happened when she was eight. I wanted to confirm with you that it didn't happen while she was living here."

"No'm. There wasn't a mark on that chile's head last time I saw her. 'Course that was days before she disappeared. I reckon it could've happened after I got the flu."

"Lia remembers being sick. She thinks she might have been in Sally Bell's home."

Maddie's brown eyes got big. "Yes'm, that's something ole Sally would've done. Lots of folks died from the flu that year. She would've risked her job to keep Miss Lia alive and keep Miss Ashton from getting sick." Maddie went to the refrigerator for oranges. "One thing's for sure. That's the first thing I'm gonna ask ole Sally when I see her in heaven."

Ellie covered her mouth to hide her smile. "When you have your answer, please find a way to share it with me."

Maddie flashed her a toothy smile. "God willing, I'll visit you in a dream."

Ellie clapped Maddie on the shoulder. "As long as you don't go haunting this house. I've had enough of restless spirits to last me a lifetime."

Maddie was squeezing oranges and Ellie was frying bacon a few minutes later when she noticed two sets of big brown eyes peeping at her from around the doorway to the butler's pantry. She set her fork down in the spoon rest. "Good morning! Come in here, you two. I want you to meet a friend of mine. Maddie, this is Bella and Mya."

Maddie registered surprise at the girls' names, but she quickly recovered. "Bella and Mya, what pretty names for such pretty little girls." Her knees cracked as she crouched down to greet them. "I knew two sisters once who named their dolls Bella and Mya."

Bella removed her thumb from her mouth. "Who?"

"Your mama and your Auntie Ellie."

The two girls looked at each other, perplexed expressions on their faces. "Do you have any Pop-Tarts?" Mya asked. "My tummy is making funny noises."

"We're fresh out of Pop-Tarts," Ellie said. "But I'm making bacon and waffles."

"Yay!" Both girls bounced a little on their toes.

Maddie hoisted the girls onto the counter and gave each a glass of orange juice to drink while Ellie removed the bacon from the skillet. "Breakfast is almost ready," she said, setting out a stack of plates. "Will one of you run upstairs and wake up your mom?"

Their brown eyes darkened. "Mama never eats breakfast," Bella said. "We're big girls. We fix our own."

This came as no surprise to Ellie. Lia didn't seem the type to worry about her daughters' nutrition. "I know you're big girls, but I like cooking for you. Will you let me make waffles and pancakes and eggs for you while you're here?"

"Yippee!" Mya threw her fists in the air. "We love waffles and pancakes and eggs."

They joined Abbott in the studio, and the four of them gathered around her pine table for breakfast. When they were finished, Ellie took the girls and Pixie across the street to the park. For the next two hours, they climbed on the Civil War cannons, rolled around with Pixie in the grass, and raced one another up and down the promenade. They returned home tired, dirty, and hungry.

They found Maddie on the terrace setting up for lunch and Lia draped over the lounge chair watching her. Maddie's face was set in a scowl. Lia had already offended her in some way.

Lia scrambled off the lounge chair when she saw them. "There you are. I've been waiting for you. Did you call your attorney yet?"

"Not yet. I've been in the park all morning with your daughters." Ellie turned her back on Lia and peered over Maddie's shoulder at the plates she was distributing to each place. "What're we having? I'm starving."

"Pimento cheese sandwiches and chips for the girls." Maddie's response was met with cheers from the twins. "And tomato basil soup and chicken salad for you."

"Yum. That sounds delicious."

Lia grabbed Ellie by the arm and spun her around to face her. "I can't stay here forever, Eleanor. This house is giving me the creeps."

"If you think it's bad now, you should've seen it when all the furniture was here. I got rid of everything, which explains all the empty rooms in case you were wondering."

"I expect to be reimbursed for half of everything you

sold." Lia was still holding onto Ellie's arm. She dug her fingers into her flesh and squeezed hard. "Now call the attorney."

Ellie jerked her arm free of Lia's grip. "I'll call him after we eat."

Abbott joined them for lunch. The sunshine had kept them warm while they were in the park, but in the shade of the table's umbrella, she felt the chill of autumn. The warm soup hit the spot. Abbott and Ellie engaged in a delightful conversation with the twins while Lia picked at her food and texted on her phone.

"Someone looks sleepy," Ellie said when she noticed Bella rubbing her eyes with her tiny fists. "Are you ready for a nap?"

Bella tucked her chin and nodded.

"Why don't I take you up for your nap?" Ellie said, rising from the table.

Lia jumped to her feet and planted herself in Ellie's way. "Let your dad do it. You have a phone call to make."

Abbott smiled at his granddaughters. "It would be my pleasure." He helped the girls down from the table and took them inside.

Ellie picked up her phone and placed the call to her attorney. When the receptionist answered, she asked to speak with Bennett's assistant, who told her that Mr. Calhoun was tied up for the afternoon but he could see her first thing in the morning. She thanked the assistant and ended the call. "I have a meeting with him at nine tomorrow morning."

"Fine, if that's the best you can do," Lia said, and left the terrace in a huff.

Ellie gathered the dishes and took them to the kitchen. She noticed Maddie was unusually quiet as they washed and dried the dishes.

"What's wrong, Maddie? What did my sister say to make you angry?"

"Ain't nothing for you to worry about, Miss Ellie."

"You're clearly upset, which means it's something for me to worry about." Ellie dried her hands on the dish towel and leaned back against the counter. "Talk to me."

Maddie groaned as she lowered herself to the step stool. "Ain't nothin' specific, just Miss Lia's attitude in general. She act like she don't remember me, even though I know she do. And she's been bossing me around all morning like your gramma used to do. 'Do my laundry for me, Maddie. Fetch me a cup of coffee. Will you bring me some fresh towels?' You were right. She ain't the same sweet little Lia I remember."

"She's plain rotten. I can smell her a mile away."

Maddie snickered. "You're so bad, Miss Ellie."

"I'm just telling the truth. What are we gonna do about her?"

She shook her head slowly. "She's family. Ain't nothin' you can do, except let it work itself out."

Ellie retired to the sofa in her studio with the mystery novel she'd purchased in the hotel lobby in Richmond. But she couldn't focus and soon drifted off to sleep.

Julian called around three inviting them to a cookout at his house that evening. "There are five of us, Julian. That's too much trouble for you."

"No trouble at all," he said. "I'm making the hamburger patties as we speak.

Her desire to see Julian outweighed her apprehension about introducing him to her sister. "As long as you promise to keep it simple. And I insist on bringing the wine and dessert."

When her nieces woke up from their naps, Ellie took

them to the market with her. "Can't Abbott come with us?" Bella asked as Ellie was buckling her car seat.

"He has to be here when the men deliver your new bed." Ellie was tired of waiting for her sister to correct her children. She didn't seem to care what they said or did. "Do you understand that Abbott is your mommy's father?"

Bella shook her head.

"Well he is, which makes him your granddaddy." She touched her fingertip to the little girl's nose. Seeing the wounded look on Mya's face, she touched her nose as well. "He's your granddaddy, too, silly. You can both call him that if you'd like. Or Gramps. Or Pops. Maybe you should talk to him about which name he prefers. I think it might make him happy to be called Granddaddy."

Ear-to-ear grins appeared on the girls' faces. They tugged on Ellie's heartstrings so much that, even though it was no one's birthday, she let them pick out a vanilla birthday cake with white icing and *Happy Birthday* written in pink frosting for dessert.

CHAPTER THIRTY-THREE
ABBOTT

ABBOTT WAS GROWING tired of listening to Lia complain. But admitting that to Ellie would be admitting he was wrong, and he wasn't ready to do that yet. They'd gone out of their way to help her, and she'd done nothing to show her gratitude. He understood she was under a great deal of stress, but he sincerely hoped this wasn't her true personality. As much as he hoped Lia had some redeeming qualities hidden behind all the self-centeredness and greed, he doubted any such qualities would be forthcoming that night based on the way she threw herself at Julian. He was good-looking, successful, and kind. And the way he responded to Lia's flirtations made Abbott like him that much more. Ellie had found herself a keeper.

"So, Julian, what do you do for a living that affords you such nice digs? I could get used to living in a place like this," Lia said, holding her tummy in, her head high, and her bust out. Although truth be told, she didn't have much bust to display.

"You say that now, but living in a house this old isn't for everyone," he said, handing Lia a glass of wine. "Most of these homes have survived too many hurricanes to count, as well as the massive earthquake of 1886. The houses lean, which means many of the floors slant. The plumbing never works the way it should, and they were built so close together you can see your neighbor's breakfast plate."

"Oh, Julian, you're so funny." Lia let out a little giggle, which, fake or otherwise, was the first form of laughter Abbott had heard come out of her mouth since they'd arrived in Charleston.

Turning his back on Lia, Julian bent down to speak to the twins. "I have a little girl, too, you know. Except she's not so little anymore. I don't get to see her very often. She lives in another part of the state. Would you like to go upstairs and see her room?"

They bobbed their heads up and down. "Then what're we waiting for?" He extended a hand to each of them. "I've set up appetizers in the garden," he called over his shoulder on his way out. "Make yourselves at home."

They wandered through Julian's downstairs rooms, admiring his extensive art and antique collections and the group of framed letters above his desk in his den from famous people whose homes he'd designed.

"Julian is an interesting man, Eleanor." Lia ran her fingers along the back of his leather sofa. "I hope you can hang on to him."

Abbott gave Ellie a half hug. "I don't think she has anything to worry about. Julian seems quite smitten with her," he said as he steered Ellie toward the French doors.

She leaned into him and muttered, "Thanks, Dad. I needed to hear that."

They sampled the antipasto tray Julian had set out on his rectangular teak table and then made themselves comfortable in the matching armchairs positioned around his gas fire pit.

"I've never been anywhere quite like Charleston," Abbott said, taking in Julian's manicured garden. "If it's okay with you, Ellie, I think I'll stay in town for a while, get better acquainted with the city. I can easily work from here."

"Stay as long as you like. Why don't you invite Tracey down for a long weekend? I'd like to meet her." Ellie looked at Lia beside her. "I hope you'll stay as well. We can get better acquainted while we explore the city."

Lia responded with a humph.

The smile disappeared from Ellie's face, but her expression remained determined. "I hope you'll at least stay for a few days. We got the new beds set up for you today. You can move your things in tomorrow. The rooms are sparse right now with only the mattresses and bed frames, but we can go up in the attic tomorrow. There's a pretty chest of drawers up there we can use and maybe an end table and a couple of side chairs."

"The girls and I are fine in the master bedroom."

"You're gonna get tired of me coming in and out for my things," Ellie said, hinting she'd like her room back. "This way the girls can have their own bed. I'm sure it's crowded with all three of you sleeping in one bed."

Lia cupped her hand around her ear. "Are you hard of hearing, Eleanor? I said we're fine where we are. I don't plan to be here long anyway."

"Where will you go?" Abbott asked.

Lia shot him a death stare. "Obviously not back to Georgia."

"I don't think going to Louisa's is a safe choice, either," he said. "Has she heard anything from your husband?"

"How would I know?" Lia snapped.

"I saw you on your phone in the garden earlier, while Ellie and the girls were at the grocery store. I assumed you were talking to Louisa."

"I told you, Louisa and I are not that close." Lia moved to the edge of her chair. "The two of you need to back off. You're suffocating me. Here's a news flash for you—we're not going to become this great big happy family you've always dreamed of. I've known you for less than thirty-six hours. I'm not obligated to share my travel plans or justify my actions to you."

Abbott could tell Ellie was struggling to control her temper.

"We understand that, Lia. We're just concerned for the girls. If you need to leave them with us for a few days while you sort out your problems, I'd be happy to take care of them."

"Just because you can't have children of your own, Eleanor, doesn't mean you can have mine."

Ellie took a gulp of wine and set the glass down on the arm of her chair. "It's not that I *can't* have children, *Amelia*. I just never found the right man to have them with."

"But Julian is that right man, isn't he? Too bad you're too old to have children of your own."

The French doors swung open, and the twins danced onto the patio in pink tutus. Julian followed, waving a plastic fairy wand and wearing a tiara on his head.

Ellie covered her mouth to hide her smile. "That's a good look for you, Julian."

"As a matter of fact, I brought this for you." He removed

the crown from his head and placed it on Ellie's. "You're my queen." He leaned over and planted a noisy kiss on her lips.

Ellie's face turned the same shade of strawberries as her hair. "In that case, as your queen, I command you to start the grill. I know two little girls who must be getting hungry."

*

Julian grilled the best burgers Abbott had ever eaten, juicy and flavorful with the right amount of pinkness. He served the twins Tater Tots with their burgers and the adults an array of roasted and seasoned vegetables. They had birthday cake for dessert, and both Julian and Abbott asked for second helpings. Mya and Bella began to yawn not long after they'd finished eating. Ellie and Abbott offered to help clean up, but Julian insisted they get the little girls home to bed.

They bid Julian good night at the door and walked down the sidewalk toward the waterfront, Abbott with one exhausted tutu-clad child draped over his shoulder and Ellie with the other.

"Do you have any red wine at the house, Eleanor?" Lia asked, walking five paces behind them. "I'm exhausted. I feel like soaking in a warm tub."

Exhausted from what? he wondered. As far as he could tell, she'd done nothing all day.

Abbott had shared a special bond with Ellie since she first came to live with him as a traumatized child. But he doubted if he'd ever have that close relationship with Lia. He didn't expect to make up for forty years in one week. And based on his observations during that short time, he neither liked nor trusted her very much, nor was he sure he wanted to waste the effort getting to know her. Jenny had turned his sons against him when they divorced, and he'd long since given up on trying to be a part of their lives when they were so blatantly disinterested in being a part of his. He didn't know them well enough to know whether he liked them or not. But he regretted not having a relationship with their children, his four grandsons. If he could help it, he wouldn't let that happen with his granddaughters. He was quite taken with the twins, with their sweet little faces and spunky personalities.

At home, he and Ellie deposited the children in Ellie's queen-size bed and left their mother to get them changed into their pajamas. He was brushing his teeth ten minutes later when he heard the water running from the master bathroom. He sneaked back across the hall and tiptoed into Ellie's room, hoping for one last peek at his precious granddaughters. He couldn't get enough of them. Just being around them made him inexplicably happy. Perhaps because he'd missed the opportunity to know his own daughters at this age.

He was kissing Bella's forehead when he saw the screen on Lia's iPhone light up with a text message from Lover Boy on the table beside the bed. The message read: *I'll wait for you here. But hurry.*

Suddenly unable to breathe, Abbott fled the room. Who the hell was Lover Boy? Her husband? Was she somehow involved in his disappearance? Or was Lover Boy another man? Was his daughter having an affair? It certainly wouldn't be her first. Whether it was true or not, according to Louisa, Lia had broken up her first husband's marriage.

He found Ellie out back in the garden, stretched out on a chaise lounge with a mug of tea warming her hands. He sat down at the foot of her chaise lounge and told her about the text message from Lover Boy.

"My sister is certainly full of surprises. Either she's cheating on her husband or Ricky is Lover Boy. If she's communicating with him, she probably knows where he is. Maybe she helped him disappear. What if he's planning to fake his death and she's planning to join him later? And here we are playing right into her hand."

Abbott studied his daughter's face through the dark and realized she was being serious. "Come on, honey. You've been watching too many made-for-TV-movies. That kind of stuff doesn't happen in real life."

Ellie shrugged. "She's got the part down right—beautiful and mysterious with a troubled past."

"Your scenario doesn't make sense. She agreed to go to the police."

Ellie shook her head. "Not at first. Not until we insisted. Going to the police legitimizes her scheme. I'm sure she realized that. And stupid me offers to give her half my inheritance, so now they have the money they need to disappear to Tahiti."

Abbott said, "I'm placing my bet on another man. Lover Boy isn't her husband. He's simply her lover."

Frown lines appeared on Ellie's forehead. "Either way makes for an uncertain future for the twins."

CHAPTER THIRTY-FOUR
ELLIE

E LLIE DREADED SLEEPING in her mother's old room. But with the faint scent of magnolias lingering in the air, she felt oddly at peace as she lay awake contemplating what to do about her sister.

She rose early, showered, dried her hair, and dressed in gray flannel slacks and a black cashmere sweater. Autumn had arrived in the Lowcountry, bringing overnight low temperatures in the forties. The day promised to be cool and overcast, weather Ellie could relate to. The twins were already awake, wearing their pink tutus and sock skating from one empty room to the next downstairs. They skated over and greeted her with a hug when they saw Ellie watching them from the bottom of the stairs.

"The two of you are up awfully early. Have you eaten breakfast yet?"

They nodded in unison. "Maddie made us scrambled eggs and sausage with a Pop-Tart for dessert," Bella said.

Ellie chuckled. "Dessert for breakfast? I think she aims to

spoil you like she spoiled me." She gave the twins a squeeze and a pat on their fannies, sending them on their way again.

She found her father working on his laptop in her studio. "Morning, Dad." She kissed the top of his head. "Is there any way I can convince you to go with me to meet with my attorney? I really want to do the right thing. I'm just not sure who I'm trying to do the right thing for—Lia, the twins, or me."

He stood to face her. "I'll go with you, sweetheart. If you're sure that's what you want."

She smiled. "I'm positive. I need you there to keep me from making a big mistake."

"In that case, let me go upstairs and shave."

"Can I fix you some breakfast?" she called to him on his way out of the room.

He paused in the doorway. "I had breakfast with the twins," he said over his shoulder. "I ate a frosted strawberry Pop-Tart for the first time since I was a kid. Brought back a lot of memories for me. You should try one."

"I've experienced all the childhood memories I can handle for a while," she muttered under her breath as she walked toward the kitchen. "I hear you're offering frosted strawberry Pop-Tarts as the breakfast special this morning," she said to Maddie, who was taking inventory of the refrigerator and making out her grocery list.

"They've been mighty popular. Better claim yours now, before the last package disappears." Maddie nodded at the box of Pop-Tarts on the counter.

"I'll just have coffee," Ellie said, pressing her hand against her gurgling tummy. "My stomach is in knots over this meeting with my attorney."

She sipped coffee and scanned the *Post and Courier* while

she waited for Abbott to get ready. Because of the chilly morning, they opted to drive to Bennett's office building on Meeting Street. They were getting into the car thirty minutes later when Lia caught up with them. "Wait for me!"

Ellie tightened her grip on her door handle. "This is a private meeting, Lia, between my attorney and me."

Lia stepped in close to Ellie, their faces only inches apart. "I have a right to be there, Eleanor, if you're going to discuss my inheritance."

"It's not *your* inheritance, Lia." Abbott came around to the driver's side of the car. "Your grandmother left everything to Ellie. She's not obligated to give you a nickel. She's doing it out of the goodness of her heart, although I don't know why she would even consider it the way you've been acting. I suggest you stay here and look after your daughters for a change."

Ellie pressed her lips together to keep from smiling. Her father had finally gotten frustrated with Lia's behavior.

"Whatever!" Lia stomped off and went back inside.

Parking was scarce, and they ended up having to walk several blocks to Bennett's office. The receptionist instructed them to take the elevator to the fourth floor, where Bennett's attractive young assistant was waiting for them. "Mr. Calhoun's ready for you now," she said, and ushered them into his office.

Bennett and Abbott hit it off right away. Bennett's collection of art from the Lowcountry marshlands prompted a discussion about wildlife. As they'd circled the room studying the paintings, Bennett complimented her father on the success of his career and asked him about his travels into the wild. Ellie cleared her throat to remind them of her presence when it appeared they might go on until noon.

"I'm sorry, Ellie. I get carried away when someone

expresses an interest in my art." Bennett led them to the seating area by the corner windows. "Let's sit down." Ellie and her father made themselves comfortable on the sofa, and Bennett took a seat in the leather chair opposite them. "Now, what can I do for you today?"

Without going into detail, Ellie explained that she'd been reunited with a twin sister she didn't know she had and that she was considering giving her a portion of her inheritance.

Bennett listened patiently until she'd finished talking. To his credit, he didn't question her motives. "Unfortunately, it's not as simple as writing your sister a check. You may have to pay gift taxes depending on how much you plan to give her."

"That's where I need your guidance."

For the next few minutes, Bennett talked about unified credits and annual exclusions. "Your net worth is quite large, Ellie. If you're a good steward of this wealth, your money will provide for your family for many generations to come. Keep that in mind when you're making your decision. Does your sister have children?"

"Yes, twin daughters, Mya and Bella. They're three years old. In the absence of children of my own, I would want to provide for them."

"And you can do that prior to your death. There are certain tax benefits to helping them with their education while you're still alive. Unless you trust your sister to handle the money properly, I would retain control of it as much as possible."

Ellie inhaled a deep breath and drew herself to her full height. "Thank you, Bennett. You've helped me make my decision."

*

Ellie parked her car in the driveway and rummaged through her pocketbook for her checkbook.

"What're you planning?" her father asked as she wrote out the check.

"I can't keep my sister here against her will, but I can give her a reason to stay." She tore the check out of the checkbook and folded it in half. "Not that I want *her* to stay. But I think the safest place for the twins is here with us."

Lia was waiting for them in her studio, pacing back and forth in front of the windows. She hurried over to them. "Well? Did you get the money?"

"This is all I can give you for now." She handed Lia the check.

Lia unfolded the check and stared down at the number, a frown forming on her face. "What do you mean this is all you can give me for now?"

Abbott's eyes grew as big as flying saucers when he saw the amount. "That's a hell of a lot of money, Lia."

"The rest is tied up, much of it in the house," Ellie said.

Lia glared at her. "Then sell the house."

"I can't until I make some improvements. But you and the girls are welcome to live here as long as you like. Where are they, by the way? I have a surprise for them."

Lia dropped to the sofa. "Outside, playing under that blasted magnolia tree."

Ellie opened the door and called the girls to come inside. "How would the two of you like to go on a horse-drawn carriage ride this afternoon?"

They looked at each other, their eyes wide. "Really, can we?" Mya asked.

Ellie smiled. "Really, we can."

"Can GoPa come too?" Bella asked, using the name the girls had decided to call their grandfather, although no one could figure out why.

"Are you kidding me? I wouldn't miss it," Abbott said and tickled each of the girls in turn.

"And that's not all," Ellie said. "I thought we'd take Julian to dinner tonight to repay him for last night."

"Yippee!" they cried, joining hands and skipping around in a circle while they chanted Julian's name.

"But we have some work to do first," Ellie said. "We're all going to help bring some furniture down from the attic for your new bedroom."

Despite their efforts to make the space cozier, Lia showed no interest in moving their things into their mother's old room and the adjoining nursery where they'd once slept. She also refused to go with them on their outings.

"Let her pout," Ellie said when her father expressed concern about Lia. "We'll have more fun without her."

Bundled up in sweaters and light jackets, they left the house a few minutes before four. The girls fell in love with the horse, Ricco, and his driver, Chip, who was careful to point out attractions and tell stories appropriate for their age. What she learned about the history of Charleston made Ellie appreciate the city even more. This fascinating city was finally beginning to feel like home.

Julian drove them to Mount Pleasant for an early dinner at Water's Edge on Shem Creek. They requested a table outside on the deck where the girls could watch the shrimp and fish boats returning from a day on the water. They lingered over dessert, not wanting the evening to come to an end.

When they arrived back home, Abbott carried the girls,

one in each arm, upstairs to bed to give Ellie and Julian a few minutes alone. She poured them each a glass of red wine, which they took outside to the garden. Sipping their wine, they stared up at the full moon. "I'm becoming attached to your nieces," Julian said. "I'd forgotten how sweet little girls can be."

"I know what you mean. I will miss them if they leave." She told him about Lover Boy and the gift she'd given Lia. "I've felt this way about very few people in my life, but I don't care for my sister. I hate to say that about my own flesh and blood, but I can't help how I feel. We're so different in looks and personality, it's hard for me to believe we're twins. Even fraternal twins have more in common than we do. I'm comfortable with my decision. I gave her enough money to make a fresh start somewhere if that's what she chooses to do. For the girls' sake, I hope she decides to stay here with us. But I don't see that happening."

"I don't know, Ellie. If she thinks she can get more money, she might stick around. Can you handle having her living under your roof if she does?"

She shrugged. "We'll have to establish some ground rules. My mother made it clear in her diary how much she loved both of us. This is what she would've wanted."

Julian took her glass from her and set it on the table alongside his. "Things will work out however they're meant to be." Cupping her chin, he kissed her lightly on the lips. "Come with me." Taking her by the hand, he led her out into the yard. Guided by the beams from his phone's flashlight, they climbed under the branches of the magnolia tree and lay down on the ground.

"I'm getting too old for this," Ellie said as she rested her head on his outstretched arm.

"Ha. We have many more years of tree climbing left in our future." He kissed her hair. "I realize we haven't known each other very long, but I'm falling hard for you, Ellie Pringle. It's too early to say the *L* word, but I never thought it would happen again for me. When you're feeling a bit more settled and this situation with your sister is sorted out, I would like to have a serious conversation about our future. I want you in my life, on whatever terms you're willing to accept me."

The bottom dropped out of Ellie's stomach at his declaration of love. She rolled over so half her body rested on his. "You're right. I need to see what happens with my sister before I can make any sort of commitment to you." She touched her fingertip to his lips. "But one thing's for sure: you're the best thing that's happened to me in a long time. Maybe ever."

*

Ellie slept in her mother's room again that night and woke before daybreak to find two tear-stained faces staring down at her. She sat bolt upright in bed. "What's wrong, girls?"

A fresh tear slid down Bella's cheek. "Mommy's gone!"

A chill crawled over Ellie's skin. She slipped from beneath the covers and grabbed her robe from the foot of the bed. With the twins clinging to her legs, she crossed the hall to her bedroom. Her sister's clothes that had been strewn across the furniture were gone, as was her cell phone and purse. After looking in the empty bedrooms for her sister, she tapped on her father's door and alerted him to the crisis before continuing her search downstairs. The doors were locked, the lights were still off, and the newspaper was on the front porch. But there was no sign of Lia anywhere. Ellie went to the kitchen for coffee and found an envelope with her name scrawled across it on the counter next to the Keurig machine. She tore open the envelope. A lump developed in her throat as she read her sister's words.

Dear Ellie,

Take care of the girls for me. How ironic that a woman as unfit as me ended up with children while you have none. Fate is twisted sometimes. I know I've been difficult these past few days. I've been under a great deal of stress.

You're lucky, Ellie. Because you couldn't remember what happened to us in this house, you've led a relatively normal life. I, on the other hand, have been plagued by those demons every single day. Maybe I inherited the crazy gene from our grandmother, or maybe living with nutcase Louisa for all those years had a negative impact on me. Either way, I'm not mentally stable, which makes me a dangerous threat to my children. If you ever tell anyone I admitted that to you, I'll call you a liar.

You are blessed to have Abbott in your life. Our father is a good man. He will be a supportive presence in the girls' lives. Don't try to find me. I need space to find my way on my own.

Lia

Her father entered the room and saw the note in her hand. "Is that from Lia?"

"It is." She handed him the letter.

She scooped the girls up in her arms, carried them to the sofa in her studio, and held them close to her while they cried.

Even though her discovery of Lia hadn't turned out the way she'd imagined, Ellie had recovered her memories and gotten the closure she desperately needed. Maddie's words echoed in her head. *Many things happened to you here, but having your sister taken away from you was the worst.* Lia would continue to be lost to Ellie, but she'd found her precious nieces in exchange. She would nurture them and love them with everything she had. She would turn this old house into a comfortable home, and they would fill it with laughter and love.

CHAPTER THIRTY-FIVE
ELLIE

JULIAN HAD BEEN to Magnolia Cemetery many times and knew exactly where to find the Pringle family plot. On Sunday, they all drove out there together. Julian and the girls gathered acorns from a neighboring plot while Abbott and Ellie visited her mother's grave. They stood side by side in silence as they stared down at Ashton's headstone. She was buried in April of 1983 next to her father, Edwin, who had died at the young age of forty-eight.

"If not for my grandmother, Mom might still be here with us today."

"We can talk about the what-ifs all day long, but it won't change a thing. When the Lord decides it's time for us to go, it's time for us to go." He grabbed her hand. "Your quest to remember your past has taught us both a lot of things. I'm so blessed to have had you in my life. And while I didn't always make the best decisions for you, I made them out of love."

"I know, Daddy." She rested her head on his shoulder. "I don't even want to think about how different things could've turned out for me, if not for you. I could've ended up in an orphanage—or worse, with Louisa."

"Don't think about it, honey. We're together now. I've decided to stay in Charleston. My place is here with you. We have each other, and we have the twins. And you have Julian. We will be one *small* happy family."

"There's nothing that will make me happier. No more obsessing about the past. From now on we're marching toward the future."

Acknowledgments

I'm grateful to the many people who helped make this novel possible. First and foremost, to my editor, Patricia Peters, for her patience and advice and for making my work stronger without changing my voice. To my literary agent, Andrea Hurst, for her guidance and expertise in the publishing industry and for believing in my work. A special thanks to my talented artist friend Johanna Carrington for sharing her knowledge of art and for her constructive feedback of the chapters of this manuscript relating to art. To my architect, Tim Galvin, for aiding my research in Charleston architecture. And to Damon Freeman and his crew at Damonza.com for their creativity in designing this stunning cover.

I am blessed to have many supportive people in my life, my friends and family who offer the encouragement I need to continue the pursuit of my writing career. To Alison and Ellen at the Gracious Posse and Leslie Rising at Levy's. For Cheryl and Mamie for your valuable feedback. And for my Advanced Review Team for their enthusiasm for and commitment to my work.

And to my family—my mother, Joanne, my husband, Ted, and my amazing children, Cameron and Ned—for your love and support and for keeping me grounded.

A Note to Readers

The idea for *Magnolia Nights* struck me while I was on one of my many early-morning walks through downtown Charleston during my recent extended stay. Many of the homes on the Battery are centuries old. Most were built prior to the Civil War when the way of life in the South was vastly different from today. I am fascinated by the families who've occupied these homes for generations. I imagine every household has at least one ghost.

Readers, please know how humbled I am by your continued support. You brighten my day with your e-mails, Facebook posts, and continuous stream of tweets. You inspire me to work harder to improve my writing skills and create intriguing characters and plots you can relate to.

I love hearing from you. Feel free to shoot me an e-mail at ashleyhfarley@gmail.com or stop by my website at ashleyfarley.net for more information about my characters and upcoming releases. Don't forget to sign up for my newsletter. Your subscription will grant you access to exclusive content, sneak previews, and special giveaways.

About the Author

Ashley Farley is the author of the bestselling Sweeney Sisters Series. Ashley writes books about women for women. Her characters are mothers, daughters, sisters, and wives facing real-life issues. Her goal is to keep you turning the pages until the wee hours of the morning. If her story stays with you long after you've read the last word, then she's done her job.

After her brother died in 1999 of an accidental overdose, she turned to writing as a way of releasing her pent-up emotions. She wrote *Saving Ben* in honor of Neal, the boy she worshipped, the man she could not save.

Ashley is a wife and the mother of two young-adult children. She grew up in the salty marshes of South Carolina but now lives in Richmond, Virginia, a city she loves for its history and traditions.

Ashley loves to hear from her readers. Feel free to visit her website at ashleyfarley.net.

CPSIA information can be obtained
at www.ICGtesting.com
Printed in the USA
LVOW03s2326190118
563260LV00001B/152/P